D0457180

Dear Reader,

When our children were young, we vacationed with friends at a cabin on a small, lovely lake in Maine. I decided God must have been in an exceptionally good mood on the day Maine was created.

We explored the stunning beauty of Acadia National Park, with its pretty beaches, incredible views from the top of Cadillac Mountain and unique rock formations. Some other special memories include trying desperately to get up close and personal with a loon (other than the ones in our canoe), visiting Bar Harbor ("Bah Hah-bah" in Maine-speak), where we launched into an impromptu circle dance when a fiddler strolled by, and introducing the kids to lobster and the joys of whale-watching.

Ever since that trip, I have wanted to return, and when I was asked to write about Marble Cove, it was the perfect opportunity to revisit the state. I could hear the roar of the surf when Diane, Shelley, Margaret and Beverly strolled along the promenade, and I could envision the cozy ambience of a small tourist town, complete with a rugged lighthouse on a spit of land. I was as thrilled as Diane to sweep away to such a place.

My story revolves around Shelley, a stressed-out young mother, and the town of Marble Cove came alive for me as I wrote this novel. I hope my words make it equally vivid for you.

Blessings,
Anne Marie Rodgers

FINDING GRACE

MIRACLES *of*
MARBLE COVE

FINDING GRACE

ANNE MARIE RODGERS

New York

Published by Guideposts Books & Inspirational Media
110 William Street
New York, NY 10038
Guideposts.org

Acknowledgments

Every attempt has been made to credit the sources of copyrighted material used in this book. If any such acknowledgment has been inadvertently omitted or miscredited, receipt of such information would be appreciated.

"Baking with Shelley" originally appeared as "Someone's in the Kitchen with Graham & Audrey" in *Angels on Earth* magazine. Copyright © 2008 by Guideposts. All rights reserved.

"From the Guideposts Archive" originally appeared as "His Mysterious Ways" by Cathy Slack as told to Skip Westphal in *Guideposts* magazine. Copyright © 1987 by Guideposts. All rights reserved.

Scripture quotations marked (NKJV) are taken from *The Holy Bible, New King James Version*. Copyright © 1997, 1990, 1985, 1983 by Thomas Nelson, Inc.

Cover and interior design by Müllerhaus
Cover photo by Veer
Typeset by Aptara

Printed and bound in the United States of America
10 9 8 7 6 5 4 3

In memory of "Vicktory Dogs" Sussex 2621,
Rose, Bonita, Seven,
Sweet Jasmine, Alf, Red and Beans,
and
in honor of the remaining survivors.
We *must* educate ourselves about dog fighting.
We *must* stop it forever.

CHAPTER ONE

Dawn was breaking in Marble Cove, Maine. Long ribbons of pink and lavender clouds hovered above the horizon as a half circle of golden rays shot its beams into the sky. From the rocking chair on her porch, Shelley Bauer smiled and cradled her hot coffee mug in both hands. She treasured the few moments of peace she stole in these early morning moments before her day began.

She gathered her bulky cable-knit fisherman's cardigan around her, curling her toes more deeply into the fleece lining of her slippers. It might be June, but Maine was reluctant to declare summer's arrival.

As she watched, the sun inched higher. Its shining fingers reached across the restless Atlantic. The ocean gently began to reveal more blue than black hues, although the weather-rounded boulders and rocks along the coastline were still dark, shrouded in wisps of low-lying fog and mystery.

Orlean Point Light was almost a cutout shape against the rich glow of the sky. She knew the old structure to be a white tower spearing upward, but now it was little more than a dark image, lightening moment by moment as the sun rose.

A rustling sound coming from the baby monitor she'd set on the table beside her was a signal that Emma, her eight-month-old daughter, would soon be waking.

Shelley stood and stretched, but a muscle in her back protested the movement. Wincing, she took a deep breath, as the memory of her recent car accident rushed back into her mind. Once again she sent a small prayer heavenward: *Thank You, Lord, for Your divine intervention.*

She still marveled at the chain of events that day. She never, *ever* left her children with anyone except Dan. But when her new neighbor Diane had offered, for some reason, one she now realized had been prompted by a heavenly directive, she had left the children at home—and saved their lives when the back half of her car was completely demolished by a speeding semi. Any other day, her two most precious gifts in the entire world would have been sitting in that back seat. The idea of it could still make her hands shake and her pulse race. She took another deep, calming breath.

As she lowered her arms, movement down near the base of the lighthouse arrested her in midmotion. What was that? She slowly brought down her arms as she strained to see. Something had definitely been moving out there—something a lot bigger than a dog. Something like a person. What would a person be doing around the lighthouse at this time of day? The lighthouse has been decommissioned for years.

She couldn't help but wonder if it had anything to do with the mysterious lights she and her neighbors had seen.

Lights they were certain meant something, even though they had been dismissed outright by Detective Fred Little. "The lighthouse must still be hooked up with the electric company," he'd said. He'd informed several other curious people around town of the same thing, and the matter had been put to rest for them. But Shelley, Diane, Margaret, and Beverly all felt the lights *meant* something.

She stood a moment longer, hoping for a better look, but whatever—*whoever*—it was appeared to be gone. And the first discontented squeak warned her she'd better hustle if she wanted to get Emma out of her crib before the baby's noise woke her older brother Aiden.

Shelley's husband Dan came into the kitchen just as she set a plate of French toast at his place at the table. He paused to chuckle at Emma's activity before crossing the room.

"Morning." He dipped his head and kissed her. "*Mm-mmm.* Looks good. I have an early shift today, so I have to get going." Dan plowed his way through his breakfast. He glanced up once and caught her looking at him fondly. "What?"

"I just enjoy watching you enjoy my food."

He grinned. "What's not to enjoy? You're a great cook." As he rose from his seat, though, he frowned. "This chair seems a little wobbly to me."

Shelley nodded. "I meant to mention it yesterday, but I forgot. Is there some way we can brace it without damaging the chair itself?" Their antique mission oak table and four chairs had once belonged to Shelley's maternal grandparents.

Although both had passed away when she was young, some of her fondest childhood memories involved them, and she treasured the dining set.

"I'll look at it when I get a chance. I'm sure I can fix it up." Dan picked up his keys and gave her and Emma good-bye kisses. "Hope you have a good day with the kids, honey."

She nodded. "You have a good day too."

Dan flashed the grin that had won her heart the first time they'd met. "See you later." And then he was gone.

Shelley smiled as she washed up their breakfast dishes. The strain that shadowed so many of their conversations these days seemed to be gone this morning. Perhaps things were looking up at Dan's workplace, but he didn't want to say anything just yet.

More than an hour passed. Shelley cleaned up the early breakfast dishes and made some pumpernickel bread dough. After she set it to rise on the warm corner of the counter beside the refrigerator, she sat down and began folding a basket of the kids' clothes.

A few minutes after eight, her three-year-old son Aiden came stumbling into the kitchen, rubbing his eyes.

Shelley opened her arms and caught him in a bear hug as she lifted him into her lap. "Good morning, my sweet boy. How are you?"

Aiden laid his head on her shoulder and snuggled in without speaking. Shelley rocked back and forth slightly, treasuring the moment. Her son was growing up, and most of the time he was far too lively and squirmy to want to sit in Mommy's lap.

"Want to count lighthouses?" she asked. Aiden shook his head. Sometimes he liked to count the strip of lighthouses that ran along the wallpaper border at chair-rail height in her kitchen.

Painted white above and a rich red below the border, the walls were accented by other lighthouses that decorated every conceivable surface: the calendar, magnets on the refrigerator, the placemats at the table, even a cookie jar and the clock on the wall. She loved that unique cookie jar; she'd never seen another one like it. The main gallery ran around the top of the jar, and the lid was composed of the tower, the watchroom, and the lens.

Shelley got Aiden started on his cereal and then picked up Emma, who had been happily gnawing on a toy in her playpen. Strapping the infant into her high chair, Shelley began to feed her some fruit she had run through the food processor. Dry Cheerios and formula were fine, but Emma needed more to eat now.

"Mommy?" Aiden banged his spoon on a glossy newspaper advertisement, spraying milk from his cereal across the table. "I want this!"

"Aiden!" With one hand, Shelley whisked the paper away from the table and grabbed a dishcloth to mop up the mess. She winced again as the quick motion irritated the muscle in her back that was still tender after the accident. "You have better manners than that, and I expect you to use them."

"But I want that." Aiden's voice was defiant. *That* was a Lego set he'd seen in the ad.

"You'll have to ask Santa next Christmas. You already had your birthday, remember?" Shelley turned back to the table to feed Emma another bite. The eight-month-old opened her mouth like a baby bird, making Shelley chuckle. "That's my sweet girl. What a good eater you are."

Emma grinned, a fat drop of drool rushing down her chin to drip onto her bib. Shelley smiled back. "Ma-ma?" she said. "Emma, can you say 'mama'?"

"I—want—that!" Aiden shouted, each word punctuated by a bang of his spoon.

"Ah-da-da-da-DA!" Apparently Emma was inspired by her brother.

Sighing inwardly, Shelley did her best to hang onto her temper. She was the grown-up, she reminded herself, and her son needed consistency and guidance, not a swat across the bottom. "Aiden, if you bang your spoon again, you will sit in time-out." She kept her voice calm and matter-of-fact, as she'd read in the child-rearing book she had bought last week...and hoped her son couldn't tell she was gritting her teeth.

Aiden, who had been hearing such words and seeing his mother follow through for a week now, finally seemed to be getting the message that tantrum-throwing didn't get him anywhere, and he subsided. "But Mommy," he said reasonably, "I *like* dose Legos."

"I know, sweetie." Shelley smiled, wishing their budget wasn't so strained, wishing she could give Aiden all the

Legos he wanted. "I see things all the time that I like, but we can't buy them all."

Aiden, clearly seeing he wasn't going to win this round, squirmed in his seat and changed direction with his demands. "I want to get down."

"May I please get down?" Shelley said automatically.

"Yeah. Me too." Aiden squirmed again, totally missing the manners cue.

Shelley had to laugh. *One thing at a time,* she reminded herself. Aiden was realizing there were consequences for misbehavior. They could worry about manners at another meal. She checked his bowl. Satisfied that he had eaten enough, she said, "All right, you may get down. You were a good eater today."

She unbuckled the strap on his booster seat with her free hand, and Aiden wriggled down by himself. "I want to play in the yard until Adelaide comes," he announced.

The Hoskinses' daughter Adelaide, who had Down syndrome, came over several mornings a week to play with Aiden, a recent arrangement Shelley had come to treasure. Those two hours without her son dogging her footsteps seeking interaction and entertainment were so helpful. There was nothing wrong, she reminded herself, with needing a break from your child for a couple of hours.

"That's fine. Put your bowl in the dishwasher first."

Aiden picked up the plastic bowl and carried it to the counter, tugging open the dishwasher door and putting his bowl on the top rack as she had taught him.

"Good job!" she said. "Now you may go outside."

"See you." Her son's nonchalant phrase made her smile.

"See you," she said.

Aiden clomped off the porch, sounding more like a moose than a small boy, and Shelley continued her breakfast clean-up.

Emma squealed. "Ay-day-day-day."

"Aiden went outside. He'll be back in a little while," Shelley told her, smiling. She set Emma in her playpen with her post-breakfast bottle of formula, where the baby immediately reached for the silky edge of the pink blanket one of Dan's sisters had given her when she was born. Emma had developed quite an attachment to it, and Shelley tried not to be secretly delighted that she preferred it to the baby blanket her mother-in-law had crocheted.

The screen door banged open. "Mommy!"

"Yes, Aiden?" Now what?

"I want a new swing. An' a new sliding board, an' a new sandbox—"

"The ones you have now are just fine." Shelley cut him off firmly. "But if you really don't like them, I can ask Daddy to take them away."

"No!" Alarm lit her son's blue eyes, and he vanished from the doorway.

She chuckled to herself as she finished clearing the table and started wiping off the counters. She finally seemed to be getting the hang of handling her son since he'd stopped being mommy's boy and had started pursuing independence.

She sighed as she walked into what looked vaguely like her living room but was buried beneath several layers of toys, laundry, newspapers and magazines, and Dan's jacket, which never seemed able to find its home in the closet. She'd been a great housekeeper before Emma was born, but even with Adelaide's helpful visits, handling two small children seemed to eat up minutes faster than she could use them. True, things had been improving lately, but some days... She sighed again.

She picked up Dan's jacket and hung it in the closet, smoothing a frayed spot along one cuff. She might be able to do a satin stitch or darn over it, but soon he was going to need a replacement. And where would that money come from?

If only Dan hadn't spent all the money he earned renovating for Diane on a new big-screen TV and Blu-Ray player. What had he been thinking? Then again, if only she'd gone to college when she'd graduated from high school ten years ago...What had *she* been thinking?

Sadly, she recalled those tumultuous days. She *hadn't* been thinking. At least, not of anything beyond her immediate situation. Her parents had divorced during her senior year. Her mother had remarried and moved away from Portland the summer after Shelley graduated. Her father had taken a job in another small Maine community and moved also. No way had she wanted to live with her dad, so she'd gotten a job and found a modest apartment with two equally poor roommates.

If only she'd gotten some further education, although she couldn't imagine where the money would have come from. But she should have tried. She could have gone to pastry school. Even back then she had loved to bake. If she had, maybe now she and Dan wouldn't be in such a financial panic.

She blew out a gusty sigh as she began to pick up the messy room. Oh, rats. There lay a sippy cup on its side. Juice had leaked out to create a cranberry-colored stain on the couch. How many times had she told Aiden no drinks in the living room?

"Mommy!" Aiden's voice and the sound of the screen door wrenching open startled her.

Clutching the cup, she hurried into the kitchen to tell him to use an inside voice in the house. Aiden was starting for the living room as she moved into the kitchen. "Hi, buddy. 'Sup?" Born and raised in Maine, she used local dialectial patterns often, although since she had met her new neighbor Diane and several other friends, she was more conscious of her speech.

"I want a puppy." Aiden danced from foot to foot, clutching at the front of his pants.

"Looks to me like you want a potty," she commented, steering him upstairs to the single bathroom in the little house.

"But I really, *really* want a puppy." In the bathroom, he dragged down his beloved Spider-Man underpants, used the toilet, and then struggled back into his clothes. Shelley knelt to tuck in his T-shirt and helped him turn on the faucet. As he soaped and rinsed his hands, her son turned hopeful blue eyes her way. "My puppy will sleep with me. My puppy will—"

"Aiden!" Her patience snapped. "Stop begging! There will be no puppy. There will be no new play set. There will be no Legos. And you need to stop that begging right this instant! The next time I hear the words 'I want' come out of your mouth, you're going to lose your television privileges after snack. Do you understand me?"

Tears instantly welled in Aiden's eyes. He shrank away from her and ran out of the bathroom. As his little feet rushed into his bedroom, she could hear her little boy sobbing.

Shelley turned off the water. Pressing the discarded hand towel hard against her own stinging eyes, she took slow deep breaths to keep from bursting into tears herself. Clearly she had a lot more to learn about hanging onto her patience.

The sound of the doorbell dragged her from the moment of self-pity. That would be Adelaide, and it wouldn't do for the young woman to see Shelley crying. Adelaide might be twenty-four years old, but she was still a child in many ways. Seeing a "grown-up" in tears would upset her.

Hurrying downstairs, Shelley summoned a big smile as she opened the front door. "Good morning, Addie!"

"G'morning." Adelaide's eyes crinkled, as a wide smile lit her face. "Where's Aiden?"

"Aiden is in his room," Shelley told her. "Let me call him, and then you two can go play in the backyard for a while."

"Okay. Need any help with Emma?" Adelaide's expression was hopeful. She was growing to enjoy Emma as much as she did Aiden.

Shelley chuckled, something inside her relaxing. Adelaide was like a cheery ray of sunshine, lightening the tense mood in the house. "Not right now, but when you and Aiden come in for snack, you may feed Emma her fruit."

"I'd like that." Adelaide beamed again, and Shelley found herself smiling as she went to the bottom of the steps to tell Aiden his playmate had arrived.

Chapter Two

While both children napped that afternoon, Shelley made a cinnamon-walnut coffee cake. She had just taken it from the oven when, over the monitor, she heard Emma beginning to stir.

Upstairs, she changed and snuggled Emma before peeking into Aiden's room. "Hey, sleepyhead."

Aiden lay scrunched into a tiny ball on his side, blinking drowsily. "I want—I mean, can we take a walk?" He'd gotten over his broken heart before lunchtime.

Shelley smiled gently. "Sure. Where would you like to go?"

"Main Street." Her son sat up with a great deal of enthusiasm. The nap seemed to have recharged his batteries completely. "Can we go see the puppies?" Aiden loved visiting the Pet Place, a small shop across from the appliance store. The shop didn't actually sell animals, but dogs on lead were encouraged to visit, and Aiden loved to see them when they came into the store.

"We can. And then we'll stop by Miss Margaret's new store. I made her a coffee cake."

"Can I have some?" Aiden looked hopeful.

"If you ask nicely she may cut you a slice," Shelley said with a smile.

Their walk downtown was pleasant. May had been a mild month, and June was following in its footsteps today, with temperatures in the midsixties and lovely warm sunshine. Shelley chuckled softly. Of course, in typical Maine fashion it could be raining buckets in the next town along the coast, but she would take today and be grateful for it.

As they walked briskly down Newport Street, Shelley paused to wave to Mr. Wheeland sitting on his front porch. "Hello," she called.

"Hello!" Aiden echoed.

Mr. Wheeland lifted a hand in greeting, and Shelley smiled as they moved on. If he wasn't on the porch, he was sitting by the front window. She waved to him nearly every time she walked, and if he wasn't there, she fretted a bit until she saw him back in one of his spots the next day.

They made the promised stop at the Pet Place, where Aiden marveled over a shar-pei drowning in velvety wrinkles and a Golden retriever who shed scads of golden hair and happily lapped at Aiden's face until he screamed with giggles.

"You must have dogs," the owner said to Shelley. "Not all children are comfortable with a dog that big right in their faces."

Shelley shook her head. "No. My neighbor recently found a stray and kept it, but Aiden hasn't been around a lot of them."

"I guess he's just a natural dog lover." The man smiled and winked as he turned to leave the shop. "A boy that loves dogs that much ought to have a dog of his own."

"Mommy! Mommy!" Aiden tugged at the bottom of her T-shirt. "See? He said we should get a doggie."

Shelley stifled a sigh and grimaced. "Let's not talk about dogs right now, Aiden. Okay?"

Lee Waters, the owner of the shop, sent her a sympathetic smile. "I can see your willpower being slowly worn away."

"Not mine." Her voice was sharper than she intended. "The last thing I need is a dog. I have enough trouble caring for two small children."

Lee looked a little taken aback. "I'm sure you do." The response was diplomatic, but Shelley imagined she saw a flicker of disapproval in his eyes.

"We have to go," she said to Aiden, who was playing with squeaky toys in a bin. "Thanks, Lee, for letting us come in and harass your clients." She made an effort to smile.

Lee returned the smile. "Any time. Maybe someday Aiden can get a job here. Then he'd see all the dogs he likes."

Aiden squealed with enthusiasm over the idea.

Heading for the door, Shelley sent Lee a final strained smile.

★   ★   ★

When they left the Pet Place, Aiden hopped into his seat in the double-wide umbrella stroller, and Shelley turned in the direction of the Shearwater Gallery. Margaret Hoskins lived diagonally across the street from Shelley. An artist who was just beginning to embrace her love of painting, Margaret recently had opened a gallery on Main Street featuring a number of artistic mediums, including her own work and her husband Allan's handcrafted furniture.

Shelley envied Margaret. Not in an unkind way, she assured herself. But, oh, wouldn't it be wonderful to have her own little business doing something she loved, the way Margaret did with her art?

But... she glanced down at her children, a troubled frown creasing her brow. She loved being able to spend each day with the kids. She and Dan had decided he would be the one bringing in the money, and she would stay home with their children. That precept was important to them both: Dan because he had been raised in a large, loving family, and she because she...well, she hadn't.

Her parents might genuinely love her and her sister, but throughout much of her childhood, they had used Susannah and Shelley as game pieces to score points off each other. One thing Shelley knew for certain—she would *never* put her children in the position of having to try not to take sides in a war between their parents.

"Shelley! Hi!" Diane Spencer was waving at her from the door of the Shearwater Gallery. Diane had moved onto Newport Street less than two months ago, but she had woven herself into Shelley's heart as if she'd always been there. And Margaret's as well. She had offered to help Margaret when

the gallery was first opening, and apparently she hadn't
given that up yet.

Shelley had been so preoccupied with her thoughts that
she hadn't even noticed Diane stepping out to hold open the
door for her. "Hi," she said. "We come bearing gifts."

"Hi, Miss Diane," Aiden piped. "I just saw a doggie,
an'...an'...an' I want one just like it." The *L* in *like* sounded
more like a *y*, a charming speech pattern Shelley expected
Aiden would soon lose.

"A doggie! He can play with Rocky." Diane gave Shelley
a quick, spontaneous hug as she maneuvered the stroller
through the door. "How's life treating you?"

Shelley shrugged. "I can't complain."

Diane's eyebrows rose. "Just because you *can't* doesn't
mean you don't *want to.*"

Shelley had to laugh. "I really don't have much to
complain about, although I was having a pity party as I
thought about what it would be like to follow my dreams
the way you two are doing." Diane had begun writing a
novel, and she appeared to be thoroughly in love with her
new profession, although she'd been a successful journalist
before her recent move to Marble Cove.

"Shelley! Hey there." Margaret came out of the small
back area that served as her studio, wiping her hands on a
rag. "I knew I needed a break, and this is a great reason to
indulge myself."

Shelley reached into the capacious bag she carried and
withdrew the coffee cake. Handing it to Margaret, she said,

"Cinnamon-walnut coffee cake. I thought maybe we all could have a midafternoon snack."

"Snack," Aiden said happily, hearing the all-important word. "Me too?"

"You too." Margaret leaned down and gently tapped the tip of his nose, chuckling. Taking the coffee cake from Shelley, she said, "Come on in. I'll get a knife and some paper plates."

Aiden squirmed, tugging at his restraint strap. "Can I help?"

Shelley shuddered, looking around at all the beautiful breakable things in the gallery. "You stay right there, Mister. Miss Margaret will bring you your cake in a minute." She plucked his favorite book from her bag and handed it to him. "Here you go."

The three women savored the crumbly, still-warm coffee cake. Aiden reduced his piece to crumbs, which he then took great delight in mashing together and eating.

"*Mm-mmm*, Shelley, you have truly outdone yourself," Margaret told her.

"Thanks." Shelley's voice was wry, as she pointed to Aiden. "Maybe I should try a new technique next time."

Diane and Margaret both laughed, and Diane's eyes lit up. "You could call it cinnamon-walnut coffee smunch."

They all chuckled again.

"Margaret," Shelley asked, "have you started on the plans for your big gallery opening?"

Margaret rubbed her hands together in a nervous gesture. "Oh, didn't you hear about the date change? I had intended to have it on the twenty-first, but the town council is having sidewalk sales that weekend."

"Sidewalk sales?"

Margaret nodded. "They've decided to kick off summer by having all the downtown merchants join in. Diane and I didn't think it would be a good idea to try to have a gallery opening in the midst of that. Too much opportunity for chaos."

Shelley rolled her eyes. "I'd have to agree with you there. So when are you having it?"

"Thursday the ninth. The big shindig will be at six in the evening, although I'm going to have special drawings and refreshments all day."

"The *ninth*?" Shelley couldn't believe she'd heard right. "Of *June*? That's only a week away!"

"Fortunately, it wasn't a problem for any of the plans I had set in place. That jazz quartet will be coming, and all my contributing artists have brought in or plan to bring in the last of the inventory. Allan has the newspaper ads all purchased." Margaret looked indignant. "Do you know how much the Augusta paper charges for a quarter-page ad? It's outrageous!"

"Ad space has gone up considerably," Diane said. "But it will be worth it." As Emma began to fuss, she got up and took the infant out of the stroller, holding her up to her shoulder and rocking from side to side.

"I hope so." Margaret's voice was missing its usual assurance. "I keep looking at my work and thinking the public won't like it. I know it's silly, but..." Her voice trailed off.

"Are you kidding?" Diane regarded Margaret with a smile, bouncing the baby on her hip. "You have beautiful paintings that will speak to people. They're going to fly out of here."

Margaret managed a smile. "I don't know why I feel so uncertain about this."

"Artistic temperament," Diane told her. "If someone doesn't like something you've created, it's like they said your baby was ugly."

Shelley burst into laughter, feeling her heart lighten as it often did around these new friends. "That's horrible."

"But true. And that's how I've felt in the past when someone didn't like an article I wrote." Diane rolled her eyes. "It's going to be a million times worse if I get this book published—"

"When." Shelley made her voice firm.

"What?"

"*When* you get it published. Think positive."

"You're right." Diane beamed at her. "*When* I publish this book, I'm going to be much more protective than I was with my newspaper work, because this is fiction. This is me, pouring myself onto the page."

"That's it exactly." Margaret pointed at Diane for emphasis. "Part of me goes into each painting, and when someone doesn't like it, it feels as if they don't like me."

"They're going to like you," Shelley said, as firm as she had been with Diane a moment earlier. "Now, back to your opening. You've got music, you've got paintings and stuff, you've advertised, and you've got a beautiful gallery. But what about food?"

Margaret grimaced. "I've successfully avoided thinking about that until now."

"Well, you can't avoid it much longer." Shelley looked around the space. "We could put one of Allan's tables there, and another over there. Snacks on one, drinks on the other."

"I like that word—*we*." Margaret took a deep breath. "It sounds much less scary than *I*."

"Okay," Diane said, "so what are *we* planning to serve?" She rubbed Emma's back and the baby's eyes began to droop.

"Some munchies—"

"Munchies?" Shelley was mildly horrified that Margaret had given the food so little thought. "Oh no, no, no. We're going to serve pretty, tasty, classy little things that will put everyone in the mood to buy fine art."

Margaret laughed. "Sounds like I need to put you in charge."

"I accept." Shelley grinned at her friend. "Why don't you worry about everything else, and leave the food to Diane and me?"

"Really?" Margaret looked stunned. "That would be *wonderful*." She turned and hurried across the room. "Let me get my purse. I'll write you a check so you can get started. You'll have to let me know if you need more."

"Oh, I couldn't—"

"Yes, you could." Margaret fixed a stern eye on Shelley as she returned. "We're not talking about a few odds and ends here. You need a budget. Now, what do you want me to bring?"

More relieved than she wanted to let on about the financial support, Shelley ticked things off on her fingers. "You and Allan can get paper products—you know: plates, napkins, and cups. It'll be finger food, so no utensils will be necessary. You can get coffee and tea ready. I'll make a fruit punch." She glanced over at Diane, who was contentedly rocking the sleeping Emma. "I guess I should have asked before I volunteered you."

Diane laughed. "No problem. You just tell me what to do, and I'll be your assistant chef."

CHAPTER THREE

It had been good to see Shelley laughing and excited again today, Diane reflected, as she walked home from Margaret's shop before dinner. She thought of Shelley dancing on the beach in the moonlight last Sunday evening. This girl needed something in her life to put that *joie de vivre* into her every day. Raising her children was important to Shelley, but Diane sensed that her young friend's soul craved something more, something that would fulfill her in a different way.

Something like she herself had, Diane thought, thinking of the novel she was writing. Although she hesitated to call it fulfilling at this very moment—more like frustrating and irritating.

Things had gone very well in the last few weeks after her conversation with her neighbor down the street, Mr. Wheeland. Beverly, she knew, had invited her to dinner in the hopes that Diane could get her father a little more interested in participating in life. But Diane had reaped as much as she had sown during their chat before dinner.

Setting a daily word count goal had worked well, and she had written the first five chapters in the first week. Since then, though, it had been slower going. Her story seemed to be veering off in a direction different than she'd initially imagined, and the outline she'd been working from no longer met her needs.

So she'd set the manuscript aside and gone back to the outline. She was tempted to just wing it, forget the outline altogether, but she was afraid she wouldn't tie up all the loose ends or finish all the threads of her story if she didn't have a road map.

And then she'd gotten distracted. First, it had been preparing for the open house she'd held for the neighborhood. Then Shelley had her accident, and Diane had simply felt too unsettled to work for a few days after that. Then she'd found a church and had immediately volunteered to serve on the Lay Ministries committee as a visitor to homebound church members.

Turning onto Newport Street, Diane briskly walked past her neighbors' homes to her own tidy little cottage. She still experienced a secret thrill every time she turned onto her pretty brick front walk and fitted her key into the red door. She really lived here! Two blocks from the ocean.

And she had a dog. She let out a fond chuckle as Rocky, the Lab/golden mix she had rescued from a tide pool, came scrambling toward her, his paws slipping on the pine floors in his haste to reach her. She knelt and buried her face in the silky coat.

"Hey, buddy. Did you miss me?" She laughed. "Or are you just hungry?" Rocky was always hungry. The dog had begun to fill out, and his coat was becoming soft and glossy. She'd realized she'd have to start vacuuming frequently if she wanted to stay one step ahead of the hair that seemed to fly every time he took a step.

The dog followed her into the kitchen and dove into the food she set down for him.

As she went to the refrigerator and began looking for something for her own dinner, a wave of homesickness swept over her. She'd been so busy and pleased with her progress settling into her new life that she hadn't dwelled too much on the changes in her daily routine. Not so very many years ago, she would have been making dinner for four. It was hard to face how fast she'd become a home for one.

Diane reheated a white sauce, boiled some spaghetti, and then slowly sat down to her solitary dinner. Seeing only one place setting on the table drove home a feeling she'd been trying to avoid. She was essentially alone. Jessica and Justin were moving on with their lives.

Suddenly, she realized what had been bugging her for the past couple of weeks. If Eric were here, she'd be hashing over these glitches in her writing process with him. He had loved the ebb and flow of a perfect sentence, the sound of a well-written tale rolling off the tongue. He would have had suggestions to help her sort out the direction she wanted to take with this story.

"What do you suppose he would have said?" she asked Rocky.

The dog cocked his head and looked at her, bright eyes inquiring.

She sighed. "I don't know either. But one thing is for sure. I need to stop fiddling around. Choose a direction and go with it."

CHAPTER FOUR

Beverly Wheeland pulled her car to the curb in front of her father's home. Now that her mother was gone, it was up to Beverly to make sure her father was doing all right.

She leaned forward and rested her head on the steering wheel for a moment before getting out of the car. Her work week had been terrifically busy, and traffic had been terrible, considering how early in the summer it was. Usually the tourist trade in Maine was reserved for the warmer months of July and August. Driving back and forth every weekend was surprisingly exhausting. How did people manage a long commute?

Refusing to dwell on the unpleasant thoughts, she let out a sigh of relief that the journey was behind her. It would be good to be here for the weekend, away from work and...and memories. Getting out, she tugged her bag from the trunk of her vehicle. She could relax and enjoy spending time with her father, and perhaps she could touch base with several of his neighbors, with whom she'd become very friendly. She'd even enjoyed the company of Dennis Calder, the grandson of her father's next door neighbor, before he'd left on a months-long business trip. Maybe life didn't need to be so lonely.

Walking to the front door, she turned the knob and entered. "Hi, Father." But though she'd pitched her voice to carry, her father didn't appear.

Beverly frowned. "Father?" she called even louder.

This time she thought she heard a faint voice.

She started out of the entry hall. "Are you upstairs?"

"Yup. Come on up."

Hefting her bag, Beverly carried it up the steps and dropped it inside the door of the guest bedroom. As she came out of the room and turned left to walk down the dark hall, she banged into a stack of empty boxes. The top two went tumbling. Quickly, she reached out and flipped on the hall light.

And was rendered speechless. Boxes—*empty boxes*—were strewn throughout the hallway. The door to the attic stood open, which wasn't a good omen. After her mother's death, Beverly had gone through hundreds of their possessions, packing away things her father would no longer use. She hadn't been able to part with them, so she'd carried them to the attic, where they were, or had been neatly stored with lists of contents on the side of each box.

Slowly she mounted the steps, noting that it was stuffy and warm up here without any windows open. "Father? What on earth are you doing?"

Most of the contents of the boxes at the base of the stairs were stacked haphazardly on the wooden boards of the attic floor, regardless of the dust and dead flies. Some items looked as if they'd been pawed through. Others had fallen over, spilling across the floor untidily. Any sense of relaxation Beverly had entered with evaporated as she stared at the mess. Straightening it all out again was going to take her all weekend—or longer.

Her father appeared from one corner of the attic, wiping his perspiring face. "Beverly! I forgot you were coming today. I was looking for...I was looking for..." Her father glanced around as if the answer might be written on a wall somewhere. "I can't recall." He seemed to rally. "But it must have been important. I'll deal with it later."

"Father! This is a huge mess."

He looked around ruefully. "I guess it is, isn't it? Maybe later you could help me put it all back?" He fanned himself. "It's hot up here. Come downstairs, and we'll have some lemonade."

Beverly resisted the urge to bean him with one of the empty boxes. Instead, she said, "You made lemonade?"

"Um, no. But you could."

Beverly shook her head, not in denial but with concern. "What got into you today? I thought I was coming home for a nice, relaxing weekend."

"I'm sorry." Her father looked genuinely remorseful. But he didn't offer any further explanation for his behavior.

With a shock of clarity Beverly realized that he couldn't explain it. She felt panic rising. Her father managed his diabetes well by keeping his diet in line, and he hadn't shown any signs that his memory was becoming problematic. Until now.

She sighed. "Come on down, Father. I'll make some lemonade while you wash up. You look like you crawled out of a coal bin."

Mr. Wheeland chuckled, looking down at his clothes and turning his grubby hands over to inspect them. "Guess I do. Guess I do," he said, nodding.

⋆　⋆　⋆

Diane left Shelley's house and went home to get Rocky for their evening walk when Shelley took Aiden upstairs for his bath and bedtime story.

As Diane and the dog strolled down Newport Avenue toward the promenade that fronted the beach along the downtown area, she spotted another person just stepping out onto the sidewalk.

"Beverly! Hello." Diane smiled, pleased to see the woman who had joined Margaret, Shelley, and her several nights ago. "I didn't realize you were visiting again this weekend."

Beverly's smile looked strained. "Yes. I'm going to be coming home more regularly. My father appears to need someone to look in on him more frequently than I had thought."

"Oh?" Diane wanted to encourage Beverly to talk without seeming obvious. The slim, pretty, dark-haired woman seemed to be wound tighter than a yo-yo. She was friendly, if reserved, and Diane hoped she would relax and share a bit more of herself over time. It would be nice to have another friend in Marble Cove.

Beverly sighed and, as Diane had hoped, spoke again. "He seems to be having some problems with his memory."

"If I can do anything during the week to ease your concerns, please let me know."

"Thank you." Beverly smiled, but Diane sensed that she already had dismissed the offer.

"How have you been since our big rescue? I have to confess, I thought about it off and on all week." Diane shifted Rocky's lead from one hand to the other. "If we hadn't seen that boy…"

"I know." Beverly's tone was as sober as the chilling thought. "He's a very fortunate young man."

"But that's just it. I am still finding it hard to believe the flash of light that showed us a struggling swimmer was just a coincidence. Doesn't it seem to you there have been far too many coincidences connected with sightings of that light?"

"I suppose it does." Beverly sounded reluctant. She always was resistant to their talk of miracles, Diane remembered.

"It occurred at *exactly* the right moment to show us that swimmer." Diane was determined to erase Beverly's doubts. "We might never have seen him if not for that light."

"Rocky was barking, though," Beverly said. "Remember? He was trying to pull you toward the water. You'd already been alerted."

Diane nodded. "But even if we'd shone our flashlights over the waves, it was far too rough to have seen anyone swimming. I have to believe that light was a deliberate occurrence. I'm not going to speculate about who or what made it." Of course she was, but that was beside the point.

The two women chatted for a moment longer, and then they said good night. Beverly headed back toward town, and Diane and Rocky continued down the beach.

It was dusk now, and most of the tourists had gone in for dinner or entertainment. Rocky saw another dog on the beach and strained at the lead, so Diane released him. He raced across the sand to do a stiff-legged face-off before the two animals began to warily sniff each other and then turned and bounded along the water's edge.

Diane smiled. She kept moving, pacing the dogs' progress. As she walked, her thoughts turned to the lighthouse and the mysterious light she and her friends had seen. What could it be? She wished there were some way to get inside. Frowning, she mulled over the recent events, trying to come up with another way to check out the lighthouse.

Just as she decided she had walked far enough, a flash of light streaked out across the water! It had been only a flash, but Diane was certain it had come from the lighthouse. Adrenaline rushed through her. Was it a sign?

"Hey! Did you see that?" A young couple paused beside Diane, and the young man looked at her inquiringly.

"I did." Diane pulled out her phone and hit the camera feature, just in case. She stared out over the water until her eyes burned from not blinking, but she didn't see a thing. Nor, she realized, did she feel the same compelling sense of urgency she had during both Rocky's and the boy's rescues. She wondered if someone else might be feeling that urgency. Surely she wasn't the only person to whom it had happened. "Do you see anything in the water?"

The couple stared out over the water with her. "Not a thing," the woman said. "Someone told me there was a rescue here a couple of days ago."

"We just arrived yesterday," added the man.

Diane nodded, never taking her gaze off the ocean. "There was." Then, realizing she had sounded much like a taciturn Mainer, she smiled. "I hope you enjoy your vacation."

"It's our honeymoon." The man looped an arm around the woman and caressed her shoulder. "We're just taking a few days away before we head back to New Hampshire to set up our first apartment."

"Congratulations!" She beamed at them both. "I hope your life together is long and happy." Then she turned away. "I have to go. That's my dog barreling down the beach without me."

The couple laughed and said farewell as she hurried off.

Diane trudged off the promenade down into the sand. "Rocky, come!" The dog wheeled immediately and began to race back toward her, the smaller black dog with whom he'd become pals at his heels.

As they neared, a man drew up in her peripheral vision.

"Hi, Diane."

She turned, surprised to see Rocky's veterinarian approaching. "Hello, Dr. Spangler. Is that your dog?"

"Leo, please. And yes, that's my dog. I owe you one. Without Rocky returning, he probably would have kept right on going down the beach." The vet was a likeable man with silvering hair that still had glints of copper in it. He'd flirted lightly with her at Rocky's last office visit.

"Glad we could help...Leo," she said.

He grinned, displaying straight teeth and two deep dimples in his cheeks that gave him an unexpectedly mischievous look. They watched the two dogs approach. Leo's dog resembled a Collie, except that its coat was solid black from stem to stern.

"He's beautiful," she said, meaning it.

"He looks even better when he's not covered with sand."

She laughed. "He and Rocky seemed to hit it off nicely. I guess they feel they have a lot in common, living close enough to get onto this beach so much."

He laughed. "That wouldn't have been the first thing I said about him."

"Why not?"

"Your dog listens. Limo is selectively deaf when I give a command."

"Limo? Now that's a little more unique than many pet names."

Spangler shrugged, his blue eyes dancing. "He was hit by a limo that was on the way to a wedding reception. The bride made them pick him up and bring him to my clinic before she would go on to the party."

Diane smiled. "What a good heart. Couldn't you find his owner?"

He shook his head. "The story even rated a mention in the paper, but no one ever came forward. I don't understand it. He's not a common breed. Someone probably paid a lot for him. And he's whip-smart and friendly and—" He stopped, looking sheepish. "And I like him."

She knelt to ruffle Limo's feathered ears. "His coat's so silky. Sandy or not."

"It takes some work. Especially after a walk on the beach."

"I'm sure that's a job." She chuckled. "One of the perks of having a short-coated dog. I rinse off his feet with the hose, dry them, and he's good to go inside." Then she thought of the flash of light. "Hey, did you see anything odd when you were coming this way?"

"You mean that flash of light?" He sent her an understanding look. "I imagine it made you a little tense after your recent experience."

Diane nodded. "But I looked out over the water and didn't see anything wrong." She hesitated. "How did seeing the light make you feel?"

He shot her a quizzical glance. "Other than a bit puzzled?"

"That's all?"

"That's all." He looked anxious, as if he wasn't certain he'd answered correctly. "How should I have felt?"

She shrugged. "The last time I saw it, I had a definite sense of…expectation or anticipation, I suppose you could say. I felt that the light meant something." She paused. "I don't feel that tonight."

Leo shook his head. "Me either. It was just a flash of light. A little mysterious, maybe, but that's it."

So the light hadn't been "meant" for him, she mused. Or for that young couple, so relaxed and content. And she hadn't felt any sense of something tugging at her to investigate. Had anyone?

CHAPTER FIVE

Midmorning on Saturday, Shelley took her children for a brisk ride in the stroller. Dan had left earlier to run over to his folks' home for a tool he didn't have in his workshop, and it was too pretty a day to be cooped up inside.

When she returned, Dan's truck was in the driveway. Aiden ran ahead of her into the house. "Daddy, we went for a walk!"

"Sounds like fun," Dan said. "It's a nice day to be outside."

"What's in there?" she heard Aiden ask.

Shelley carried Emma into the kitchen to find that Dan had set a large box in the middle of the kitchen floor.

"It's a surprise." Dan began to lift the flaps.

"For me?" Aiden demanded.

"For you," his father confirmed.

Shelley frowned. They had talked about not spoiling their son by constantly giving him gifts. Why hadn't Dan—"

Aiden screamed and clapped, dancing from foot to foot as Dan reached into the box. "Mommy-Mommy-Mommy, it's a *puppy!*"

A *what?* Flabbergasted, Shelley stood riveted to the floor, barely remembering to keep Emma held to her shoulder.

Dan held up a small, fuzzy ball of fur, black and brown with a little white and ridiculous floppy ears.

Aiden threw himself down beside Dan and laid a gentle hand on the puppy. "I wished and wished and wished for a puppy, and you came," he informed the little creature.

Grinding her teeth together to keep from screaming, Shelley avoided eye contact with her husband. "Aiden, maybe you'd better take her out in the grass so she can go potty. Puppies like to play outside."

"All by myself?" Her son sounded awed by the prospect.

If she hadn't been struggling to contain a volcano of anger, Shelley would have been charmed by his delight.

"All by yourself." She walked to the door and held it open. Dan set the puppy on the floor.

Aiden said, "Come on, puppy," and started outside.

Shelley opened her mouth to explain that puppies didn't understand words, but the animal followed Aiden through the door. With infinite gentleness, Shelley closed the door and turned to her husband. "Stay." Her tone betrayed her exasperation, and Dan nodded with wary eyes.

She turned and marched into the living room to lay Emma down in the playpen. The baby's eyelids were drooping, and Shelley covered her with her favorite blanket. Then she straightened, took a deep breath, and marched back to the kitchen.

She folded her arms and glared at Dan. "Explain yourself."

"Shelley, I promise you I wouldn't have done this without consulting you—"

"But you did!"

"It was so strange though. We were all at Greg's for lunch, and he showed us his new litter. One of them got free, and she kept following me around. Of the seven of us, she followed *me*."

"What were you thinking?"

"I don't know!" He let out an exasperated sigh. "Greg said if I wanted her, I'd have to decide then because he was selling the litter. It was like the puppy found *me*," he said quietly. "Besides, I thought Aiden would love a dog. He's always talking about them, and he loves seeing Rocky and the ones down at the Pet Place." He lifted his hands. "We always had a dog when I was growing up."

"Yes," she snapped, "and a supermom who, no doubt, could take care of it with one hand while cooking a meal with the other and folding laundry with one big toe."

Dan's shoulders fell. "I know my mother can be a little overbearing—"

"A little?" It was nearly a shriek. A muffled cry from the living room reminded Shelley to keep her voice down. "Never mind. I don't want to fight about your mother. I want to fight about the fact that you went out and brought home a dog that *I* will have to take care of, that *I* will have to walk and feed and pick up after. A dog that will chew the kids' toys, our shoes, the furniture, and anything else it can when I'm not looking."

"I'll help. You won't have to do it all."

"A dog," she went on, "that we'll have to feed and buy supplies for and take to the vet, when we can barely manage to cover our expenses already! And dogs don't train themselves. How can we pay for obedience classes? *What were you thinking?*"

Dan looked completely abashed. At the mention of their finances, he flushed a deep red. "Believe me, I know that I can't care for my family the way I'd like. I just wanted to do something nice for Aiden, but Legos and play sets are expensive. The puppy was free." He looked away. "I honestly hadn't thought about the cost of pet care."

His pleasure in the surprise had been replaced by a defeated expression, and Shelley felt a pang of guilt. But she still was too angry to relent. "I'm sorry to spoil your surprise," she said in a stiff tone, "but I know nothing about pets. And I don't have time to learn."

Dan didn't speak.

"Plus, I refuse to get sucked into the trap of giving the children something every time they ask—"

"Shelley, let's talk about this calmly for a minute—"

"*Calmly?*" She pointed to her own face. "This *is* calm. You want to see agitated? Dan, I want you to return that puppy."

"I can't." Dan looked even more miserable.

"What do you mean, you can't?"

"Greg won't take it back. He said if we didn't want her, we could give her away."

She stared at him, disturbed by the idea that a puppy was just an item to be passed around. "To whom?"

"I don't know. Look, I get it." He held up a hand. "I'll take her to the humane society. They'll find a good home for her."

"The humane society? What if she doesn't get adopted?" Shelley was aghast. "Besides, Aiden's already seen her."

"I can do it while he's napping this afternoon." Dan set his jaw. "We can tell him she ran away."

"No, we cannot." Shelley stood silently, feeling as if there was steam escaping from her ears. "I'll learn to deal with her."

"Are you sure?"

Shelley nodded slowly. "We might as well try to make it work, now that she's here."

"All right. Thank you, honey." Dan embraced her, but she held her arms stiffly at her sides.

*   *   *

Margaret finished placing the last painting on an easel in the window display she'd created for the gallery opening. An elegant array of handmade ceramic wares, baskets, delicate lamps, fabric art, and many other things covered the floor and lay across pieces of Allan's furniture. Several of her paintings and those of other artists were propped up, and one graced an easel near the back of the display, lending a pleasing vertical aspect to the arrangement.

Walking out to the street, Margaret studied everything with a critical eye. It was stunning, even by her exacting standards. The colors were complementary, and the varying textures invited one to come in and touch and explore.

"Are you thinking of buying something?" A middle-aged man stopped beside her on the sidewalk. The camera bag, ball cap, and sneakers screamed *Tourist!*

She smiled at him. "No, I was just looking at the full effect."

"Good."

"Pardon?" Surprised by the comment, she turned and looked at him.

The man grinned. "I'm glad you aren't going to buy, because I want that painting right back there." He gestured to the canvas she had just placed on the easel. "My wife has been looking for something for over our couch, and that would be perfect. The colors will be a great accent. But even better, it's extremely well done."

Margaret couldn't prevent the wide smile that felt like it spread from ear to ear. The watercolor had been one of her recent experiments in that medium, and she'd liked the end result. "Thank you. I'm the artist, as well as the owner of the Shearwater Gallery. Please come in and look around."

"I'd love to," the man announced, "just as soon as you put a 'sold' sticker on that watercolor."

As she wrapped the painting securely in brown paper and carefully padded a box for a ceramic vase the man also had decided to purchase, she wanted to pinch herself to make sure this was real. She'd just made a great sale to someone who had raved about her work! Thank heavens she had been building her personal inventory for a while. She'd have to go in the back and see what she had to replace the watercolor she'd just sold.

Walking home from work later, Margaret saw Shelley Bauer out in her yard with her tots and...a puppy!

"Hey there! Is that yours?" Margaret called.

Shelley smiled and helped Emma wave, and then she made a face. "Yes, she's ours. Dan got her from one of his co-workers."

Margaret let herself into Shelley's yard and knelt. The puppy ran to her, ears flopping and tongue lolling.

Aiden skidded to a stop beside her as she rubbed the puppy behind its ears and patted its belly when it rolled over. "Her name is Prize."

"Prize?" Margaret echoed.

"Yeah." Aiden nodded vigorously. "Because my daddy brought her home for a s'prise."

"Ahh." Margaret glanced up at Shelley.

Shelley nodded and adjusted Emma on her hip. "Only the real surprise was on me!"

"Oh dear." Margaret tried not to smile. "I remember one time Allan thought it would be a good idea for Adelaide to have a ferret to take care of. He said it would be a good learning experience."

"A ferret?" Shelley giggled, eyes wide. "Suddenly I'm feeling much better. So was it a learning experience?"

"You'd better believe it." Margaret nodded, her tone wry. "I learned that ferrets will steal anything they can carry, including socks, car keys, wallets, and cutlery."

Shelley's eyes grew wide. "Oh my," she said faintly.

"They can get into just about anything you think you've closed tightly. They need a lot—and I do mean a *lot*—of attention. And they can be quite nippy."

Shelley looked down at the puppy. "I'm growing fonder of you by the minute."

Margaret chuckled. "This puppy is precious. She looks like a beagle, but her coat's wavy. And so are her ears."

Shelley explained Prize's parentage. "I don't know anything about either breed. Dan says beagles will follow their noses anywhere, whatever that means." She sighed. "I just wish he'd given me a little warning, at the very least. I had to send him to the store for puppy food, a collar, and a leash. And when he got home, a few toys had sneaked into the bag too."

Margaret chuckled. She watched Aiden run giggling through the yard, the puppy gamboling along behind him. It wasn't nipping at his clothing but simply enjoying the exercise. "Looks like a nice puppy."

Shelley nodded. "She seems to be. Although the person who told Dan she was housebroken is going to get an earful the next time I see him!"

"Oh." Margaret ran her tongue over her teeth. It would be unkind to laugh. Especially since she knew the new pet was going to add to Shelley's stress level and workload. And thinking of workload reminded her of something she had been meaning to talk to Shelley about for a few days. "So how's work going for Dan?"

Shelley grimaced. "Not so great. His hours were cut even more. Now he's barely working twenty-five hours a week."

Margaret sucked in a breath of dismay. "Oh, Shelley, I'm so sorry."

The younger woman shifted baby Emma to her other hip. "We're soon going to get to the point where I'll have to take a job, whether Dan likes it or not." She sighed. "Although I can't imagine what type of job I could find that would pay me enough that it would make sense for me to hire a babysitter."

"Perhaps you could find something you could do during the hours Dan is home. Then you wouldn't need childcare."

Shelley chuckled. "And then *he'd* have to deal with the puppy."

The women shared a knowing smile.

"Actually," Margaret said, "I wanted to talk to you about work. Allan has been getting so many orders for his custom furniture from tourists that he is having trouble meeting the demand. And it's only June! The high season hasn't really begun yet."

"Wow. That's both a good and bad problem to have."

"It is. I was wondering..." Margaret hesitated. She would cut off her right arm before she would knowingly offend her young friend, and some people could be sensitive about money matters. "Do you think Dan would be interested in doing some work with Allan on the side? Diane was so impressed with Dan's attention to little details when he did the work for her last month, and I know he's quite proficient at woodwork already—"

Shelley reached out and touched her arm, stopping the flow of words. "Margaret, you are so thoughtful. Thank you for thinking of us." Her brow furrowed. "Dan's never done anything like that except as a hobby. I'm not sure..."

"Would you like to mention it to Dan? No pressure. If he's interested, just tell him to pop in and see Allan in the next few weeks."

"Okay." Shelley whipped her head around, as she heard a telling noise behind her. "Aiden Bauer, you do *not* open that gate. Ever."

Aiden jumped and turned away from the front gate with a distinctly guilty look. "I was just looking, Mommy."

Margaret laughed. "I suspect you hear that plenty of times every week."

"Every week? Try every day," Shelley said, grinning.

Chapter Six

Perhaps it would help to rework her outline. After dinner on Monday, Diane decided to spend a little more time working on her novel.

She had taken an online course on plotting, and the author who ran it had many good tips for helping a writer clarify plots. One suggestion had struck a chord with Diane, because she was a very visual learner. Didn't it stand to reason that she'd be able to plot more effectively if she had some visual cues?

Diane stacked several piles of index cards atop one another and carried them over to the floor near the fireplace, where there was the largest empty space. With meticulous care, she laid them all side by side: pink, blue, lavender, yellow, white, green, and orange. Then she laid each stack in chronological order with events in that plotline from first to last.

It felt good. It felt promising. She finally had decided she had to do something to break through whatever barrier was keeping her from moving forward with her story. If she couldn't get through it, she'd go around it until she found the right direction again.

Scanning the index cards, she found the one that detailed the first scene of her story, and she laid it in a separate location. Then she found several more "opening scenes" from other piles representing other subplots, and laid them carefully below it in the order she wanted them. Going back to the columns of colored cards, she repeated the process, trying to keep the events in her story moving forward in a logical fashion that still would surprise the reader occasionally. She found that using the colored cards gave her a strong visual assist: She could easily see when she'd lingered too long in one character's point of view.

An hour later, she had finished although something still didn't seem right. Before she began to number them so she could keep them in chronological order if they got separated, she shuffled several cards around to different spots. *Better? No. Hmm...* Again she moved cards around, and again she sat back on her heels and looked. She couldn't put her finger on it, but she knew something didn't work.

And then... a scrabble of claws was the only warning she got.

Diane glanced up in time to see a mouse scuttle along the floorboard and vanish beneath a door. "Aaah!" She leaped to her feet and shuddered. She wasn't afraid of mice— exactly—but she certainly didn't want one in her home.

Rocky, who was rapidly regaining strength and energy, tore after the mouse a moment later, limbs, ears, and tail flying in ten different directions.

"Rocky, stop!" she yelled, too rattled to think about any sensible obedience command.

But it was too late. The yellow dog tried to put on the brakes, but he reached the leading edge of the freshly organized index cards and skidded wildly. Cards and yellow dog hair flew every which way, and Rocky's solid body thumped against her with a force that knocked her right off her feet. Both of them went sprawling across the floor to fetch up against the ottoman in front of the easy chair.

Ooomph! Either the body-block from Rocky or the ottoman knocked the wind out of her, and she lay there for a moment, sucking in gasps of air. Rocky whimpered, and she automatically put out a hand and scratched behind his ears. "It's all right, buddy. I'm not mad at you...although I may send you to bed without any supper for destroying my hard work."

Slowly she sat up and looked around.

Index cards—*unnumbered* index cards—had settled in new locations all around the room. As dog hair drifted toward the floor, Diane pushed the weight of a warm, furry body off her legs and sat up. Rocky looked up at her with as sheepish an expression as she had ever seen on a canine face.

"Off." She needed only the one word, and the dog fell over himself to move. He started to take a step. Then he froze, and she realized he was trying to avoid stepping on any of the index cards.

Diane sighed. She hauled herself to her feet, dusted off her pants, and used the tip of her stockinged foot to haphazardly sweep index cards aside until there was a path to the back door. Opening the kitchen door, she pointed. "Out."

Rocky couldn't get out fast enough. Although he did cast her one more look that she would swear was "I'm sorry."

When he was gone, she turned and walked back into the living room to survey the carnage. She shook her head and slumped into the easy chair in dejection. All that work down the drain. Tomorrow, she supposed, she'd start over. And she'd have to get some mouse traps while she was at it.

★　　★　　★

"He's really cute." Adelaide Hoskins knelt to pet the Bauers' new puppy, who was nestled on Aiden's lap while Aiden watched television before his bath Monday evening. Adelaide had been nearly as thrilled as Aiden about the puppy, and she came over to pet Prize for a few minutes every time she got a chance.

"Yeah. She's sleeping," Aiden told her, as if that fact weren't obvious.

Prize stretched and hopped down off the couch...which she wasn't supposed to be on in the first place. Shelley hastened to open the back door and shoo her out, having learned the hard way that puppies are much like children when they wake from naps: They have to go. A few minutes later, Adelaide left.

Aiden came into the kitchen, frowning. "Where's my Prize?"

Shelley pointed to the bowl on the floor, and the puppy who was currently slurping down enough water to guarantee another trip outside. "Right here."

"Good girl." Aiden walked over and patted her on the back. Then he turned away. Prize instantly followed. They had had the puppy for only two nights, and already she and Aiden seemed to have formed a close bond.

So close, in fact, that their first two nights had been miserable. Both times, the puppy had cried and howled in her kennel on the porch. Dan finally couldn't take it the first night and had brought her kennel into the kitchen. But she'd continued to whine and whimper and bark— short, unhappy, somebody-come-and-get-me barks—for the rest of the night. Neither Shelley nor Dan had gotten a good night's rest, and Aiden had cried because he said Prize was sad. Emma was probably the only person in the house who'd gotten enough rest in the past couple of days.

"Aiden, bath time." Shelley went up the stairs, entered the bathroom, and began to fill the tub.

Aiden came romping in a moment later, Prize at his heels. He was dragging one of the dog toys Dan had purchased, and Prize was leaping at the already bedraggled thing. Each time Aiden dropped it, she pounced on it, shook it madly, and then dropped it and eyed it expectantly. Clearly she was waiting for it to move again. Finally, she would lie down in front of it and eye it mournfully until Aiden picked it up and waved it before her again.

"Prize needs a bath too," Aiden announced.

"No, Prize does not need a bath." Shelley shook her head. This argument was going to get old fast. They'd been having it each evening now. "And if you continue to fuss about it, Prize will have to go down to her kennel until your bath is over."

Aiden sized her up, clearly trying to determine whether he should say anything else. Finally, he started shucking off his clothes. "I have to hurry with my bath."

"I'll go as fast as I can," Shelley promised him.

She kept her word. Bath time and dressing in PJs was accomplished with record speed. Dan read Aiden a story, with Prize snuggled in Aiden's lap.

Shelley sighed as she paused in the doorway after laying Emma in her crib. There was going to be dog hair everywhere. She worked hard to keep the house clean, even if it wasn't always the most organized. And what about the smell? Wouldn't Aiden begin to smell like dog? She already had decided Prize really would have to have a bath. She smelled. She would *not*, however, be indoors in the bathtub. They could fill the little wading pool and bathe her. *They*, meaning Dan and Aiden.

Dan finished the story, and Aiden sleepily climbed under his covers. Prize began to settle down beside him.

"Oh no, you don't," Shelley said. "Say good night to Prize, honey, before Daddy takes her down to her own bed."

"But she doesn't want to be in a cage." Aiden's eyes filled with tears.

"She's getting used to it." Shelley smoothed his hair. "She will be all right, and you can get her out again first thing in the morning." She signaled Dan, and he gathered up the puppy.

"Good night, Aiden," Dan said in a squeaky voice. "I'll see you in the morning." He waved one of Prize's paws at Aiden.

The little boy giggled. "'Night, Prize. I'm sorry you can't sleep with me."

Dan carried Prize downstairs, and Shelley joined him in the living room when she had finished tucking Aiden in. Dan was sitting in his easy chair watching the big-screen television, and the puppy was fast asleep in his lap.

Shelley sighed. "Do you really have to have her on the furniture?"

"She's not on the furniture. She's on me." Dan smoothed a hand over the puppy's head.

"Our house is going to smell like dog." She flopped down in the armchair. Dan was watching a ball game as usual, so she couldn't even enjoy the television without going up to the one in their bedroom.

Dan looked over at her, a steady, patient look she finally couldn't take anymore.

"What?"

"There are worse things than having a dog in the house. It's made Aiden so happy."

"For the moment. In six months, he'll have moved on to some new love, and I'll be stuck taking care of her."

"I don't know about that. I had a dog when I was just a kid, and he was my best buddy. I fed him and bathed him and played *stick* with him for thirteen years. The day he died was the worst day of my life up to that point."

Shelley stared at her husband. "I've never heard that story before."

Dan smiled ruefully. "Well, we haven't exactly had tons of time to share conversation that isn't related to kids or money lately."

"I know." She eyed the puppy. "Do you think she'll sleep tonight?"

"I don't know. She really seems to hate being down here alone. Maybe we should put her carrier in Aiden's room. That would be a compromise, wouldn't it?"

"No." Shelley was not going to yield on that point. Dogs did *not* belong in bedrooms. "I don't want that dog sleeping in Aiden's room. Everything in here is going to smell as it is."

"No, it's not. We'll bathe her. And we don't have to let her on the furniture."

She eyed the spot where Prize was, at that moment, already on the furniture, and she gave Dan an *Oh, really?* look. "Aiden's had her on the couch with him too."

"So we'll tell him she can't get on the couch, but he can sit with her on the floor if he likes."

"Oh." She hadn't thought of that approach. "Good idea." It seemed so simple. "Do you want some citrus pinwheel cookies? I tried a new recipe today."

Dan's eyes lit up. "That sounds good. I'd love some."

Shelley went into the kitchen. She heard a little thump as the puppy jumped down from Dan's chair and padded straight to her water bowl. "Not too much," Shelley cautioned. "A lot of liquid before bedtime is no better for puppies than it is for little boys."

She got down the tin of cookies she'd made and arranged a few on a plate for Dan, along with a glass of iced mint tea, which she knew he loved. Remembering that the cookie jar was empty, she went to the far counter and picked it up. If she washed it out, she could put some of the cookies in there for Aiden and Adelaide to find tomorrow.

As she turned toward the sink, a small, furry body scampered between her feet, startling her and knocking her off balance. Shelley gave a small screech of surprise, bobbling the cookie jar as she tried to regain her balance. Prize yelped and scrambled away. Before Shelley's horrified gaze, the beautiful lid of her lighthouse cookie jar slid off. It hit the floor with a thunk, breaking into two pieces.

"Oh no!" Shelley knelt and set down the jar, staring helplessly at the broken lid.

Dan rushed into the kitchen. "Honey, are you okay? What happened?"

"Your dog is what happened!" Shelley plunked down on her bottom, as hot tears began to roll down her cheeks. "She tripped me, and I broke the cookie jar." She cried harder, as she remembered the little shop in Michigan where they'd purchased it. "You got me this when we were on our honeymoon."

Dan knelt and picked up the pieces of the lid. Examining them, he said, "It didn't shatter. This is a clean break. I think I can repair this so you won't even see it."

Whimpering, the puppy came to stand beside him, eyeing Shelley. Prize's tail was down, her face clearly anxious. She shied back a few steps, sinking to her belly.

"She didn't mean to do it." Dan's voice was gentle. "It was an accident. I'm just thankful it wasn't worse. You could have been hurt."

"I wasn't, but what if I were Aiden?"

"If you were Aiden, you wouldn't have been carrying the cookie jar, *and* you wouldn't have nearly as far to fall." He set the cookie jar and the pieces of the lid up on the counter and put his arms around her. "Come on. Let me help you up."

Shelley put her arms around his neck, letting him lift her to her feet. He rubbed her back and then reached around her for the tissue box in the kitchen drawer and offered her one.

"Thank you." She felt so defeated, and she didn't really know why. It was just a cookie jar, she told herself. She glanced down at the puppy, who was still lying on the floor as if she knew she were in disgrace. "Is she okay?"

"Yes. It just scared her." Dan bent and picked up the puppy, who still looked frightened. His big hands stroked over the soft fur and gently trailed over one ear. "I'll take her out and then put her in her kennel for the night."

Shelley blew her nose. Tossing the tissue in the trash, she took a deep, steadying breath. Deliberately turning away from her damaged cookie jar, she washed and dried her hands. Then she picked up Dan's snack and took it into the living room, where she set it beside his chair and took a seat. The television was on, but she didn't really see the program. *Baseball. Yuck.*

Dan came in a moment later. Instead of sitting in his easy chair, he sat beside her and put his arm around her. "I'm sorry." He dropped a kiss on her hair. "You were right. A puppy was a lousy idea."

She sighed. "It wasn't totally lousy. It's made Aiden very happy. And you were right. We can't afford to give him many things, and this was something you knew he would love."

"Yeah, but with what she's going to cost us in total expenses, it seems like saving up for a big set of Legos would have been a lot smarter." He sounded so woebegone that she had to chuckle a little.

"You're right. But you also were right about something else."

"What's that?"

"You had a dog for thirteen years. Giving the kids something like that is beyond price."

"Maybe, but not at the expense of your happiness." He heaved a sigh. "I'm sorry about the cookie jar."

"I'm sorry too," she whispered, ducking her head and laying her forehead against his chest. "I wasn't always such a shrew. I used to be happy and fun, remember?"

Dan's chest moved, as he chuckled. "You're not a shrew, and you're still happy and fun a lot of the time." He tipped her chin up and kissed her. "You're still the person I want to spend my life with. And I definitely deserve to be hit over the head for being so obtuse. I wasn't thinking at all about the money, just about Aiden's face when he saw that puppy."

"He was over the moon," she said, smiling a little.

"Thrilled. But I apologize again for not discussing it with you first. My dad used to surprise us kids all the time, and nothing ever seemed to faze Mom."

The warmth and closeness she'd been feeling vanished. *Of course not,* Shelley thought. *Supermom.* But she didn't say it aloud. Sliding out from under Dan's arm, she stood and gathered up a handful of toys that had been dragged down from Aiden's room during the day. "I'm heading to bed," she said. "Emma gets up so early that it's hard to stay up late anymore."

CHAPTER SEVEN

On Saturday morning, Beverly made her father a hot breakfast. Afterward, he went into the living room to watch the morning news. She carried a cup of tea to him and then headed upstairs to start putting the attic to rights.

She sighed, surveying all the junk in the hallway. He never had remembered what he'd been searching for. She didn't have the heart to bring it up again, since knowing he'd forgotten something upset him.

As she picked up old photo albums, hatboxes, and ancient Christmas decorations, she thought again about her father living here alone. It seemed it could rapidly become a significant problem. Even if she visited every weekend, which really hadn't been her plan, he still had five whole days to muddle through. For the first time, glancing around at the mess, she realized just how much trouble he could get into on his own.

Several hours later, someone knocked on the front door. She needed to take a break anyhow, so she went down the stairs. Her father must not have heard the knock, since she could still hear the television blaring in the living room.

When she tugged opened the door, she found Diane standing there, wrapped plate in hand.

"Beverly! What a nice surprise. I didn't realize you were going to be here this weekend." Diane stepped forward and hugged her before Beverly could move out of the way. "These are Neapolitan cookies for your dad. I remembered he loved them at my open house."

Beverly forced a smile, although Diane's eager-beaver friendliness made her want to take a step backward. "He would have licked the plate if he'd thought no one would notice. Would you like to come in?"

"Sure."

"Daddy's in the living room. Go right on in. I'll put some of these on a plate."

Beverly took the cookies to the kitchen and arranged them on a pretty luncheon plate of pink Depression glass with apple blossoms on it. There was a whole set of the stuff that her mother had gotten from *her* mother. Beverly hadn't thought about it in years, but she loved those plates. The way the pink in the cookies complemented the plate pleased her eye. Beverly picked them up and took them to the living room.

Her father and Diane were chatting animatedly. Beverly heard him say something about "Twain's best work," and Diane laughed. Her reply was muffled, but Beverly could swear she'd said something about frogs.

Shaking her head, she decided she'd better have her own hearing checked. "Father," she said as she entered the room. "Look what Diane brought."

"Oh ho! My favorites." Her father's eyes twinkled as he winked at Diane. "I guess you noticed who cleaned your cookie plate at the party."

Diane laughed. "I'm glad you enjoyed them."

Beverly sat quietly with a cookie, watching her father and Diane chat easily about writing and life in Marble Cove. How nice that there was someone close by who cared enough to check in on him. Guilt rose, almost choking her. She should be taking better care of her father. If only she could afford to move back to Marble Cove.

When Diane got up to take her leave, Beverly debated with herself for a moment. Then, shuffling aside her desire for solitude, she beckoned Diane upstairs. "Come up here for a minute."

Diane followed, stopping at the top to exclaim, "Holy cow. Did we have a tornado?"

Beverly sighed. "My father was the only tornado around these parts, I'm afraid."

"What was he doing?" Diane picked her way through some of the stacks and boxes to peer up the attic steps.

"Looking for something," Beverly reported. "He tore open boxes and scattered things everywhere. All this is stuff I had gone through and organized after my mother passed."

"Wow." Diane shook her head. "I guess whatever it was he was hunting for was important."

"I don't know." Beverly spread her hands. "He can't remember what he was looking for."

"Are you kidding?" Diane's eyes went wide as she looked around again.

"I wish I were." Beverly ran a hand through her dark hair, dragging it back from her face. "Have you noticed if he seems confused lately, or if he's having trouble remembering things?"

Diane shook her head, her eyes sympathetic. "I see him nearly every day when I walk Rocky, but I rarely stop and chat. And I don't know him well enough to determine if his memory is impaired or not. There's nothing obvious to me. He certainly doesn't have trouble recalling literary tidbits."

"My mother used to tell people he loved his books as much as he loved her. Not possible, of course. They were incredibly devoted." The memory was bittersweet. She paused, looking back into her past. "When I married, I was certain I would have that kind of lifelong connection to someone."

"But...?" Diane prompted when Beverly fell silent.

Beverly shrugged. "But it didn't work out that way."

"I'm sorry." Diane looked like she understood.

There was a moment of awkward silence.

"Well," Diane said, "I should run along. I have to make a home visit to a church member, and then I promised Margaret I'd come in this weekend."

"So you're still helping Margaret?"

Diane nodded. "The gallery opening was moved to the ninth, and there's a lot to do. We've been receiving a great many pieces from other artists."

"The ninth! But that's next Thursday."

Diane nodded.

"Darn it. I was hoping to attend." Beverly felt inordinately disappointed. "Perhaps I'll drop by tomorrow and see how it's going. I could lend a hand for a bit." And perhaps she would check her schedule and see if there was any way she could work a half day on Thursday the ninth and also take Friday off, so she could come down for Margaret's big debut. She'd been there for the initial launch, and she felt surprisingly invested in the older woman's business venture.

"That would be great!" Diane sent her a genuine smile. She glanced at her watch. "And now I really must go. Good to see you."

"You too. Thanks for bringing Father the cookies. See you tomorrow."

As Beverly closed the door again, she reflected that only a fool would set aside the friendship Diane offered. She would go over to the gallery tomorrow afternoon and make an effort to be more friendly. It wasn't that she didn't like Diane, Margaret, and Shelley. But...she wasn't used to sharing confidences, dreams, and disappointments with others.

And there were some things she didn't want to share with anyone. Ever. No matter how close a friendship developed. Some things were just not meant to be told.

*   *   *

On Sunday afternoon, Margaret was kneeling in front of a packing box, carefully unwrapping a shipment of stunning pottery with a lavender and mint design and iridescent glaze from an artist down in New Haven, when Diane and Shelley came through the door.

"Well, hello." She rose from her knees and stretched, feeling her muscles protest after being compacted into such an uncomfortable position. "What are you two up to?"

"We came to help," Shelley announced.

"But you were here yesterday." Margaret directed the statement at Diane. "I don't want the gallery to take over your life."

"It won't," Diane assured her. "But Shelley and I would like to help with the opening, and helping you clean and get organized is something we can handle."

"I can't paint," Shelley said. She picked up the broom behind the door. "But I can clean."

"And you can bake," Margaret said. "Boy, can you bake!"

Diane grinned, as she took the utility knife to the tape securing yet another carton. "I can— Beverly! Hi!"

The other two women turned and smiled as Beverly came through the door. "I heard there might be a work party here today."

"You heard right." Margaret beckoned her in, delighted to see her. "I didn't know you were coming this weekend."

"It was sort of a sudden decision." Beverly made a wry face. "And a wise one. I've realized that my dad is slipping a little."

Margaret winced. "Oh, I'm sorry. I didn't realize."

"I didn't either." Beverly shrugged. "So what can I do?"

Seeing that her friend didn't want to discuss it further, Margaret pushed a polishing cloth into her hands with a grin. "Here. You can go over the frames for fingerprints."

All four of them got to work, but after a moment, Diane paused and smacked herself in the forehead. "Oh my gosh, I cannot believe I forgot to tell any of you—I saw the light again Friday night!"

"What?"

"You did?"

"What happened?"

Diane nodded. "I took Rocky for a walk on the beach Friday evening. And just like before, a flash of light shot out across the water. There was a young couple nearby who both saw it too. And so did Ev—Dr. Spangler."

"Dr. *Leo* Spangler?" Margaret's curiosity was aroused. The vet, a widower in his midfifties, was known to be a kind and thoughtful person. "Was he walking with you?"

"No." Diane shifted from foot to foot, and red crests appeared on her cheekbones. "He was just…there. With his dog. Who was playing with Rocky." She cleared her throat. "Anyway, I asked all of them—the people, not the dogs—if they saw anything in the water. We all looked but didn't see a thing." She pursed her lips. "And here's something weird. Before, I felt a sense of urgency. This time, I didn't feel anything."

"I know what you mean." Margaret remembered the insistent feeling she'd experienced. "Before we rescued that boy, I felt compelled to look out over the water."

"Right!" Shelley exclaimed. "Compelled. That's exactly the right word. I felt the same way." She cleared her throat. "I have something to share about the lighthouse too. This isn't exactly the same thing, but Wednesday at dusk I saw something moving near the base of the lighthouse. I could swear it was a person."

"That's not really that surprising," Beverly said. "More and more tourists are arriving each week."

Diane looked thoughtful. "Yes, but it's not easy to get out there, and what would a tourist be doing skulking around there at dusk, anyway?"

"Was there a light then?" Margaret asked.

Shelley shook her head. "That's why I thought it was strange. Who would go out there when it's getting dark without a light?"

"Again," Beverly said, "odd, but not really so extraordinary. I imagine someone was just fooling around."

"Going back to Friday night," Diane said, "I've been asking around, but no one has reported any extraordinary events, rescues, or anything like that. Have any of you heard of any miracles like ours?"

Margaret and Shelley shook their heads. Beverly said, "I haven't been here."

"You know," Shelley said, "since I married Dan and moved here, I have seen lights several times, and so have other people. And sometimes after those sightings, something miraculous happens. Someone being saved from the water or living through a bad accident, things like that. Last year, Dan's folks' neighbor fell off his ladder in January while he was taking down Christmas lights. He might have frozen to death if someone hadn't walked around to the back of his house trying to get a better look at an unexplained light coming from the lighthouse."

"I remember that!" Margaret said. She felt a shiver work its way up her spine to lift the fine hairs at the back of her neck. "And before that, a woman fell off the cliff road, and her boyfriend fell too when he tried to rescue her. A light flashed several times right at the spot where they'd fallen, and when the sheriff drove up to investigate, thinking it was smugglers, he found them."

"Neither one of them had any sort of flashlight with them," Shelley said. "The woman lost her backpack when she fell, and his was at the top of the cliff. It's what led the sheriff to look over the edge."

"There have been other things like that over the years," Margaret told them. "I'm sure some of them are documented in local writings and the newspaper."

Diane looked awed. "So, finding Rocky and saving that swimmer aren't the first miracles to happen near the lighthouse!"

Beverly cleared her throat. "I hate to be the voice of reason, but the more I think about it, the more I've realized that maybe Fred Little is right. Maybe we're using the word *miracle* too loosely. It was certainly strange, but a miracle?"

"What would you define as a miracle?" Diane didn't sound confrontational, just puzzled.

Beverly shrugged. "I probably would have to hear the voice of God saying, 'Go save that guy!' to consider it a miracle."

Shelley chuckled. "You do have high expectations, don't you?"

"I just don't think seeing some lights before a rescue happens qualifies as a miracle," Beverly said. "They could be totally unrelated. Just because a person thinks something miraculous happened to them doesn't automatically mean they were saved for some special reason."

"I agree that the word should be used sparingly," Diane said. "But something is miraculous about the lighthouse. I just know it."

"How? How do you know?"

Diane hesitated. "I can't explain why I'm so sure. But I'm certain these things aren't just coincidental. I feel it deep within myself. If that sounds all woo-woo and mystical and makes me weird, so be it."

"It doesn't make you weird," Shelley said. "Mystical and woo-woo maybe, but we can live with that."

CHAPTER EIGHT

Shelley fed the children and the puppy earlier than normal on the day of Margaret's grand opening. Dan had promised to be home by five so she could go down to the gallery to lend a hand. But five o'clock arrived and passed with no sign of Dan. She tried his cell phone twice, but he didn't answer, and she began to get a bit worried. That wasn't like him. He might be late, but he was too considerate to leave her high and dry.

Just as she was about to try his cell again, Dan's truck pulled into the driveway at five-twenty. He came striding into the house, saying, "I'm sorry. The boss called me into the office, and I couldn't get away any faster."

"What did he want?" Shelley was instantly filled with dread. They both lived in fear that Dan might lose his job completely.

Dan looked utterly dispirited. "They're cutting everyone's hours again. I'm only losing a few, but..." He shook his head.

Shelley sighed. "I'm sorry, honey. Try not to worry. Something will work out." She thought fleetingly of what Margaret had said about Allan needing help, but now wasn't the time to get into that. "I have to go. I'm really sorry, but I promised Marg—"

"It's all right." He pulled her to him and pressed a quick kiss to her lips. "Wish Margaret good luck for me. Hope your food is a big hit."

She managed a smile. "Thanks. Me too." She grabbed her handbag and checked one last time to be sure no baby food or other unmentionable substance was decorating her flowered sundress and lacy crocheted cardigan. All good.

She left the house and slipped into the used minivan that had replaced her car after it had been totaled in an accident last month. She shivered, thinking once again of the divine protection that day. "Thank You again, dear Lord," she whispered.

Outside the gallery, she hefted one of the trays of cookies she had stacked in the back of the van and headed for the front door.

"Shelley's here!" Allan called, opening the door as she approached. He rubbed his hands together. "And I smell cookies."

Shelley, Allan, and Diane carried in the cookies and hors d'oeuvres she had made. Quickly, she plugged in her fondue pot and placed a block of chocolate in it to melt while she arranged the other plates and platters. Diane had made several items as well, and Shelley felt pleased as she stood back and viewed the display.

"It looks lovely." Margaret stepped up beside Shelley and drew her into a hug. "Thank you so much."

"You're welcome so much." Shelley glanced at her watch. "Only ten minutes to go. What else needs to be done?"

Margaret shrugged. "I think we're in pretty good shape." Her daughter Adelaide was happily wielding a broom on the sidewalk in front of the store, and Allan appeared to be double-checking to see that everything had price tags attached discreetly.

The door opened, and Margaret tensed. "I'm sorry, but we're not quite o— Beverly!"

"What are you doing here?" Shelley blurted. "It's only Thursday."

Beverly smiled. "I couldn't miss the grand opening, could I?" She held out a fistful of helium balloons she'd carried in. "I thought we could attach them to the sign out front."

"Thank you so much for coming." Margaret looked as if she was on the verge of tears.

"That's a great idea." Diane wrapped an arm around Beverly affectionately. "Glad you're here."

Shelley noticed that Beverly stiffened a bit under Diane's hug. "I'll help with the balloons," Shelley said, smiling. As she and Beverly walked outside, she said, "This means a lot to Margaret that you came."

Beverly shrugged. "I just thought it might be nice to be here."

They tied the balloons to the sign and went back inside. Just a few minutes now until Margaret turned the "Closed" sign to "Open" and propped the door wide.

"Okay, everybody, we're ready. Thank you all so much for your help and for your support." Margaret took a deep breath. "Diane, you're keeping an eye on the food, right? Addie, honey, you help Diane with anything she needs. Shelley, you know most of the locals, so would you meet and greet again?"

Shelley nodded. "Of course."

"The rest of us will circulate, meet and greet, and answer questions. And if anybody says anything bad about my work…"

Diane hitched her thumb toward the door. "Out they go on their keisters."

Everyone laughed, and Margaret took one last deep breath.

Twenty minutes later, it was Beverly who made the first sale of the evening—one of Allan's lovely little tables. She was especially good at finding just what a customer was looking for. By the time the first hour had passed, several pieces had been sold, and the gallery was filled with guests.

Shelley was delighted on Margaret's behalf. And more than a little touched to see that a number of other downtown merchants had put in an appearance to publicly welcome Margaret.

Margaret checked in with Diane several times, and Shelley overheard Diane reporting that she'd heard many wonderful comments about the art while people lingered over the food.

"And I heard a whole bunch of comments about the food itself," Margaret said, turning to Shelley. "They talked about what terrific food we're serving. In fact, two people have already asked me for the name of my caterer!"

Shelley laughed. "I wish."

Diane and Beverly came up beside them in time to hear the last exchange. Diane gave Shelley a searching look. "Do you really?"

Shelley was about to answer when Margaret murmured, "Hottie alert at two o'clock."

Shelley turned to look, and she saw the local vet standing in profile, studying a painting. Her eyebrows rose. He was a cutie, no doubt, but he was kind of old... But then again, Margaret had close to forty years on her, and Diane had twenty, maybe. So perhaps the two of them would find him attractive.

Beverly... well, she wasn't so sure of Beverly's age. Her figure and attractive face made her look quite youthful, but close up, Shelley could see fine lines, particularly when Beverly smiled.

"Who is that?" Diane gestured to a woman in a navy suit with white piping who carried a little notepad and was speaking to some of the guests. The suit was quite smart, but the white sneakers the woman wore spoiled the effect.

Beverly sniffed. "Someone with no fashion sense."

"That's Harriet Malcolm. She works for the local paper," Margaret told them. "She does the social news and writes about art and literature." She looked surprised. "I guess Harriet's here to critique my work. What do you think she's going to say?"

"That it's terrific," Shelley said firmly.

"I hope so. She has a reputation for being awfully critical."

"She may just be here to report on the opening in general," Beverly said. "And even if she does critique it, she's going to say it's great. Why, you've sold four paintings already, and we have two hours yet to go!"

Margaret smiled, but she still looked anxious.

"Hey, I just realized something." Diane gestured around them. "This is the perfect opportunity to ask if anything unusual occurred in town last Friday evening. I've asked a few people this week, but no one's mentioned anything so far."

Beverly crossed her arms. "And how do you propose we do this? Just walk up and ask if they saved anyone's life recently?"

"I think if anything like that had happened, we'd have heard about it," said Margaret, always a peacemaker. "Working downtown like this, I usually get the scoop from someone."

"So there probably is no scoop," Shelley said.

"Maybe not. But we won't know unless we ask." Diane turned her back and sailed off to the food tables.

Beverly sighed. "She's determined to find miracles here, there, and everywhere."

"You might be too," Margaret said gently, "if you'd been diagnosed with terminal cancer and then suddenly learned you were cancer-free or had some equally miraculous event occur."

Beverly's shoulders sagged a little. "You would think so."

She sounded so forlorn that Shelley experienced a ridiculously maternal instinct, even though she was the youngest of the group. "Come on," Shelley said, guiding Beverly toward the back of the room. "Diane could use some help refilling the platters on that small oak table."

But as the pair started across the room, Harriet Malcolm stepped right into their path. Shelley gave Beverly's arm a quick squeeze, inclining her head. Getting the silent message, Beverly continued on.

Shelley stopped beside the sneaker-clad woman, who was scowling up at one of Margaret's largest seascapes. "Isn't that lovely?" Shelley asked brightly. Maybe she could figure out how Harriet felt about Margaret's painting.

"*Hmm.*" Harriet didn't agree or disagree.

Shelley tried again. "I'm a big fan of seascapes. Especially ones with lighthouses."

The woman snorted. "You can find those in every art gallery from the Florida Keys to the tip of Maine. I prefer different things. Unique things. Artists with unlimited imagination."

"I think it takes a lot of imagination and skill to paint at all." Shelley forced a chuckle. "I'm not artistic in any way. Are you?" She extended her hand. "I'm Shelley Bauer."

"Harriet Malcolm." The art critic gave her hand one quick, limp shake and then let her hand slide away like a wet dishrag. "I'm not artistically inclined in the traditional sense," she said. "My gift is more along the lines of being able to discern truly great pieces of art."

Eyebrows rising, Shelley asked, "But how do we know what's great? I mean, you might love a piece, and I might prefer something else."

Harriet sniffed. "Perhaps, but my opinions have been honed over several decades of viewing many, many pieces."

Shelley felt out of her depth. "I know what I like."

"Most have simple tastes. It's not what I tend to prefer," Harriet said, before she walked away.

Shelley headed for the food tables, where she recounted the exchange.

"She said what?" Diane's eyebrows snapped together.

"I bet most people know what they like, and they don't really care if it's a masterpiece or not," Shelley said, the pitch of her voice rising two octaves.

"Exactly." Diane frowned. "Love of art is in the eye of the beholder. Your opinion is as important as anyone else's." She sighed. "I hope that's not representative of what that woman will say about Margaret's work." But now seeds of worry had been planted, and Shelley could see Diane wasn't going to forget it any more than she would.

The rest of the evening passed quicker than a finger snap. Shelley wasn't sure how many people had jammed into the gallery, but it was a far larger crowd than the Shearwater's unofficial opening last month.

As Margaret locked the door behind the very last guest-turned-customer, she pivoted around and leaned against it with an exaggerated sigh. "Whew! Am I ever glad I don't have to have a grand opening again. That was exhausting."

Shelley was helping Diane pick up leftover dishes and napkins. She pointed to the food table. "It looks like a cloud of locusts descended."

Diane laughed. "That's how it felt too. Your food was a huge hit."

"The whole evening was a huge hit," Beverly declared. "I don't know how many things we sold, Margaret, but you've got a lot of bare spots on your walls and display tables."

Margaret smiled. "And it would never have come together without all of you. Thank you so much."

"No thanks needed," Diane told her. "That's what friends are for."

*　　*　　*

On Sunday morning, Dan left early on a day fishing trip with his brothers, so Shelley fed both children and cleaned up the kitchen before dressing them and herself for church.

As she scrambled around trying to pack a diaper bag and another bag with enough things to amuse Aiden, she automatically reached for the desk drawer and withdrew an offering envelope. Their church kept track of monetary donations with the envelope system.

Perching on the chair at the desk, she reached for the checkbook and dashed off their usual check to the church. But her fingers slowed as she began to write her signature. Laying down her pen, she gave a resigned sigh and drew from the drawer the budget sheet for the week.

Unfortunately, she'd printed it at the end of the previous month...before Dan had brought the puppy home. She'd saved a little extra on groceries last month, and the money had gone to purchase the leash, collar, and food Prize needed. This month, she didn't expect to be so lucky. And that meant she had to see how they could tighten their belts to feed this new mouth.

She sighed as she reviewed the columns of numbers, though she knew them by heart. It had been over a week since Margaret had mentioned Dan working for Allan, and she had yet to mention it to Dan. Partly because she was so tired by the end of the day when they had time to talk that she forgot, but partly because Dan might think she'd been talking to the neighbors about money problems, and she knew that would upset him. But she was going to have to tell him.

Slowly she took the check she had just partially written and tore it in half. Although she really preferred giving on a weekly basis, it appeared that Light the Way Chapel was going to have to wait until the end of June to receive her contribution. Abandoning her efforts, Shelley latched the children into their car seats and headed for church.

She loved attending Light the Way. Dan's whole family went to another church and had done so for generations, but Shelley hadn't felt comfortable in a staid congregation with few young families to whom she wasn't related. Light the Way had caught her eye because of her affinity for lighthouses, but it had kept her attention and interest because the small congregation had a large percentage of people her age with children, and the two pastors were young and dynamic. Dan attended with her infrequently. He seemed to enjoy it, but Shelley suspected he felt guilty about not going to his family's church.

She arrived at the church parking lot and got the kids inside.

"Hi, Shelley." Wanda Bacon, a young mother she knew from her class, stopped to greet her. "We miss seeing you and Dan at Sunday School."

"I miss it too. Dan's schedule changed. He works every Sunday morning now. Well, except this time, but he's fishing with his brothers."

Wanda smiled. "You can still come to class on your own. We'll save a seat for you if you let us know you're coming."

"Thanks, Wanda. I'll remember that. It's mostly a time issue. Me trying to get anywhere on time with two small children." She and Wanda shared a laugh of agreement as they parted. Shelley did appreciate the thought, but there was nothing enjoyable about walking into a room full of people alone.

"Hey, Shelley." Lee Waters, who owned the Pet Place, greeted her and then stooped to give Aiden a high-five. "How you doin', buddy?"

"Good!" Aiden reared back and gave Lee a mighty smack in the palm, and Lee pretended to be staggered by Aiden's strength, which made the little boy giggle uncontrollably.

"Are you visiting? Welcome to Light the Way," Shelley said.

Lee nodded. "My sister's little girl is singing in the junior choir today, and I didn't want to miss it." He grinned. "So you got a puppy, eh?"

She nodded, forcing herself to show some enthusiasm. "She and Aiden have become inseparable. In fact, she was howling in her kennel when we left."

Lee grinned. "She'll settle down soon, once she realizes howling isn't going to get her what she wants."

"I hope so," Shelley said. "She does it at night, too, when Aiden goes to bed and Dan puts her in her kennel."

Lee nodded. "I imagine this is the first time she's ever had to sleep alone. Until you got her, she probably was sleeping with her brothers and sisters and mommy."

Instant sympathy—and guilt—squeezed Shelley's heart. "I never thought of that. Poor little thing."

Lee nodded. "Dogs are pack animals. They don't much like being alone. It always breaks my heart when I see a dog tied outside all alone. Why would you get a dog if you're just going to tie it out, you know?"

Shelley wasn't sure if the question required an answer. She didn't want the dog in the house, and yet it seemed there was no way they could be good dog owners unless she let it come inside. Or unless they got more four-legged companions—which was *not* an option. She sighed inwardly, wishing for at least the one-hundredth time that Dan had never brought home that puppy.

Lee smiled. "Sorry. I get a little hot under the collar on that topic. What did you name your dog?"

"Prize." Shelley explained the name.

Lee grinned. "I like originality. Guess you're going to be needing dog food and some other stuff."

"Dan already got her a leash and a collar." Shelley shifted Emma, who was growing heavy. She wanted to take her to the nursery for infants and toddlers before the service started.

"I meant like toys and bedding, stuff like that. Maybe a jacket for her wintertime walks. You come see me whenever you're ready, and I'll bargain with Aiden so you get a good deal."

Shelley smiled, although the thought of spending even more money on the puppy made her cringe. How were they going to manage it?

That afternoon, while both children were napping, Shelley sat down at the computer and pulled up the online version of the *Marble Cove Courier*, the local paper. It was published biweekly on Mondays and Thursdays from Memorial Day to Labor Day, and the rest of the year just once a week, in accordance with the tourist trade that descended upon the town during the summer months. She clicked on the *classifieds* link and began to scan the employment opportunities. She didn't want to work, but she might not have a choice.

Then she remembered Margaret's words about Allan's furniture business. She had to talk to Dan about that.

Chapter Nine

Diane was up bright and early on Monday morning. Today was the first edition of the *Marble Cove Courier* to come out since Margaret's opening. Diane was determined to hurry out and get a copy hot off the press. She couldn't wait to see what the paper said.

Rocky was delighted that they were going to go for a walk first thing in the morning rather than just a quick trip outside. He pranced along at her side, leaving no doubt that he was pleased.

The Cove, a charming coffee shop on Main Street, had a newspaper stand right outside the door. Diane fed in the coins and, when the latched door opened, slid out a copy of the paper. There was nothing on the front page, which didn't really surprise her. She was a little surprised to see that there still was no mention of any accident or water incident or *anything* to explain the light she'd seen the other night.

It was too breezy to try to open the paper on the street, so she tucked it beneath her arm and headed home. As she walked along Newport Avenue toward her cottage, she saw Shelley outside her home heading up the street. This early, her children probably were still sleeping.

"Hey, neighbor," Diane called. "Where are you off to so early?"

"Downtown." Shelley caught a lock of her long blonde hair and shoved it carelessly behind her ear. "I want to see what the paper says about the gallery opening. We stopped having it delivered at the end of the month, and I hate not getting the morning news. Dan's still home with the kids, so I told him I'd hurry."

Diane grinned. "Your trip may be shorter than he thinks." She displayed the newspaper she had tucked beneath her arm. "Want to come in for coffee, and we'll read it together?"

Shelley glanced over her shoulder at her home with a mischievous grin. "Why not? Dan expects me to be gone for fifteen minutes or so anyway."

They were almost to Diane's door when Diane heard someone call her name. Turning, she saw it was Margaret. "Good morning. Want to join us for coffee?"

Margaret came hurrying along the sidewalk. She was already dressed for the gallery in a rose-colored sweater that matched the flowers splashed across her flowing printed skirt. "I saw you had a paper," she said. "Does it say anything about my opening?"

"I don't know yet. I haven't looked at it." Which was mostly true. "Come on in, and we'll see."

The three women turned into Diane's brick walkway and went into the house.

Diane got down three mugs. Filling one that displayed a lighthouse on it first, she handed it to Shelley.

"Thanks." Shelley wrapped her hands around the warm mug.

"Have you talked to Dan about working with Allan?" Margaret asked her.

Shelley shook her head. "I keep forgetting. I promise I will, though. Let's look at the paper." She scanned the front page and made a moue of disappointment. "I thought maybe your grand opening would be the lead story. I mean, it's not every day a new business opens in Marble Cove."

Diane laid the paper on the table. As she peeled off her light jacket, Margaret grabbed it and began to flip through it.

"Nothing, nothing, nothing...Here we go! 'Shearwater Gallery Opens.'" She sniffed. "Couldn't they have come up with a title with a little more pizzazz?"

"They need a good journalist," Shelley said to Diane, tongue in cheek.

"Not me," Diane said absently. She was trying to see the article over Margaret's shoulder when she realized Margaret's body had grown stiff. "What's it say?"

Margaret sucked in a breath. "She didn't like my work."

"What?" Shelley's eyes widened in alarm.

Margaret began to read. "While Hoskins has some unique selections of local artwork in the gallery, her own efforts are very much the typical fare served up and down the East Coast."

"What?" Shelley sounded outraged. "That horrible woman had her mind made up before she ever walked in."

"What do you mean?" Diane asked.

Shelley again recounted her brief conversation with Harriet Malcolm at the opening. "She came in there prepared not to like your work."

Diane was reading the rest of the review. "'She lacks seriousness and depth'? Harriet Malcolm wouldn't know depth if someone dropped her in a quarry." She felt sick. That rotten little art critic—if that's what she really was—had gone out of her way to hammer Margaret's work.

"Oh, Margaret, I'm so sorry." Shelley placed a hand on Margaret's shoulder. "You know she's wrong, don't you? Think about all the paintings people bought and the nice things your customers said. Doesn't that mean more than one silly woman in sneakers?"

Margaret was sitting motionless at Diane's table, hands lying loosely on the newspaper. She didn't appear to have heard her friends' words.

"Your work is wonderful," Shelley said. "Just look at how much of it sold. Obviously she doesn't know what she's talking about."

Finally Margaret lifted her head, and Diane could see the devastation the review had inflicted. "She must." Margaret's voice was flat and dull, completely unlike anything Diane had ever heard from her. "She's got her own column in the paper."

Diane crossed her arms. "I'm writing a letter to the editor today."

"No. Don't." Margaret looked up at her, and Diane's heart squeezed at her friend's bleak expression. "Acknowledging it will just give her another opportunity to say more nasty things." She squared her shoulders. "Even if she didn't like me, she said some nice things about the gallery itself and the other pieces I have there. Let's hope people will focus on those." But Diane could see her friend didn't really believe her own words.

"Everyone who knows her said the only thing she's notable for is having a grandiose view of how much her opinions are worth." Diane spread her hands in appeal. "Margaret, you sold more than you'd hoped in your wildest dreams on Thursday evening. People loved everything in the gallery. And that includes your work."

Margaret sighed. "I know. At some level, I know that. But like you said the other day, it's as if someone told me my baby was ugly. It really hurts." Tears welled in her eyes. "Why do harsh words have so much more impact than kind ones?"

"Because they speak to our inner critic," Diane told her, "that little inner voice that's always trying to shake your confidence. Look at how much weight you're giving one person's opinion." She held both hands palm up, mimicking a scale. "On one side you've got Harriet Malcolm. On the other...," Her hands moved, lifting one side higher and higher while the other dropped, "...you've got at least fifty people, and probably many more, who told you how much they loved your work. Not the gallery's other items, as nice as they may be, but *your work.*"

Margaret nodded. She squared her shoulders. "I know." Quietly she added, "It's just so disheartening to hear someone speak that way of my work. Every single painting I displayed was one I thought was among my best pieces. If she didn't like those, just imagine what she'll say if she ever sees the others."

"Let's *not* imagine it." Shelley's voice was firm. "Instead, let's imagine how happy all those buyers from the opening are with their new paintings."

★   ★   ★

Several hours later, both her children were napping. Once again, Shelley sat down at the computer. Taking a deep breath, she went to an Internet site she had bookmarked and opened a new document. At the top, she typed her name, address, and contact information.

Then she hit the Caps Lock key and, on a new line, wrote, "QUALIFICATIONS."

"Oh boy," she muttered. In many of the sample résumés she'd studied, the first category was a statement of the job-seeker's special skills and abilities. What could she put there? Retail sales experience. Good cook. In-home child care experience...for herself. Her fingers fell away from the keyboard. She had no education, no marketable skills.

Someone knocked on her door, a welcome interruption. Rising, Shelley snagged the puppy's collar to hold her back and opened the door.

Diane stood there, looking exhausted.

"Come in and sit down." Shelley took her arm and urged her to a seat, still holding off the bouncing puppy. "Are you all right?"

Diane smiled wanly. "I was at the gallery with Margaret. I just realized I forgot to eat lunch. No wonder I feel faint. Got a crust of bread for the starving?"

Shelley smiled. "I've got more than that. Here." She tugged the top off a tin of almond spritz cookies. "Have a few of these."

"They smell heavenly." Diane smiled. "My guardian angel."

Prize calmed down as she got used to Diane's presence. The puppy approached Diane, her favorite stuffed toy in her mouth. After a moment of cuddling and a "What a pretty girl you are," the dog flopped down at Diane's feet and proceeded to chomp on the toy.

"Aw, you must be teething," Diane said. She checked the puppy's mouth. "Have you found any baby teeth, Shelley?"

"I didn't know she would lose any. But I guess that makes sense."

Diane nodded, stroking the short coat that still carried traces of baby fuzz. "I've been doing some research on canine development, and apparently they get their adult teeth anywhere between three and seven months."

Shelley chuckled. "You crack me up. Do you research everything?"

Diane looked sheepish. "Pretty much. When I tackle something new or even just learn something I've never heard before, I often check it out online to familiarize myself with it."

"Like the lighthouse?" Shelley asked.

Diane shook her head. "I haven't done that one yet. I figured a trip to the local library might be more valuable than online research. But between Rocky, getting settled, and my novel, I just haven't had time." She wore a determined look. "But I'm going to."

While they were talking, Prize got up and went to the door. Shelley noted the behavior absently, but when the pup squatted and began to pee, she realized what it had meant. "Prize! No. Bad puppy."

By the time she reached the door, the puppy was finished. "Oh, you little stinker." Stepping over the puddle on her vinyl floor, she took the puppy and set her outside in the grass. "It's probably too late for that," she said glumly. "Everyone says you're supposed to catch them *before* they go. But they can't talk, so how am I supposed to know?"

Diane tried not to smile and failed. Seeing her amusement, Shelley had to laugh as well.

"I'm no dog expert," Diane said, "but I think it's like training a child. You have to learn their signals and get them outside."

"What signals?" She imagined the puppy dancing in place as Aiden frequently did when he waited too long.

"She went to the door," Diane pointed out. "Really, she's a pretty good pup to give you that kind of notice. One lady at the dog park where I take Rocky says her dog circles once, just once, and that's all the warning she gets."

Shelley sighed. "It sounds so simple in theory." She pinched two fingers almost together in a gesture indicating a teeny-tiny amount. "What I know about dogs would fit on the head of a pin. I was never allowed to have a pet when I was growing up."

Diane's face took on the intent look that Shelley had learned meant she was about to launch into reporter mode. "Is your family in Maine? You've never mentioned them."

"My father is. He lives up in Jonesport."

Diane tilted her head. "That's a pretty quiet area, isn't it?"

Shelley smiled. "If quiet is a euphemism for 'nothing to do,' it sure is."

"So your mom's not in Maine anymore?"

Shelley's smile faded. "No. They divorced when I was in high school, and she remarried right away."

"That must have been tough."

Shelley shrugged. "We aren't close. And I have Dan's family, which makes up for the lack of relatives on my side." She sent Diane a long-suffering look. "Whether or not I want them, I have Dan's family."

Diane laughed. "Ah, in-laws. Always a tricky path to negotiate."

Shelley thought of her mother-in-law, who seemed to have more advice to share than Dear Abby. "You said it perfectly."

*   *   *

Diane was enjoying caring for the gardens around her sweet little cottage. The first time she'd seen the house, it had been buried under a thick layer of snow. She'd liked the exterior and the promise of spring bulbs and summer blooms all around the yard, almost as much as she'd loved the interior. Initially, it hadn't been exactly what she needed, but after a little paint and a few renovations, she couldn't be happier.

On Tuesday afternoon, she was clearing out her flowerbeds, dividing overgrown perennials, and making room for new things. This year she had planted some annuals in front to give it some color. Most were bright shades that went well with the geraniums in the big planter on her porch.

"Diane!" The call came from her front gate.

Getting to her feet, Diane saw Shelley waving. She had both children with her, probably beginning or finishing one of their frequent walks. "Hello." She walked over and opened the gate, snagging Rocky's collar when he came to investigate. "Where's Prize?" She greeted Aiden and bent down to nuzzle Emma's neck, making her squeal and giggle. As she did so, Aiden went tearing off to greet Rocky.

"In her kennel. She gets under my feet too much to manage when I have the stroller." Shelley didn't even bother with a greeting. "Have you seen Mr. Wheeland recently?"

Diane's eyebrows rose. "No. But I don't see him every day." She thought back over the last couple of weeks. "I saw him Saturday when I brought over some cookies for him and Beverly. And I stopped to chat for a minute Sunday morning when I saw him on the porch waving good-bye to her. She had to get back early for a co-worker's retirement party. But I don't believe I've seen him since then. Why?"

"I see him nearly every day," Shelley said. "He waves at us when we walk. I didn't see him at all yesterday, and he wasn't out again this morning or just now."

Diane's level of unease rose. "Why don't I try to call him? I don't think he'll mind." Retrieving her phone, she found Mr. Wheeland's number in her contacts and hit the button to dial. It rang and rang . . . and rang some more. After perhaps the tenth ring, a recorded voice broke in to tell her the party was not available at this time and to call back. "No answer." Diane tried again, with the same result.

Shelley's eyes were anxious as she watched Diane try to contact Mr. Wheeland. "Maybe we should go check on him." She twisted her fingers together. "I just don't know what to do. I don't want him to think that we think he's feeble."

"It's a fine line to travel with elderly folks." Making her decision, Diane nodded firmly. "I think we should go make sure he's all right. I believe he'll appreciate our concern, and I *know* Beverly will." She glanced down at her hands, dirty despite the gardening gloves she had just peeled off. "Give me a minute to wash and change clothes."

As Diane hurried through her ablutions and tossed on clean clothes, she sent a prayer winging heavenward. *Dear*

Lord, please let Mr. Wheeland be all right. But if he's ill or incapacitated, reassure him that someone's coming.

A few minutes later, the two women took both children and hurried to the end of Newport Avenue. Diane left Rocky behind, and she could hear his unhappy whining. "Stay, boy," she said and firmly closed the door.

It took only a minute to reach Mr. Wheeland's home, which was situated on the opposite corner from Mr. Calder's and right past Fred and Cindy Little's house. Diane preceded Shelley and the children up the walk and mounted the steps of the elaborately shingled old Victorian, while her friend got the baby out of the stroller. Modest by some Victorian standards, the house had a single wide porch stretching across the front and a steeply pitched roof. It was painted a soft cream, with equally soft green and butter trim.

Diane lifted the front door knocker and rapped it several times against the solid wooden door. Mr. Wheeland had never appeared to be terribly hard of hearing, but if he had the television on, she knew it would take quite a racket to distract him.

They waited a long moment, and Diane rapped again. Still no answer. Nor, more ominously, was there any sound from a person moving around within.

Brow furrowed, she turned to Shelley. "You stay here in case he comes to the door. I'll walk around back and see if I can get any answer at the rear door."

Shelley nodded, and Diane descended the porch steps. Walking around to the back porch, she repeated the knocking process, except she used her knuckles since there was no doorknocker.

Still no answer or movement. Frowning, Diane cupped her hands around her eyes to decrease the bright outside light and peered through the window in the top half of the door. It appeared Mr. Wheeland was home. A half-gallon of milk stood on the counter beside a mug, and a chair was angled away from the table as if someone had just walked away for a moment.

The hairs on the back of her neck rose, and a sudden, deep sense of unease struck her. She tried the door, but it was locked. She hurried back to the front of the house where Shelley waited on the porch.

"No answer," Diane said. "It looks like he's home, but I didn't see him. I tried the door, but it's locked."

Shelley reached out and opened the front screen door, twisting the large front doorknob, but it too was unyielding. "What are we going to do?"

"I think we should call Beverly right away," she told the younger woman. "Maybe—"

"Yoo-hoo!" A high-pitched voice sounded from somewhere off the porch.

Diane turned and saw another neighbor, diminutive Mrs. Peabody, standing on the sidewalk and waving at them. She wore a familiar plaid Pendleton wool jacket despite the mild weather, and her curly white hair framed her face, wisps occasional breaking free to wave in the breeze.

"Hello, Mrs. Peabody." Diane's eyes met Shelley's, and she saw her own thoughts reflected there. Their elderly neighbor was sweet, but she could talk a tin ear on a person, and she was the repository of every tiny piece of local gossip, which she loved to share regardless of how short one might be on time. "How are you?"

"I'm fine, dear," the old woman called. She made her way along the walk to the foot of the stairs. "Are you trying to get in touch with Harold Wheeland?"

Diane nodded. "Yes. Yes, we are. I knocked at the front- and backdoors and didn't get any answer. He might just be watching TV, but Shelley hasn't seen him in a couple of days, and we got a little concerned."

Mrs. Peabody frowned. "You know, now that you mention it, I haven't seen him since his daughter left either." She turned and slowly began to retrace her steps. "Let me get my key."

"Your key?" Shelley and Diane spoke the words together.

Mrs. Peabody turned back. "Oh yes. We exchanged keys years ago when his wife was living. Just in case we ever locked ourselves out or needed the other to water plants while we were on vacation, that sort of thing. Why, I remember—"

"Why don't you get the key first, and then we can chat?" Diane hated to be rude, but it was possible there was no time to lose.

"Oh, of course." Mrs. Peabody waved a hand in the air as she turned and began to walk again. "Sometimes I just don't know when to turn off my talker."

Shelley and Diane looked at each other while the old woman made her way across the street. Despite the gravity of the situation, Diane snickered. Shelley giggled. And then the two of them laughed aloud. Really, Mrs. P was priceless.

*　　*　　*

While they waited for her to return with the key, Shelley called the Hoskins home. Allan answered, and Shelley asked if Adelaide could walk down the block to meet her so she could play with Aiden in Mr. Wheeland's yard. Shelley didn't know what might be waiting inside, and she thought it might be better if Aiden was otherwise occupied when they got inside.

Probably everything was fine, she assured herself. Mr. Wheeland might be sitting happily in front of the television and she, Diane, and Mrs. Peabody were worrying for nothing. She stood in front of the Wheeland home and waved when she saw Adelaide, waiting until the young woman had crossed the street and joined her. Then, extracting a promise from both Aiden and Adelaide that they would play in the backyard until she came for them, she sent the pair off. And just in time, too, as Mrs. Peabody traipsed back across the street from her pretty lavender home with the key to Mr. Wheeland's house.

Diane took the key and fitted it into the lock. When the door opened, she hesitated for a moment and then stepped forward. Shelley followed with Emma on her hip, feeling Mrs. Peabody crowd in at her heels.

"Mr. Wheeland? Mr. Wheeland." Diane called his name as the threesome moved through the main floor of the house. The television in the living room was turned off, but an afghan straggled from one arm of a recliner over the edge and across the floor, and a half-finished mug of something dark—tea or coffee?— was sitting on the end table.

The kitchen was a mess, she saw now that she could get a better look at it. Mugs, bowls, plates, and utensils were piled in the sink and scattered over the counter and table. A cupboard hung open, and a dish towel had fallen to the floor. Diane turned to Shelley and Mrs. Peabody. "I don't like the look of this. Let's check upstairs."

Then Shelley heard a sound. "Listen!"

All three women froze. They definitely could hear a sound coming from above them as though something was scraping along the floor.

Diane sprinted for the doorway. Mrs. Peabody and Shelley, who was carrying Emma, were somewhat slower. Diane was pounding up the stairs by the time Shelley reached for the banister. Shelley heard her footsteps racing down the hall.

"He's up here!" Diane called seconds later.

Shelley rushed the rest of the way up the stairs. Emma thought this was a great game and giggled happily. The second door on the right stood open, and Shelley hurried toward it.

When she arrived in the doorway, Diane was bending over the bed, lifting Mr. Wheeland's legs back onto the mattress. In the moment before she pulled the sheets over the old man, Shelley saw that he wore a very crumpled pair of pants and a white button-front shirt with some brownish stain dribbled down the front of it.

"Mr. Wheeland, what's wrong?" Shelley cried.

Beverly's father croaked something, and Diane turned to Shelley and Mrs. Peabody, who had arrived as well. "He says he thinks he has the flu. You two probably shouldn't come any closer, just in case." Then she stepped away from the bed, and her gaze locked with Shelley's. "Call 9-1-1 and then call Beverly. Tell her that her father's very ill, and we need her to come down right away. He could have had a stroke or some other serious health problem. I'm afraid to make any changes, even though he keeps saying it's just the flu."

Shelley nodded. "Of course."

"Mrs. P," Diane went on. "Is it possible for you to clean up downstairs? Beverly is going to have a lot to do to help her father when she arrives, and it would be really helpful if that kitchen was cleaner."

Mrs. Peabody nodded vigorously. "Of course, dear." The old woman turned and began to make her way back down the hall.

Shelley stopped just outside the bedroom door. She took out her phone and called 9-1-1. The emergency operator repeated the address, assuring Shelley that help was on the way and asking her to stay on the line until the EMTs arrived.

While she waited, Shelley found Beverly's number beside Mr. Wheeland's large wall telephone downstairs. When the EMTs arrived, she directed them upstairs and then called Beverly.

"Hello?" It was Beverly's voice, sounding both cautious and slightly alarmed.

"Hi, Beverly. It's Shelley."

"I know. I saw your name come up. What can I do for you?"

Shelley cleared her throat. "Your father's ill." She figured the faster she explained, the better. "We hadn't seen him since you left, so Diane and I came to check. But he didn't come to the door, so Mrs. Peabody got her key—"

"The key to *our* house?"

"Yes. Your mother gave it to her way back when, Mrs. P says. So we all went in and found your dad half fallen out of his bed. He told Diane he thinks he has the flu, but we called 9-1-1 because we just weren't sure."

"Oh dear. How does he seem?" Beverly's normally cool, calm voice hitched and rose.

"Diane?" Shelley called, "Beverly wants to know how he seems."

"Dehydrated," Diane said. "And a little confused. He says he hasn't been able to keep anything down for a while. And I'm pretty sure he's running a fever."

Shelley repeated the information and explained the state of the house.

"Okay," Beverly said. "I'm getting my things together right now. I should be there in about an hour if the traffic's decent."

Beverly paused, and Shelley could hear high heels clicking on a hard floor. Beverly quickly explained where her father's insurance information could be found. "Thank you so much, Shelley. Please thank Diane and Mrs. Peabody. I'll see you soon."

CHAPTER TEN

Beverly's heels clicked on the tile floor of the hospital corridor. Shelley had called again while she was on the road to say her father had been admitted. Fear clogged her throat.

When the elevator doors slid open on the second floor, Beverly quickly oriented herself, turning left down the hallway toward the room number the front desk had given her. Then she took a deep breath and stepped into the room. "Father?"

The way her father's face lit up nearly broke her heart. "There's my girl," he said in the same raspy whisper.

Diane rose from the chair beside him.

Beverly crossed to the bed and bent over, hugging him carefully as she kissed his cheek.

"I...don't want to...be in the hospital." He clutched her hand. He might be sicker than he'd been in years, but her father hadn't lost any of his stubbornness. "It's just the flu."

"It'll only be for a little while," she told him, although she hadn't spoken to a doctor yet. On the other side of the bed, Diane was nodding vigorously. "They'll probably give you some fluids. You have to have fluids, Father, to keep you from a-gettin' too dehydrated."

It was a sign of how sick he was, she thought anxiously, that he didn't continue to argue.

Diane picked up her handbag. "I'm going to go now." She hugged Beverly, whispering, "The doctor should be in soon," and then took the hand Mr. Wheeland was extending, gently holding it. "I'll come back and read to you tomorrow if you like."

The moment Diane departed, Beverly's father turned to her again. "Want to go home."

"I know, Father. Soon."

Her father's eyes fluttered closed, and he appeared to sleep. But only minutes later, his eyes opened for a moment. "Olive?"

Beverly's heart contracted. Olive was her mother's name. She stepped forward. "Father, it's me. Beverly. I'm right here." She took his thin hand and patted it gently.

A fretful frown pulled at his features. "Where's your mother? I have to talk to her."

"She's not here. Don't you remember?"

The frown deepened. "Well, where'd she go, eh? Be a good girl and go find her, will you? I have to talk to her."

She opened her mouth to remind him that her mother had passed away four years ago. But then she closed it again. Really, what was the point? He'd remember eventually. Why upset him now? "Okay. You close your eyes and take a little nap, all right? I'll go find her."

Her father smiled, his eyes fluttering closed. "Always were a good girl," he mumbled.

Beverly sat on the side of the bed, her heart aching nearly as fiercely as it had in the dark days right after her mother's death. Unaware of her anguish, her father began to snore lightly. She brushed a hand over his silver hair, smoothing it back from his forehead. *I promise I'll take care of you.*

A short time later, a young man whose ID tag hanging around his neck proclaimed him a doctor, stepped into the room. "Oh, good," he said. "Are you Mr. Wheeland's caregiver?"

Taken aback, Beverly frowned. "No, I'm his daughter. My father doesn't need a caregiver."

"I'm sorry." The doctor looked chagrined. "I meant that only in the broadest terms. Your father isn't going to be able to go home unless he has someone there to help him, at least for a while. He's got one of the most severe cases of the flu I've seen in a while. He's extremely dehydrated."

Beverly swallowed the lump that had risen in her throat. "He's so independent that I don't take very good care of him, I'm afraid. I live in Augusta."

"Is there anyone who could look in on him each day, perhaps help with a meal or two until he's fully recovered? It's going to take a while before he's back to himself."

Beverly thought of Diane and the other women on her street who were becoming her friends. But no, each of them was busy, and she couldn't ask them to take on a time-consuming task like this on a daily basis. She shook her head. "Not really."

The doctor's brow furrowed. "I can give you the names of some agencies that specialize in in-home eldercare. If all goes well, he can probably come home by the weekend. Perhaps in the meantime, you can find someone to help out a bit."

After the doctor left, Beverly sighed. Even if they got through this crisis, she was kidding herself to think that her father could live alone for much longer. She ought to look for a job down here and move home. After all, there were two more bedrooms in the house. She'd live rent free, which would certainly help. And one of those rooms could become a home office. Her job was too demanding to permit many of these emergency absences, but what if something happened to her father during an especially busy time? She could have much more difficulty just dropping everything and rushing home than she had today.

★   ★   ★

Margaret closed the gallery at six and walked the short distance home. She supposed it had been a good day at the gallery. She'd sold a piece of Allan's furniture and a pottery bowl and some smaller items. Tourists were beginning to arrive in ever-growing numbers as the calendar crept toward July.

A week ago, she would have been thrilled by the sales, and she already would have been looking forward to the next day. This evening...not so much.

She hadn't felt the smallest urge to paint since the critical review in the paper yesterday. What direction did she want to go in now? Despite her friends' encouraging words, good sales weren't enough. She wanted to be known for the quality of her work as well as its popularity.

"Margaret!" Her young neighbor Shelley's voice dragged her from her introspection. "Have you heard about Mr. Wheeland?"

"What about him?" Margaret set her artistic concerns aside as Shelley came across the street to meet Margaret in front of her walk.

"This morning Diane and I realized we hadn't seen him in a while..." Shelley went on to tell the entire story. "So Beverly has decided to stay through the weekend. We all hope he'll be on the mend by then."

There was an awkward pause. Margaret, usually able to put anyone at ease, cast about for an appropriate response. She felt oddly off-balance, as if she were observing the chat with Shelley rather than participating. "Um, I hope so," she finally said.

Shelley gave her a searching look. "Are you all right?"

Margaret nodded. "Sure."

"I was thinking that perhaps the four of us—you, Diane, Beverly, and I—could have another get-together like we did the night we saved the swimmer. That was really amazing."

Margaret nodded. She couldn't seem to work up much enthusiasm for the idea. "Yes. Maybe we can." She cleared her throat. "I'd better get going. I haven't even thought about dinner yet."

"I thought Allan cooked when you had to work late."

"Ah, right. He does. He does." She was desperate to get away from her chatty young friend. "I'll see you. Have a good evening."

"You too." Margaret was aware that Shelley stood looking after her as she made her way into her home.

"Hi, Mom. See what I'm doing?" Adelaide was working on a puzzle at a table in the living room.

"Very nice, sweetheart." Margaret angled over to kiss her daughter.

"Hi, honey." Allan stuck his head out of the kitchen, smiling at her. "How does chicken casserole sound?"

"Fine." She managed to smile at him. "I'll be there in a minute. Just have to change my clothes."

But she didn't. Once in her bedroom, she sat down on the edge of the bed and folded her hands in her lap. Thoughts about painting floated through her head. She really should start another canvas tomorrow. But what would she paint? She'd done all the seascapes and local landmarks, scenes of dunes and beaches and rocky cliffs...all the typical, predictable stuff tourists loved. She supposed if she wanted to be taken seriously, she needed to try something new. Something meaningful and deep.

She sighed. Right now, the only color paint she felt like using was black. What would that critic say if she just slapped black paint all over a canvas and gave it some silly name? Maybe she should try that next.

CHAPTER ELEVEN

In the Bauer house across the street, Shelley stood in shocked silence, holding Aiden's beloved Spider-Man pajama pants that she had saved up to purchase for his last birthday. There was a three-cornered tear in one leg.

Aiden stood in front of her, tears in his big blue eyes. "I didn't do that, Mommy. Prize did."

"Prize?"

Her son nodded. "I was running, and she chased me and pulled on my jammies, and they teared."

Shelley stared blindly down at the garment, trying not to give in to tears. She had cut corners from their grocery budget to save for the pajamas because Aiden had seen them in a catalog and wanted them desperately. Even then, she'd waited until they'd gone on sale at the nearest store, and she'd gone early so she could get in the moment the doors opened. She couldn't afford to replace them right now. Quietly, she said, "How about if I sew this up? You'll hardly even notice it if I use the same color thread."

Aiden nodded. He gulped and knuckled tears from his eyes. "Okay. That would be good." And off he trotted, with everything well in his little world again.

Shelley heaved a sigh and then turned and carried the pajamas to her sewing basket. She'd have to get to them tomorrow.

It just wasn't going to work, she decided. Prize simply couldn't stay. Dan was going to have to find a new home for her.

As if thinking of him had brought him home, she heard Dan's truck pull to a halt in the driveway. Moments later, the truck's door slammed, and Dan's footsteps crunched across the gravel.

"Hi, honey," she called, as she heard the back door open. She took a deep breath and rose, letting the pajamas lay atop the basket. It wouldn't do to jump down his throat about the dog first thing. "How was your day? My goodness, you worked some serious overtime today, didn't you?"

Dan slumped into a kitchen chair. "Not exactly." His glum tone alerted Shelley that he wasn't very happy.

"What happened?" She took a seat at an angle to his, so she could see his face. And when she did, her heart sank.

"My hours got cut again. I worked extra today because they fired another guy and needed someone to do his job until it's reassigned, but I'll only be working two-and-a-half days a week from now on."

Shelley's throat felt tight, almost too tight to speak. "Wha...what about your benefits?"

Dan didn't even raise his head. "We're covered for the next sixty days, but then I'll officially be part-time, and we'll have to find our own insurance."

Shelley sucked in a breath of dismay. Dear heavens. *Find insurance?* "What are we going to do?"

Dan leaned forward and put his head in his hands, spearing his fingers through his hair. "I don't know." His voice was low and flat. "I just don't know."

Shelley stood and walked to him, reaching up to embrace his broad shoulders gently. "We'll work it out. Together, we'll figure it out."

While Dan went upstairs to change out of his work clothes, she pondered dinner. One of his favorite meals was her herb-stuffed chicken breast served with mushroom cream and roasted garlic smashed potatoes. She'd read that smashed potatoes were all the rage in restaurants at the moment because they were easier to make than mashed potatoes. She didn't really care about that, but she knew Dan liked the chunkier dish in which he could taste the potatoes. And the cream sauce recipe called for cremini mushrooms, which she didn't have, but she could substitute some canned ones. Add snow peas and some chocolate drop cookies for dessert, and she would have a meal.

Inspired, she set to work. The meal would only take about forty-five minutes if she got the chicken in quickly. And Dan liked to relax with the kids before dinner anyway.

As she worked, she heard Dan's deep tones in the living room, along with Aiden's much higher ones. Emma squealed in her playpen, rocking on her hands and knees. Shelley set her on the kitchen floor in her tiny footie pajamas and said, "Go find Daddy." Dan loved it when she came crawling toward him. Since she'd begun to crawl about two weeks ago, she was no longer content to stay in one place. Her style of motion always made Shelley laugh: Emma dragged herself along on her elbows as if she were doing an Army crawl.

The baby made a beeline for the living room, and Shelley could hear her squealing and giggling when she reached Dan. Aiden still exhibited a trace of jealousy sometimes, and he extracted a promise from Dan to play Legos after dinner.

Finally everything was ready. Shelley called her family to wash their hands and come to the table. Then she set out the meal. Aiden appeared first, and she helped him into his booster seat and buckled the strap.

Dan carried Emma in and placed her in her high chair. "This looks great!" he said.

Shelley smiled. "I thought you could use a little something special."

Dan's face clouded, and immediately she was sorry she'd reminded him of his impending pay cut and their insurance crisis. Silently she served and cut up food for the children, mashing Emma's potatoes so they would be easier for her to eat.

The meal was a quiet one, punctuated by Aiden's chatter as he told his daddy about playing with Adelaide and Prize today. Guilt shot arrows deep into Shelley's heart. Her son was really going to miss the puppy. Then she thought of the pajamas as well as toys Prize had chewed. And Shelley's treasured cookie jar. Really, there was no choice. She just could not manage with a puppy underfoot all the time.

"Daddy?" Aiden repeated the word until he had his father's attention. "I'm going to play with Legos. You come soon, okay?"

Dan nodded. "Okay."

"Aiden, don't you want a cookie?" Shelley asked.

Her son shook his head. "Legos." He turned and started for the living room. "With Daddy."

Shelley rolled her eyes. "He's got Legos on the brain lately. It's all he talks about."

Dan smiled, but she could see that his heart wasn't in it.

"How was your meal?" she asked.

"It was terrific." Dan looked chagrined. "Sorry. I appreciate your hard work. That chicken is great."

"I'm glad you liked it," she said, as she cleaned off Emma's tray and went to the sink to wet a washcloth to clean the baby's face and hands. "I'm sorry you're so worried about your job. Do you think I should look for part-time work?"

"No. We agreed that you'd stay home with the kids. They need you." Dan's voice was inflexible. "My mom stayed home when we were little, and I think it makes a difference. I still remember coming home from school to milk and cookies."

Okay. This probably wasn't the time to mention her efforts to write a résumé. Shelley didn't sigh, but it took some serious effort. Dan's mother had done everything in the world, it seemed, and done it well. "It's not that I want to work," she said. "I agree with you. I just thought that if we need the money—"

"I'll figure out a way to support this family. Just give me a little time, all right?"

"Of course." Something was niggling at the back of Shelley's memory, something important, but she couldn't— "Oh!" She smacked the heel of her hand to her forehead.

"'Oh' what?" Dan sounded impatient.

"I completely forgot to tell you this." Shelley smiled at her husband ruefully. "And I can't believe I forgot. Margaret told me that Allan's furniture business is going even better than he expected. Apparently he's getting more orders than he can fill." She paused, hoping the offer would appeal to Dan. "Margaret knows you're a woodworker, and she asked me to find out if you'd be interested in working with Allan. I know it's not full-time employment, and I don't know what he'd pay you, but you could go talk to him."

She waited expectantly.

Dan was still and silent, his gaze on the table.

"Honey?" She probably sounded as puzzled as she felt. "What's the matter?"

Dan raised his gaze to hers, and she was stunned to see that his eyes were filled with anger. "What's the matter?" It clearly was a rhetorical question, but she had no clue what the answer was. "I'll tell you what's the matter, Shelley. It annoys the heck out of me to know you share details of our financial situation with all your neighborhood pals. I do not need any more charity jobs from your friends, do you understand me? And I'd appreciate it if you'd quit talking about our problems behind my back."

Shelley stared at Dan, completely stunned by his outburst. She wasn't sure she'd ever heard him speak so harshly before. Growing up in a large family of squabbling siblings, Dan was more a peacemaker than a fighter. Usually.

Hurt made her breath come faster as the words sank in. "Diane did not ask you to paint for her out of charity," she said, her voice trembling. "She needed to hire someone to do the work. I suppose she thought it would be nice to have someone she knew in some context helping out since she'd just moved here and knew no one else."

"Even so, I don't need the Hoskinses dreaming up some job for me," Dan said, his jaw set.

Shelley didn't often get furiously angry, but her husband's pigheaded assumptions about her friends' motives got under her skin. Before she could censor her words, she said, "Well, I didn't *need* a dog or a TV with a Blu-Ray player. But I got them anyway."

Dan's eyes widened, as her words hit home. "I didn't—"

"That's right: *You didn't*. Didn't ask me, didn't even tell me what you were thinking. You knew how tight our budget was! And that puppy...You didn't even know whether I might be allergic to dogs. You just went ahead and did what you wanted." A tear rolled down her cheek, and she angrily dashed it away. She *hated* that she always cried when she got mad. "At least I didn't accept Allan's job without even talking to you," she said bitterly.

Dan opened his mouth. Closed it again.

She grabbed plates off the table, spun, and marched to the sink.

"Shelley—"

She didn't turn around. She just held up one hand in a *stop* gesture.

Dan made an unintelligible sound of frustration. There was a taut pause. "Fine," he said angrily. He grabbed his jacket off the back of his chair and bolted out the door. Moments later, she heard the sound of the truck starting. Then he backed out of the driveway and was gone.

Gone. Stunned, she looked at Emma, whose little lip was trembling as she prepared to howl.

Aiden rushed into the room. "Where's Daddy? He's going to play Legos with me. He *promised.*" Her son's face looked as stricken as his tone sounded.

"Daddy left," Shelley said. "Maybe he'll play with you when he comes back."

"*Daaa-deee!*" As Aiden began to shriek, he startled Emma, whose little face crumpled as she too began to sob. Shelley, completely overwhelmed, turned around and rested both hands on the edge of the sink so her children wouldn't see the tears in her own eyes. She and Dan had argued before. Didn't all couples? But they'd never had a nasty fight like this.

And Dan had never stormed out of the house before. As she turned to comfort the kids, anger rose so fast she nearly choked on it. How dare he leave? These were his children as much as hers. She couldn't imagine ever walking away from them, furious as she might be.

She took a moment to compose herself. All she knew to do was the next thing in front of her.

"Up you go, sweetie." She hauled Emma out of the highchair and rested her on one hip. Then she held out a hand to Aiden. "Honey, I know I'm not Daddy, but I will play Legos with you if you like."

Aiden was still sobbing. "You p-p-promise?"

"I promise."

Shelley vowed to herself that she would never break a promise to either of her children without an extremely, *extremely* good reason.

And a fight with Dan would never be a good enough reason.

CHAPTER TWELVE

The hours passed. Shelley played with Aiden and gave both children baths. Afterward, she put them to bed, cleaned up her kitchen and folded two loads of laundry while watching an evening television drama.

As the evening evaporated and night took its place, her anger cooled, and concern began to supplant it. Had something happened to her husband? His cell phone lay on the counter untouched, so she had no way to contact him. Several times she picked up the phone to call his parents, but each time she put it back down, unwilling to alarm them needlessly. She considered calling the police to ask if there had been any accidents. But Marble Cove was a small community, and she was afraid Dan's family might hear of her concern. Same with the medical center. They could say all they wanted about confidentiality, but there was no keeping that kind of secret in Marble Cove.

Once she let it enter her mind, the thought of an accident refused to go away. Memories from her own accident a few weeks ago tormented her. *Dear God, please keep Dan safe, wherever he is.* She glanced at the clock. It was nearly eleven. Where was her husband?

Midnight passed. To occupy herself, she baked. Just before one o'clock, when she was about to call the police regardless of how the news might spread, she heard the sound of a vehicle turning onto Newport Street. She ran to the window and watched as headlights approached. The engine sounded like Dan's truck. And to her relief, it turned into their driveway.

Thank You, Lord, she thought as she saw Dan's tall form walk across the yard to the back door.

As he came in, he stopped uncertainly on the braid rug inside the back door. "I thought you'd be in bed," he said, looking down at the floor.

"I was too worried to sleep." She tried not to let any hint of accusation color her tone.

"I'm sorry, honey." He started across the floor toward her. Shelley crossed her arms defensively, and he stopped. "I shouldn't have blown up at you and left like that without telling you where I was going."

"I was afraid something had happened to you." She clamped down on the tremor in her voice.

Dan looked alarmed. "I'm fine. I was over at my folks' place."

"At your parents'? Until after midnight? What did they say when you showed up at dusk without any warning?" Her chest felt even tighter, as she struggled not to sob aloud. She was mortified, absolutely mortified, that Dan's folks knew they'd been fighting.

Dan shrugged, clearly uncomfortable, as he realized he'd made another blunder. His mother and Shelley were far from being close friends. "They didn't really say anything. Mom had made butternut pound cake, and she knows it's my favorite, so, of course, she made me have some."

Shelley glanced at the lovely baked goods she had made while she was all alone at home. Dan hadn't even mentioned them, much less asked to taste them. Usually he could hardly wait to dive in. Hurt rose again, and so did more anger. The knot clogging her throat turned to a lump of lead. Spinning away, she whipped several containers out of her cupboards. A key lime pie went into a shallow woven basket. She set her red velvet cake in a deep box.

"What are you doing?" Dan sounded wary.

"Just putting a few things away." A tear rolled down her cheek.

"Honey..." He hesitated.

She didn't look at him, too churned up and upset to trust herself to speak.

"I apologize again. I can't explain how it feels to be afraid you can't provide for your family. When you talked about Allan Hoskins' offer, I felt you were criticizing me."

Her mouth fell open, and she turned to stare at him, her eyes brimming with unshed tears. "That wasn't it at all!"

"That's what Mom said."

She couldn't believe her ears. "You talked to your *mother* about us? About me?"

"I only told her about Allan's offer." He looked sheepish. "I totally overreacted. It was nice of him to offer. I'll go talk to him tomorrow."

Shelley was silent. She was relieved that Dan was going to speak with Allan, but she wondered if he ever would have considered it if he wasn't trying to worm his way back into her good graces. Or if his mother hadn't suggested it. "Do whatever you want."

"But it should be our decision together."

"Just like talking about our private affairs to your mother was *our* decision? And getting the puppy and the TV?" This was pointless, she realized. She was just too furious and hurt to be rational.

Dan sighed. "Those were all wrong."

It seemed he suddenly was realizing a lot of things were wrong. Her lip quivered, and she bit down hard. Making a snap decision, she grabbed her house key and shoved it into her pocket. Then she slung the pie basket over her arm, picked up the cake box, and headed for the door.

"Where are you going at this hour?"

"Over to Diane's." Shelley grabbed her jacket and sailed out the door without looking back.

Slamming it would have been childish, so she very carefully closed it quietly behind her. Then she set down her burdens and shrugged into her jacket, grateful she'd seen it hanging there. Otherwise, she'd probably have come out without it, and it was chilly, even if it was June.

It was really dark outside. She hadn't realized exactly how dark until she was standing there with no porch light, no light of any kind to guide her. There wasn't even much moonlight. *Rats,* she thought. She couldn't possibly go back in for a flashlight after that dramatic exit. She sighed, standing on the back porch waiting for her eyes to adjust to the dark.

As she stood there, the light went off in the kitchen. All that was left burning was the small light over the stove that they used as a nightlight. The lump rose in her throat again. She and Dan had been so happy together when they'd first met—

What was that?

She carefully negotiated the steps off the porch and hurried around the side of the house and out to the sidewalk where she would have a better view.

A small flash of light seemed to float in the air out near the harbor. It had to be coming from the lighthouse. She stifled a squeal of excitement as she rushed across the street and knocked hastily on Diane's front door.

Inside, Rocky began to bark immediately. Shelley turned around and looked down the street toward the lighthouse. But the light had vanished, and the night was dark and still.

Inside, footsteps approached. Diane called, "Who's there? *Quiet,* Rocky! Who's there?"

"It's me. Shelley." Suddenly she felt rather foolish. "I, um, was out and—"

Diane's door flew open. Clad in a T-shirt and baggy flannel pajama bottoms, Diane stared at Shelley in astonishment. "What on earth are you doing at..." She turned and checked a clock on the mantel above her fireplace. "Holy cow, Shelley, it's after one in the morning!"

"I know. I'm sorry. I should go. But…oh, wait! I just saw a light from the harbor. I'm almost positive it came from a window in the lighthouse. But it's gone now."

Diane's eyebrows shot up, and she grinned. "Want to take a walk?"

Shelley smiled back, feeling her heart lighten for the first time since things had blown up with Dan. She held up the things she carried. "Sure, but can I set these down first?"

Diane reached out and took the pie basket. "Come on in. What is all this, anyway?"

Shelley described the goodies as she followed Diane into the kitchen, taking the key lime pie from the basket and stashing it in the fridge. The red velvet cake stayed on the counter.

Diane rushed up to her bedroom. She came back down wearing fuzzy Ugg slippers with sturdy soles and a Boston College sweatshirt over jeans. "Ready?"

Shelley nodded.

Pulling Rocky's leash off the row of coat hooks inside the door, Diane said, "Let's go. And while we walk, I want to know why you have all that food and why you're out at one in the morning."

★   ★   ★

Diane glanced at her young friend from the corner of her eye as they walked down the slight incline of Newport Street toward the promenade along the beach.

Shelley looked a little odd. She was still dressed in the clothing Diane had seen her wearing earlier that day—well, yesterday, actually—when she'd had the children out in the yard, although she'd added a lightweight stone-colored windbreaker. She should have looked sleepy. Instead, she radiated tension, like a spring that was too tightly coiled. She seemed to be just waiting to fly apart.

"I don't see it," Shelley said. "But I swear to you, it was there a few minutes ago."

"What did it look like?"

Shelley described the light, very different from the large flashes that had streaked out across the water before.

"So it was more like a light in a window."

"Maybe. It wasn't the same as the one you described that looked like a lighted window. It was just tiny, repeated flashes. And only for maybe half a minute or even less."

"But no one lives there, and Fred Little swears it hasn't been used in years." Diane strolled along at a leisurely pace. Rocky, no doubt wondering why he'd been dragged from a sound sleep for a trot along the promenade, stayed at her side.

"Not as far as I've ever heard." Shelley sank down on one of the benches that faced out over the ocean. She looked dejected and defenseless.

Diane decided not to fight her natural instincts. Settling on the bench beside Shelley, she slid an arm around the younger woman and briefly hugged her.

"What was that for?" Shelley turned and looked at her.

Diane shrugged, smiling a little. "You looked like you needed a hug."

To her surprise, Shelley bowed her head, clearly fighting tears. "I did," she confessed. "It's been a terrible evening."

Diane listened as the story of Dan and Shelley's argument spilled out.

"So I left," Shelley said. "I feel like such a mean person. I wanted Dan to see how it felt to be stuck there with two little kids and no help."

"That's not so bad. Every woman I know has felt like that at some time in her marriage." Diane chuckled. "Besides, they're sleeping. He's getting off easy."

Shelley managed a ghost of a smile. "We were so happy when we got married."

"How did you two meet?" Diane could no sooner resist asking questions than she could breathing.

Shelley smiled. "Dan was visiting his brother, who lived in Augusta at the time. That's where I lived."

"Did you grow up there?"

Shelley shook her head. "No. We lived in Belfast when I was a kid. After my mom remarried, we moved to Augusta. My dad said I could live with him, but his place was tiny, and the town was tiny, and I hated it. So I moved in with Mom and Ron in Augusta. Then I realized that wasn't going to work either. Ron was a real control freak. Honestly, my sister was twenty and I was eighteen, and he was trying to give us a ten o'clock curfew!"

"Wow." Apparently Shelley's stepfather hadn't known much about teens. "I guess that made for some confrontations."

"And how," Shelley said in a vehement tone. "My sister took off, and I didn't want to stay there with just Mom and Ron, so I got a retail job and found an apartment with two roommates."

"And that's when you met Dan?"

Shelley shook her head, blonde hair flying around her head in the light breeze. "No. I met him three years later, when I was twenty-one." She smiled, a soft, gentle curve of lips that told Diane how good the memory was. "He came into my store for something, and I thought he was the sweetest man I'd ever met. He came by three more times before he worked up the nerve to ask me out. We didn't get engaged for two more years, but when we did, I moved here. I got an apartment and worked as a waitress until we got married, and then I stopped working." Her smile faded. "I was happy at first. I'm still happy most of the time. But Dan's family is so big and...and loud, and I never quite feel I belong."

Diane's heart ached for the young woman. "I imagine that's hard for Dan to understand. People who have families like that just sort of assume everyone fits somewhere, I think."

Shelley nodded with a rueful smile. Then she grabbed Diane's arm and pointed out across the water. "Look!"

Diane looked, and sure enough, there was a quick pinpoint of light in the window of the lighthouse, just as Shelley had described. As it flashed into the night repeatedly for a few moments, Diane began to see a pattern. "What *is* that? It looks like Morse code."

Shelley nodded.

Diane scanned the bit of beach that she could see in the dark, but nothing looked out of place. She reached into her pocket and grabbed her cell phone, but when she glanced back in the direction of the lighthouse, all was dark again. "Rats!" She held up the phone. "I was going to try to take a picture of it."

Unsettled, Shelley turned to her friend. "Do you think someone's in trouble again?"

Diane tilted her head, as she considered her words. "Maybe, maybe not. I'm not feeling any sense of danger. Look at Rocky." She pointed at the dog. "He's not in the least disturbed. I think if someone was out there at this time of night, he'd notice it. Still..." She rose. "Do you think we should walk a little more?" *And look for someone or something in trouble,* was the unspoken subtext.

"Maybe a little, as long as we don't leave the promenade."

They continued along the promenade. Both women strained to see and listen for anything unusual, but there was only the velvety darkness, the white curl of the waves meeting the beach, and the hypnotic rhythm of the surf.

"Diane, do you believe God is sending the lights as signs?"

Diane pondered the question, wondering how to explain the way she felt. "I don't know if it's quite that direct."

"See a light, save a life. If that's not direct, I don't know what is."

Diane had to laugh at Shelley's droll tone. "You may have a point. We never would have seen that swimmer if the light hadn't illuminated him." She paused, pressing a fist against her heart. "I don't presume to know what these unusual lights mean. But I feel very strongly that we are meant to see them and, at least in some cases, respond. I don't feel the same urgency tonight that I felt when we found the swimmer."

The two women walked on in silence for a while after that, but no more lights appeared. Finally, they strolled back the way they had come. The dark felt peaceful to Diane. She sensed that Shelley was significantly calmer than when she'd knocked on her door.

Shelley paused when they reached Diane's front walk. "Thank you for humoring me. I can't believe I had the nerve to wake you in the middle of the night."

Diane smiled. "I'm glad you did. It was a pleasant walk. And just wait until we tell Beverly and Margaret we saw another light." She gestured over her shoulder. "What do you want me to do with your baked goods?"

Shelley shrugged. "I don't care. Eat them. Just bring me back the containers later."

"But I couldn't eat all that alone even if I wanted to," Diane protested. "Why don't you take some of it home?"

Shelley shook her head. "No. That stuff will just bring back memories I'd rather forget. Just take it to the gallery tomorrow."

CHAPTER THIRTEEN

First thing Thursday morning, Margaret prepared a slim vase with an arrangement of puffy-headed purple alliums she had brought from her garden. As she set them on a table in the front so they could be seen through the large plate-glass window, she saw Diane coming through the door.

"Good morning!" Diane practically sang the words. She wore aqua capris and a pretty aqua-patterned short-sleeve blouse and was carrying two containers that looked as if they might have food in them.

"Good morning." Margaret didn't feel nearly as enthusiastic, but she forced herself to smile. "What's that?"

"Stuff Shelley made." Diane licked her lips in an exaggerated fashion. "Key lime pie and red velvet cake."

Margaret's eyes widened. "Is someone having a birthday?"

"No occasion," Diane told her. "Shelley was in the mood to bake. She thought you could offer them to customers today."

The two women set out the snacks on one of Allan's tables near the door, along with some napkins left over from the gallery opening. The sight of the food table was enough to bring back vivid memories of that evening, and Margaret felt her spirits plunging. She needed to work. She needed to produce paintings. But she surely wasn't in the mood.

She forced herself to go to the back of the gallery and uncover the canvas she'd started yesterday. But before she took a seat on her stool, she froze. Normally, she didn't care who watched her paint. In fact, Diane often peeked over her shoulder and offered encouraging comments. But today, Margaret didn't want anyone to see her work. As she had decided, she was trying something new. It wasn't fun, and it wasn't going well, and the last thing she needed was comments from her friends or customers. Hefting her easel, she turned it to face the back of the room. Then she moved her stool and her supply table where she could reach them. Finally she was ready to continue her painting. She glanced up—and immediately saw Diane's speculative gaze.

"What are you working on?" her friend asked.

Margaret shrugged. "Just trying something a little different."

"Like what?" Diane started for the back of the room.

But Margaret put out a hand to block her access to the easel. "No. I mean, um...I'd rather not share this one until it's done."

Diane's eyebrows shot up practically to her hairline. "All right," she said slowly. "I'll look forward to seeing it."

Thankfully, a couple of tourists entered at that moment, saving Margaret from having to face the hurt in Diane's eyes. *Really, what was so wrong with wanting a little privacy? Nothing.* So then why did she sit with her paintbrush largely idle for the next hour, feeling rotten about how she'd treated Diane?

In the same hour, Diane was busy. A number of tourists stopped in, and in her usual friendly fashion, Diane chatted with them, showed them the inventory, subtly steered them toward pieces she thought they might like, and made several sales.

Those same tourists stopped to taste the desserts laid out on the table near the door, and the comments were so positive that Margaret grabbed a pen and a slip of paper and quietly began jotting them down. Shelley deserved to know what a huge hit her food was.

"Hey, Margaret, got some mail here for you." Ham Levesque, named by long-ago fellow high school wrestlers who had faced his enormous hands, came strolling through the door. He wore the US postal workers' summer uniform with shorts, and he waved a fistful of envelopes at her, grinning. Ham stopped dead when he saw the desserts. "Hey, whoa, what's this? Ladies," he said, "tell me I can have some of those, and I'm yours forever."

Diane laughed. "You're welcome to try them. Shelley Bauer made them."

Ham grabbed a slice of cake before walking to the back and handing the mail to Margaret. "What are you working on today?" He started around toward the front of the canvas, but Margaret held up her paintbrush in warning.

"No, no peeking." She tried to be more playful in her rejection than she'd been with Diane. She couldn't deal with any more hurt feelings today. "I'm experimenting."

Ham shrugged. "Hope it's another one of those lighthouse paintings. Beth has her heart set on one of them for her birthday." Ham's wife was as petite as he was large, but everyone in town knew who ruled the Levesque home.

Margaret smiled. "I have a few in the back. Come in when you have time, and you can choose the one you want. I'll wrap it and set it back for you."

"It's a deal. Thanks." Ham trekked back to the door, stopping to wolf down a piece of pie. "That Shelley sure can cook, can't she? She brought a pineapple upside-down cake to the church social last summer, and I'm telling you, it was the best thing I've ever tasted." He winked. "But don't tell my wife."

Diane grinned. "I'll pass your compliments on to the chef."

As Ham left, a slender woman in a gorgeous blue twinset worn with a stylish pair of navy trousers and matching low heels waited for him to pass.

"Hi, Beverly!" Diane said. "How's your father?"

Beverly shook her head. She untied the arms of the sweater that had been draped around her neck and then retied them. "He's still in the hospital."

"Oh, shucks." Diane was instantly sympathetic. "I was hoping he'd be released today."

Behind her easel, Margaret set down her paintbrush and began to clean off her hands. A hug might be in order, and it would never do to get paint on Beverly's lovely outfit. "What's going on?" she asked as she joined them.

Beverly shrugged. "He just couldn't keep anything down. They put him on antinausea drugs to get his system straightened out. This morning, he was keeping breakfast down, so I'm hoping he can be released tomorrow."

"I'm so sorry." Diane immediately moved to the younger woman's side and slipped an arm around her shoulders. "Is there anything we can do to help?"

Beverly shook her head. "Not really. Just keep saying prayers."

"That's all?" Margaret spread her hands. "I'd do that anyway. I thought you meant a real favor."

Beverly's face relaxed, and she almost smiled. "Prayer is a real favor."

"Well, we've certainly got that covered." Diane gave her a cheeky grin. Then she sobered a bit. "So how did he seem when you left?"

Beverly sighed, her shoulders wilting. "He's very confused. He keeps asking for my mother."

Diane winced. "Oh dear."

"The doctor thinks he'll be more himself once he's feeling better."

Margaret could tell Beverly was trying to convince herself of that fact. "I'm sure he will. Another day of rest will straighten him right out."

"The doctor wants me to get someone to pop in every day at home, maybe make him a meal or two and generally straighten things up and see how he's doing."

Diane opened her mouth immediately. "I could—"

"No," Beverly said. "You could not. I appreciate the thought, but you already have enough on your plate, Diane. This would be a daily commitment that would take a chunk of time."

"She's right." Margaret loved the way Diane instantly jumped in to help anyone in need, but Mr. Wheeland was going to need a lot more than a neighbor sticking her head in to say *Hi* every day. "There must be someone in town who does that type of work."

"I'm a little afraid to hire a perfect stranger. Father isn't going to be comfortable unless it's someone he knows."

"Well, that limits the pool considerably," Diane said. "I don't imagine he knows that many folks in Marble Cove anymore."

Beverly shook her head. "No. He knows the waitresses at the Cove and the librarians and the postman. But he doesn't attend church anymore, and the friends he meets for breakfast once a week at the Cove are all beginning to have their own health and mental acuity issues."

"*Hmm.* Let us think about it this week. Surely we can come up with something," Diane said.

"And don't wear yourself out," Margaret advised. Beverly was awfully thin already. "If you get sick, that will compound your troubles."

"I don't have time to get sick. I'm trying to do a massive cleaning job on as much of the house as I can this week before Father comes home." Beverly checked her watch. "I'd better get going." She gave them each a hug before striding out of the store.

"I know that feeling," Margaret said, walking back toward her easel.

She narrowed her eyes and stared at what she had done so far with the canvas on which she was working. Hiding a shudder, she resumed her seat and picked up the Filbert brush she had been using. She glanced from color to color indecisively, finally dipping the paintbrush into a deep midnight pool of oil paint. All right. She was committed to trying something different. She couldn't stop now.

CHAPTER FOURTEEN

Aiden wanted to play with Prize in the yard before lunch time, so Shelley checked to be sure the gate was shut and then let the pair out the back door. They practically exploded into the yard, making her glad it was a pleasant day and she didn't have to deal with all that energy cooped up inside the house.

Emma was napping. The baby had been up since six-thirty, and by midmorning she was sleepy-eyed. Shelley had read to her—even though her mother-in-law said reading to a baby was silly—and let the baby turn the pages of the board book before putting her down in her playpen for a snooze.

While both children were out of her hair, she tackled one of her least favorite tasks: reviewing their budget. Where was the money going to come from to buy dog food and get the vaccines the puppy needed? Since the night of their big fight, Dan had not mentioned Allan's offer, and she had no intention of bringing it up again. But if he didn't find some other way to bring in some money, he was going to have to get past his aversion to having a working wife.

But what kind of jobs was she suited for? She'd been a salesclerk all her short working life before she'd married.

Plenty of sales positions were available in a tourist town like Marble Cove, but many of them were seasonal because extra employees were unnecessary in the off-season. In addition, she would have to pay for day care and still earn enough to help with their finances, unless Dan became a house husband and took care of them.

She shook her head and began to write checks to cover at least the minimum balance on some of their outstanding debts. She was dreaming. The only way she could make any kind of reasonable money would be to find something she could do at home.

A shriek from the living room made her snap her head up sharply. Adrenaline flooded her system and her maternal instinct kicked in. She flew into the other room, frantically searching for her son. What had happened? Was he hurt?

Aiden was sobbing his little heart out as he walked across the living room. Prize bounced around his feet, nearly tripping him several times.

Shelley ran to him and dropped to her knees, pushing aside the puppy, who was eager to get in on the new game. "Honey, what happened? Are you hurt?"

Aiden shook his head. "Prize...Prize..." He was crying too hard for her to understand what he was trying to tell her.

She turned her attention to the puppy. Surely Prize wouldn't be so lively and happy if she were hurt, would she? There was no blood visible, and the little animal didn't seem to be limping or in pain. "What about Prize, Aiden?"

Aiden gulped. "Prize chewed up my Lego train." He began to wail again. He held up one hand, showing a small item dangling from it.

Shelley took the small toy. It was the engine from a Lego train set she and Dan had given Aiden for his birthday. The tiny vehicle was dented and battered, with puppy teeth marks clearly visible. One axle was broken.

Shelley drew Aiden into her arms, relieved that he hadn't been hurt and angry at the damage. Just like those pajamas Prize had damaged, she had saved and saved to get that train set for his birthday. Tears stung her eyes. Prize continued to circle them, tongue lolling as she cavorted.

"Bad puppy." Shelley took the train and shook it in front of the puppy's face. "You are a *bad puppy.*"

"Bad puppy," echoed Aiden.

The little dog backed up a step or two, confusion taking the place of her customary happy expression.

"Go lie down in your kennel." Shelley pointed sternly in the direction of the kitchen.

But the puppy didn't know that command, so Shelley surged to her feet and grabbed the puppy's collar, hauling her along until she had shut Prize in her kennel and slammed the door.

Prize cowered in the back of the kennel, and Shelley looked in at her, blowing out a breath of frustration. "I'm not going to hurt you." *She doesn't understand the words,* Shelley reminded herself.

Still too frustrated to gentle her tone, she hurried back to the living room to cuddle Aiden and examine the sad little train to see if there was any hope of salvaging it. Unfortunately, it was beyond repair. Shelley set it on the counter so Aiden wouldn't see it go into the trash.

Rustling and cooing heard through the baby monitor announced Emma's awakening, and Shelley hurried upstairs to get the little girl from her crib and change her. Then she carried her down and set her on the floor while she prepared lunch. She cast a critical glance at the kitchen floor as she mixed canned tuna with chopped celery and a pinch of salt. The floor was going to need a good washing again this afternoon. Since Emma had been crawling, Shelley had been trying her best to keep the floors clean.

Her mouth was set in a stern line as she spooned tuna salad onto English muffin halves and topped each one with grated sharp Cheddar cheese. She was about to pop them into the oven for a few minutes when the back door opened and Dan walked in.

"Hey," he said.

"Hello. What are you doing home in the middle of the day?" She searched her memory, but she was pretty certain Thursday was a day he was supposed to work until two.

Dan shrugged. "They didn't have much work, so they sent me home early."

"Have you had lunch?"

Dan held up the lunch box she had packed that morning. "Yes. I ate it all. But if that's an offer, I'd be happy to take one of those tuna melts off your hands." He was smiling, but his eyes were watchful.

Since their fight the other night, their conversations had been purely surface concerns. Who did what household chores, what child needed something, the time for an upcoming meal...It appeared that neither of them knew quite what to say, so neither had brought up anything deeper than a puddle.

"Sure." Shelley quickly added an extra tuna melt to the baking sheet before placing it in the oven. Then she walked to the counter. She picked up the little train, took it over and set it in front of Dan. All the while she kept an ear out for Aiden, who hadn't yet realized his daddy was home. The last thing she wanted was for him to see the destroyed toy again.

Dan picked it up, eyes questioning.

"Puppy." She didn't need to say more.

Dan closed his eyes and exhaled, shaking his head. "Darn it. Can we get another one?"

"Not the exact one that came with that set." She sat down across from him. "Dan, that's not the point." She spread her hands. "That puppy cannot stay. I just can't deal with a dog as well as two small children and household chores. Aiden isn't old enough to remember to pick everything up without my supervision, and I can't manage it every minute."

Dan exhaled. He sank lower in his chair, scrubbing both hands over his face. "Aiden's going to be heartbroken."

She nodded, wishing Dan had thought of that possibility before he'd brought the dog home.

He looked at her over his hands, still covering half his face. "What if we made her an outside dog? She can live on the porch, and I can run a line from there to that tree by the fence so she would have some room to run. And I could build her an insulated kennel so she'd be snug and warm even in winter."

Shelley hesitated. She recalled everything she'd read and learned about dogs since Prize had joined them. She would be all alone out there a great deal of the time, with a limited area in which she could move.

The plan bothered her a great deal more than it would have a few weeks ago. Dogs were pack animals, she now knew. Prize would be so lonely. She loved lying near them or hanging around underfoot. "I don't like that idea," she said. "It's not really fair to Prize." But then she thought of how devastated Aiden would be without Prize. "But I guess...I guess we can try it."

★　　★　　★

Beverly called the hospital on Friday and learned that her father had had a restful night and could be released. She spent the morning cleaning the last of the attic windows. Shortly before two, she headed for the hospital.

As she approached his room, a woman came out and walked toward her.

It was Diane. "Hi, Beverly. Are you here to take your father home?"

She nodded. "I am. Were you visiting him?"

It was Diane's turn to nod. "He knows he's going home, and he's getting impatient, so I kept him company for a while. He will be happy to see you."

"Thank you." Beverly knew she sounded stiff and standoffish, and she tried to relax. She really did like Diane, even if the other woman's talk of miracles could be a little wearing. "Thank you for looking in on him. I appreciate it." She smiled. "And I appreciate you."

Diane looked a little surprised. "You're welcome."

"Being demonstrative is hard for me," Beverly admitted slowly. "But friends like you are worth the effort."

Diane laughed and hugged her fast and hard before stepping back. "I'm glad. You're worth it too. Now get your father out of here before he drives the nurses bonkers."

Beverly smiled and stepped into the elevator. It was good to have friends at home.

Home? When she realized what she had just been thinking, she was a little chagrined. She hadn't lived in Marble Cove, but after a small taste, it felt as if she could belong here. Maybe she always had. Once again she wondered if she should consider moving.

The door to her father's room stood ajar, and she forgot about everything but seeing him. Hurrying forward, she entered just as a nurse was leaving.

"Hello," the woman said. "Are you his daughter?"

Beverly nodded.

The woman rolled her eyes and grinned. "Are we ever glad to see you. He's been telling us to look for you for about six hours now, ever since the doctor said he could go home."

The way her father's face lit up when he saw her made a lump rise in her throat, and she felt the sting of tears at the backs of her eyes. "Hi, Father." She bent and kissed him. "Are you ready to break out of this joint?"

Her father grinned. "You bet. I want to go home." He sobered. "I left an awfully big mess. Got a lot of cleanup to do."

Beverly smiled. "I believe an elf has been hard at work. There won't be anything for you to do except enjoy all the food the neighbors brought you."

His faded eyes twinkled with delight. "Dessert?"

"Some," she said. "But you can't have that until we're sure your tummy is settled. First you'll have to make do with some of the chicken-noodle soup Shelley Bauer brought."

He beamed. "That sounds just about right. Will you stay and have some with me?"

"Sure." She cleared her throat. "It's Friday evening. I'll be here until Sunday evening."

"That's good," he said. "Your mother will be happy."

Standing slightly above him, he couldn't see her face and it probably was a good thing, she decided. She knew she hadn't been able to hide her shock at the way he'd slipped so easily into the past. There was no point in trying to remind him that his wife was gone. It would only upset him. He would recall it for himself soon enough.

But she realized now more than ever, that she was going to have to devote some serious effort to finding a part-time caregiver to visit him during the weekdays.

CHAPTER FIFTEEN

Dan put the puppy's kennel on the back porch on Friday. Since it was mid-June, a blanket over the top and one inside would keep her warm enough for the time being, and Dan promised to build an insulated doghouse with a door flap. He also promised to stock some hay, because Lee at the pet store had mentioned that hay was warmer than blankets in the winter. He hadn't told Lee that Prize would be living outside permanently now. Dan knew what his reaction would be, and he simply didn't have another argument in him.

Aiden and Prize crawled in and out of the covered kennel several times. Aiden thought the outside kennel was a great idea—until he realized that Prize was not going to be allowed in the house anymore. "But she's my friend, Mommy," he explained through sobs, as fat tears rolled down his cheeks.

"I know, sweetheart, but remember what happened to your train? Prize doesn't know how to behave inside."

"I don't ca-a-are." He was having a total meltdown, partly due to genuine distress and partly because it was nap time and he had played hard all morning.

Shelley carried him up the steps, something she rarely did anymore, and placed him in his bed. He immediately rolled away from her. She reached out and patted his back; then she slipped the rail into place so he wouldn't roll out. "You rest for a little while, and when you get up you can play with Prize again."

"Inside?"

Shelley sighed. "You know the answer to that."

Aiden's response was another wail. She gently rose and walked across the floor, closing the bedroom door behind her.

He slept for his usual two-hour nap and woke up sunny and cheerful. But he insisted on having his snack outdoors at the picnic table so Prize could be with him. He even argued with Dan when it was time to come in for dinner. Dan finally had to get stern, and Aiden came inside with a mutinous expression that lasted throughout the meal. Then out he went again until time for his bath.

After the bath, Aiden said, "Can I go say good night to Prize?"

Shelley thought it was a bad idea. But before she could speak, Dan said, "Sure, buddy. Just for a minute."

The two males went downstairs. Shelley, cleaning up Aiden's room, listened intently. Sure enough, after a short pause, Aiden began to sob. Dan came back upstairs with a crestfallen expression. Aiden, crying and squirming to be released, practically leaped from Dan's arms into his bed. He rolled over onto his tummy, buried his face in his pillow and cried so hard Shelley was afraid he might make himself sick. She sat on the edge of the bed and patted his back, pat-pat-pat-rub in a little circle. She'd done it since he was an infant, a nonverbal sign to his body to relax and fall asleep. But he shrugged away from her hand and cried harder.

Sighing, Shelley looked at Dan and raised her hands. Then she stood and put the bedrail in place, and they left the room together. After Dan quietly closed the door, they sat on the top step together, waiting for Aiden to calm down.

Suddenly a mournful howl split the night, combining with Aiden in a heartbroken duet.

Dan dropped his head and ran a weary hand over the back of his neck. "I never should have brought the puppy home."

She patted his knee. "It will get better." She was trying to convince herself as well as her husband. "Remember the tantrums he threw when he was two? We just had to wait them out." *Loving, but firm. Stick to your resolve.*

They went downstairs, turning on the television to one of their favorite programs. Aiden continued to cry off and on, and Shelley was surprised at how long he was able to keep himself awake. Prize continued to howl occasionally too. Finally Dan said, "I can't concentrate, and I think I'm more exhausted than Aiden. Might as well go to bed."

Shelley nodded. But as she rose, she hesitated. "Do you think we should check on the puppy?"

Dan grimaced. "Bad idea. She's finally gotten a little quieter. If we go out there, we're going to start the whole cycle again."

"You're right." But as she turned out the lights and preceded her husband up the stairs, she felt a gnawing sense of guilt as she remembered Lee's words. *Dogs don't much like being alone.*

Aiden had finally stopped crying by the time Dan and Shelley went to bed. Prize was still making a little whining noise, but Dan turned on a ballgame on the TV in the bedroom, and she couldn't hear it any longer. When he shut off the TV and turned out the light, the house was blissfully quiet.

See? This will work. I just have to stick to my guns.

★　★　★

Margaret was getting ready to close at six when Diane came strolling along the sidewalk on Main Street.

"Howdy, neighbor," Diane called.

Despite the unproductive day she'd had, Margaret had to grin. "I think you're in the wrong part of the country for that greeting."

"It'll broaden your cultural experience." Diane waved a book she'd been carrying beneath her arm. "I got this out of the library."

"What is it?"

"Stories of Marble Cove Light." Diane's eyes sparkled. "I glanced through it. Looks like an awful lot of fiction, but still, I'll enjoy it."

"I've read that book. It *is* fiction." Margaret picked up her handbag. "Are you walking home?"

Diane nodded. "Thought you might be done for the day."

"Done for the decade is more like it," Margaret muttered beneath her breath.

"I heard that. Are you having trouble with your work?" Her friend was too perceptive, as her next words proved. "Margaret, you can't let one self-important meanie destroy your faith in yourself. You're a wonderful painter. Your work is flying out of the shop."

"Just because something sells doesn't mean it's good. Haven't you ever read a terrible best seller that only sold well because of the name of the author?"

"Of course. But this is different, and you know it. People aren't buying your work and then regretting it. They're buying it because they *love* it. Remember that couple yesterday who were so thrilled to meet the artist? They couldn't believe you were actually painting right there in the shop."

"Technically, I wasn't." Margaret didn't even try to hide the dejection in her voice. "I was sitting there staring at a blank canvas, thinking about all the things I should be doing instead of painting."

"Such as?"

"Making new curtains for the kitchen. Stripping the wallpaper in Adelaide's room and putting up something more adult. Turning that swampy patch at the bottom of our little hill into a water feature with a bridge and some koi. Trimming my toenails. Oh, I could list a dozen chores I've been wanting to tackle. Every day when I think about painting, the list grows longer. I'm going to start calling it the *Reasons Not to Paint* list."

Diane's eyes were both troubled and sympathetic. "So why are you following this path if you don't enjoy what you're painting?"

Margaret shrugged. "I'm not really sure I can explain it." They walked in silence for a moment. "When you get your novel published and people begin to read it, how will you feel if they say they thought it was fantastic?"

Diane shot her an incredulous glance. "Are you kidding? Fabulous."

"And if it hits the top of a best-seller list?"

"Not going to happen with a first book, but yes, I would be over the moon."

"And then how will you feel when you read a review that says it's terrible and your work is a joke?"

Diane's eyes widened. She fell silent. "Okay, I admit it. It would shake my confidence a little. Probably more than a little."

Margaret didn't say anything. That was exactly it. Her confidence had been shaken.

Diane cleared her throat. "But if my work is selling well and making best-seller lists, it's touching the hearts of people. And that's what matters, right?" She pressed her lips together tightly for a moment before going on. "I'm not saying the critical review wouldn't hurt; it would. But I guess I'm just too bullheaded to let one person's opinion cut me off at the knees."

"I'm not. Bullheaded, that is. I suppose I'm soft. Easily devastated."

"No, you are not." Diane looked stunned. "A soft person would never have had the courage to open a gallery in the first place, especially one that showcased her own work. An easily devastated person would not have raised a handicapped child to be so incredibly well-adjusted, one who functions to the best of her ability."

Margaret managed a smile. "You make it sound as if those things are extraordinary—"

"They are."

"But there is something inside me that wants to earn critical acclaim. It's important to me. I can't tell you why, but I'm having a really hard time just shaking those comments off."

"I know." Diane's eyes softened. "I know. Give it time, okay? Just don't stop painting."

"I won't." But she didn't tell Diane about her deliberate change in style. She wasn't enjoying it, and she certainly wasn't sure it was anything she wanted to display or share.

Chapter Sixteen

Emma's happy babble on the baby monitor awakened Shelley and Dan the next morning. They grinned at each other as they hauled themselves out of bed.

"I could wake up to that sound for the rest of my life," Shelley said.

Dan chuckled. "We could record it and make it the sound of our alarm."

"There you go. A recordable alarm clock. That's how we'll make our first million."

Dan sobered. "I imagine there's already something like that on the market. And I don't need a million—just enough to pay our bills, set some aside for the kids and take you on a vacation once in a while."

She smiled at him. "We'll get there." She had to let go of her anger about the dog, she knew. And Dan seemed more than willing to meet her halfway.

Dan dressed and went for Emma while Shelley made their bed. As she left the room to head downstairs and start their morning routine, an odd whimpering sound stopped her in her tracks.

Dan came into the hallway, carrying a happily drooling baby girl in one arm. He stopped at the look on her face. "What's wrong?"

"I thought I heard Aiden," she whispered. "Something didn't sound right."

Dan frowned. Together they moved to their son's closed door. Shelley quietly opened it without making noise, and they looked across the room at their sleeping son.

Shelley sucked in a sharp breath. "What on earth...?"

Aiden lay on his back, one little arm flung above his head in a position in which he often slept. Lying beside him, her head resting on his tummy, was Prize. When she saw Dan and Shelley, her stubby tail began to wag until it was doing a lively dance.

"Where did that dog come from?" she demanded, keeping her voice low. "Dan, I told you how I feel about that dog sleeping—"

"I didn't put her there!"

They stared at each other.

"Then who did?" Shelley asked.

"You don't think Aiden got up and got her, do you?" Dan looked as if he couldn't believe that possibility.

"Of course not." Shelley couldn't either. But...there was no other explanation. "I can't imagine it."

Aiden stretched and rolled to his side, his eyes slowly opening. Behind him, Prize stood and began to whine.

"I'd better take her out." Dan handed Shelley the baby and picked up the puppy.

"Daddy, can she come back in?" Aiden's eyes were pleading. "She's afraid out there alone."

Dan sighed. "Okay. Just for now." As he passed Shelley, he muttered, "I'm a total pushover."

Shelley heartily agreed with that assessment. Her optimism flew out the window. Once again, she knew she was going to be the "bad cop."

While her husband took the puppy downstairs and outside for her morning duties, Shelley set Emma down and helped Aiden wash his face. These days she had to close the bathroom door or Emma would be out the door and down the hall before she knew it.

Dan and Prize were in the kitchen when she came down with the children. "Hey, buddy," Dan greeted his son. "You want to feed your dog?"

Aiden eagerly opened the cupboard door and dragged the bag of dog food out. Dan handed him a scoop, and Aiden carefully poured it into the puppy's bowl. Prize watched expectantly, waiting politely before nosing into the dish.

"Look at me, Mommy. I feeded my dog." Aiden sounded like he'd leaped a building in a single bound.

Shelley had to smile. "I see. Very good job." It was hard to work up the appropriate enthusiasm.

As their son scrambled into his booster seat, Shelley put Emma in the high chair and buckled her in. Shelley got out bowls and utensils, while Dan set other cereal choices on the table and set out the milk. "I wonder if we should get some kind of container for the dog food so Aiden could open it himself," Dan said. "We could leave a scoop inside so he always would feed the right amount."

"I could feed Prize all by myself." Aiden's voice was matter-of-fact.

"That's a good idea," Shelley said. "Aiden, how did Prize get in your bed?"

Aiden's gaze slid to one side. "She came and hopped in."

"No stories," Shelley said, "or you'll have to sit in time-out. How did Prize get into your room?"

Aiden paused, and then apparently decided he'd rather face his mother than sit in the corner. "I went and got her."

"When?"

"Last night. When it was dark."

"All by yourself?" Shelley was staggered at the thought of her son finding the courage to sneak downstairs, open the back door—*in the dark,* unhook the puppy, and bring her in without anyone hearing them. "Where were Daddy and I?"

"In bed. You were watching a grown-up show." Aiden was allowed to watch only the programming that Shelley and Dan thought suitable for children.

"You went downstairs in the dark and opened the back door?" Dan whistled. "That was a pretty brave thing to do." The males beamed at each other until Shelley cleared her throat. "But you broke the rule, buddy," Dan added hastily.

Aiden's face fell.

"Honey, Prize chews things, remember?"

"I don't care." Aiden crossed his arms, and she could see another impasse coming.

Time to play the mother card. "I care. Prize has to stay outside."

"Why?"

"Because I'm the mother, and I said so."

Several hours later, Dan was working in his workshop area in the garage—hopefully working on a doghouse—when the back door opened without warning.

Shelley whipped around from the counter, putting a hand to her heart. "Wha—? Oh, hello, Frances. You gave me a scare." *In other words, could you please knock?*

Shelley's mother-in-law, Frances Bauer, waved a hand in the air as if sweeping away the statement. "Family never knocks, dear. You should be used to it by now."

Shelley wasn't sure she would ever get used to it. She and Dan had married more than four years ago, and she still hated it when people just walked into her home unannounced. Even Diane and Adelaide, who were frequent visitors, always knocked, but Dan's large and informal family had yet to get that memo. "What brings you by today?"

"I just wanted to snuggle my grandchildren." Frances helped herself to a seat at the table and beamed as Emma spotted her and army-crawled at top speed across the floor. "Look at you go, missy." She bent and picked up the baby, snuggling her into her generous lap. "Gracious, do you think these floors are clean enough for her to be crawling around on?"

"I've been mopping them every day since she began to crawl." Shelley tried to smile and keep her tone light, although she resented the implication.

"Mopping is all well and good," Frances replied, "but a mop will never replace good old-fashioned elbow grease. I still scrub my floor on my hands and knees." She took Emma's little hand and spread the fingers wide.

Checking for dirt, Shelley assumed. Since there was nothing good she could say in response to that, she didn't speak. Instead, she went to the back door to call Aiden, who must not have seen his grandmother arrive.

Glancing toward the sandbox where he often could be found, she didn't see him. But she did see Prize standing beside their picnic table, tail wagging happily as she looked up.

Up? Aiden was standing atop the table reaching in vain for a branch of the overhanging tree that was just out of his reach.

"Aiden Daniel!"

Her son whipped around with an incredibly guilty look plastered across his face.

"I don't want to see you trying to get up in that tree." Shelley shook her head in exasperation. Aiden had just discovered tree-climbing, courtesy of his older cousins, and now he was constantly trying to figure out how to scale the trees in their backyard, the limbs of which, thankfully, he couldn't reach. "Your grandmother is here. Come say hello."

"Hey, Meemaw!" Aiden leaped off the table and came running. "Come see what I got." He dragged her to the door to show her his new puppy.

"Daddy got you a dog, eh?" Frances sounded as unpleasantly surprised as Shelley had felt.

Aiden chattered away about the new puppy.

When Aiden paused for breath, Frances glanced around. "Dan working today?"

"No," Shelley replied. "He's in the workshop."

"What's he doing out there?"

Shelley shrugged. "He has several projects going. You should let him know you're here."

"I will, I will." But her mother-in-law made no move to rise.

"Would you like something to drink?" Shelley finally asked.

Frances nodded. "Iced tea would be good. And maybe some cookies or something? I always tried to keep home-baked snacks around when my children were young."

"I have chocolate drops." Shelley took a tin from the counter and arranged a few on a plate. She set it on the table before getting the tea from the fridge. When she turned back around, Frances had unsnapped Emma's little one-piece outfit and was sticking her finger down the back of the diaper.

"Just checking to see if she's dry," Frances said.

Shelley tried desperately not to grind her teeth together. "I checked her right before you came in, and she was fine."

Her mother-in-law stayed for thirty minutes, about twenty-five longer than Shelley would have preferred. It was hard to feel close to someone who criticized every single thing she did. Sometimes it seemed as if that was Dan's mother's favorite sport.

When Dan finally came in from the workshop, Frances said, "Hello, Daniel. I thought you were going to ignore my presence."

"Hi, Mom. What's up?"

"Nothing in particular. I just stopped by to see my grandchildren. It's been a while since you brought them out to see us. You know, Aiden would benefit quite a lot from being shown how to start working with his hands. You really should be taking him with you when you fiddle around out there."

Dan got himself a glass of iced tea. "Thanks for stopping by."

Aiden, who was apparently as oblivious to Frances's criticism as his father was, dragged Frances into the living room to see his toys. From the kitchen, Shelley heard him explaining what had happened to his locomotive.

"You mean the dog had it in her mouth? Did she touch any of the rest of this?"

Aiden must have nodded, because a minute later, Frances was back in the kitchen. "I need some disinfectant and paper towels, dear."

Shelley raised her eyebrows. "What for?"

Frances shuddered. "Aiden says that dog you got him was putting his toys in its mouth. Who knows what germs it could be carrying?"

Shelley made no move to hand over the requested items. "I've washed and disinfected them since that incident." She set her jaw, refraining from pointing out that Frances's son had been the one to bring the dog home.

"Oh well, that's good. Can't be too careful." Frances waved an admonishing finger at Shelley. The twinkle in her eyes was probably meant to take the sting from the words, but it didn't succeed.

After a few more minutes of listening to Aiden ramble and snuggling Emma, Frances said, "Well, I guess I'll run along. I have to get some groceries and get home to fix lunch. Dan, I sure hope they call you back to work full-time soon."

"So do we." Shelley was pleased to find a topic on which they could agree.

"I know your finances are tight," Frances said to her. "Have you thought about anything you could do to bring in some income? Surely there's something you're qualified to do."

Shelley blinked, taken aback by the personal question. Dan stepped in to answer. "Shelley and I agreed when we decided to start a family that she would be a stay-at-home mother. It's something we both feel strongly about."

"Oh, I understand completely." Frances absently ran a finger along the molding on one of the cabinets and examined her finger, brushing away a little dust. "*Hmm*."

What did *hmm* mean? Without uttering a word, Frances implied that Shelley wasn't a good housekeeper.

"You know I agree with your position," her mother-in-law said. "Why, I was an at-home mother all my life, and I believe it's one reason the kids all turned out so well. But back to this question of income, you really should consider what you could do from home. Why, when my children were

little, I dried sea grasses and searched for shells to make
dried wreaths that were sold in a local shop. It was lovely to
take the children walking on the beach every day. Fresh air
is so good for them, you know. I would work on my wreaths
when the children napped..."

Shelley had heard every word of this speech before. Facing
the sink, she silently recited each sentence as Frances went
on and on.

Dan cleared his throat. "Actually, Mom, Allan Hoskins
asked me to work on some of the furniture he's selling in his
wife's new gallery. I talked to him a little while ago, and I'm
going to do it."

"Daniel, that's wonderful!" His mother beamed. "Wait
until I tell your father! I'm leaving right now to go tell him."

Shelley stared at him, too dumbfounded to speak.

"You must be thrilled about that!" Frances beamed at
her. "Thank you for entertaining me, dear, and for letting
me barge in here and play with the children."

"You're welcome." Shelley felt uncomfortable with
the gratitude, especially after she'd been thinking such
ungracious thoughts.

"You think about what I said." Frances put a hand on the
doorknob. "I know it's nice not to have many responsibilities,
but if you had even a little money coming in, it would take
so much weight off Dan's shoulders. After all, who knows
how long that gallery is even going to be open." Before
Shelley could respond, she waved good-bye and sailed out
the door.

Okay, so maybe her guilt had been a little misplaced. Frances certainly had a way of making her feel inadequate. Shelley shook her head as she mixed up batter for banana bread. Then she bit her lip, thinking of Dan's job. Of course, if he lost his job altogether, who knew what they would have to do?

"Sorry to spring that on you while Mom was here." Dan made an apologetic face. "But I wanted to get her off your back about finding a job."

Shelley nodded. "It's all right. What did Allan say?"

Dan shrugged. "I'm going to start next week. First he wants to teach me the tongue-and-groove method he uses. I've always wanted to make furniture that way."

"That's great." Shelley smiled. She was pleased that Dan had found more work, and she felt at least as pleased that it was something she thought he would enjoy.

CHAPTER SEVENTEEN

S aturday afternoon, Shelley, Beverly, and Diane walked down to the Shearwater Gallery. Margaret had called and asked if they could stop in. Curious about the request, Diane dropped everything and called Beverly to take a short break from her father's care. When she called Shelley, the younger woman had put the kids down for naps, and Dan was home, so she also was free.

Diane stepped onto the sidewalk, looking to see if either of her friends was out yet. It was a glorious early summer day. Everywhere she looked, irises were blooming in stunning colors with ruffled edges and pansies spilled from barrels and baskets and pots, providing a new focus now that the rhododendron and azalea blooms were over. Hydrangeas were just forming fluffy snowballs, and more than one homeowner along their walk was out weeding or mulching tender young annuals.

Moments later, Shelley and Beverly joined her, and they walked downtown. Main Street was getting busier as more tourists arrived. School was out in many places now, and families were beginning their summer vacations.

"Goodness," Diane said as they threaded their way along the narrow sidewalks toward the gallery. "I forgot what summer is like around here."

Beverly smiled. "Busy. All the resort towns are. When I was a kid, I worked every summer as soon as I was old enough."

"Doing what?" Shelley asked.

"I was a waitress for several summers and school holidays." Beverly ticked the jobs off on her fingers as she spoke. "One year I worked at the bookstore, and another I worked at the Five and Dime."

"So they were all retail jobs?"

Beverly looked at Shelley with raised eyebrows. "Yes. High school and college kids aren't qualified for much else, unless you want to work for a lawn service or paint houses, neither of which appealed much to me. Some of the boys work on the water with their families, and sometimes there's extra work picking crabs. If you're lucky, you might get work as a tour guide with one of the park services or museums. You thinking about looking for work?"

"Not really." Shelley shook her head. "Although my mother-in-law thinks I should."

Beverly snorted. "No offense, Shel, but your mother-in-law has opinions about how to run almost everyone's life."

Shelley laughed. "You've got that right."

The three of them were still chuckling as they walked into the gallery. Margaret had propped open the door in deference to the lovely weather, and there were tourists browsing.

"Hello," Diane said, as they crossed the room. "Business good today?"

Margaret nodded. "I sold that drop-leaf table Allan just finished last week. He's going to have a fit. I know he was hoping not to have to make another of those anytime soon."

"If you have to have a problem, that's the best kind," Beverly pointed out.

"It certainly is." Margaret beckoned to them. "Come with me. I have something I want to show you."

The other three women followed her to the back of the shop.

Diane noticed immediately that Margaret had the easel covered. Normally, she would have mentioned it, but Margaret had been acting so secretive about her work since the opening and that horrid critique that Diane didn't want to draw undue attention to it. Maybe that wasn't what Margaret wanted them to see.

But to her pleased surprise, Margaret led them right to the easel.

"Have you finished the project you were working on all week?" Beverly asked.

Margaret nodded. "I'm going to show it to you, but you have to promise to be honest. If you don't like it, it's fine. I just want to know what you really think. I'm trying a new style."

She herded them into a better viewing position, and then drew the sheet off the easel. "What do you think?" Her tone was apprehensive.

Diane studied the painting. Done in oils, it was a significant departure from Margaret's previous work. It was painted in a much starker, more modern style. The painting depicted something Diane thought most resembled a storm over the ocean. The colors slipped seamlessly from one shade into the next in some places, and in others, there was an abrupt change of color family that was almost jarring. The technique was different too. It looked as if Margaret had used a sponge or a rag to apply the paint.

Beverly stepped a pace closer. "Margaret, this technique is excellent," she said. "I had no idea you were so proficient in this style." But Diane noticed she didn't say she liked it.

Shelley cleared her throat. "I love the colors, especially the way you blended them here." She pointed at one area. "To be honest, though, it's a bit dark for my taste. I'm more of a sand-dunes-and-sunshine-type of art lover."

Margaret turned to Diane. "What do you think?"

Diane studied it a bit longer. "I think it's extremely well done, as Beverly said, and that it will sell easily to the proper person. I also think it will be more difficult for most people to fall in love with, because most people prefer a more traditional look, like your earlier work." She turned and speared Margaret with a direct gaze. "But the most important question, to my mind, is how do you feel about it? Are you happy with the finished product?"

Margaret cleared her throat. "I think perhaps that critique was a wake-up call for me. Painters need to explore new avenues in order to grow as artists. If this is what the public wants, then this is what I'll produce. After all, my painting isn't just for fun. It helps put bread on the family table, so to speak."

"But Margaret, your other paintings have sold very well, haven't they?" Shelley had twin grooves of worry between her eyebrows.

"I'm not sure this *is* what the public wants." Beverly cleared her throat. "Like Diane said, I'm not sure a lot of your target market—tourists—will connect with pieces like this."

"I agree," Diane said quietly.

Margaret's expression changed. In the blink of an eye, she lost the sweet, open smile with which she normally greeted the world. Instead, they were faced with an unsmiling woman with wary eyes. "Maybe not, but it's what the art world wants."

"I guess. But the art world doesn't have to pay the bills. Your goal is to sell your work, isn't it?" Shelley was normally the least outspoken among them, so Diane was surprised at the vehemence in her tone. "You have a gift with a certain style, and you have an audience that loves it. I just don't understand what your goal is with this change."

Margaret blew out a breath of frustration. "I don't have a clue what my goal is anymore. I'm sorry I ever had a gallery opening. I was much happier before."

Diane put a bracing arm around her friend's shoulder. "You'll work it out."

A customer interrupted then to ask a question about a woven bowl Margaret had gotten on consignment. When she returned, Diane decided it was time for a change of subject.

"So there's something I haven't told you." She looked at Margaret and Beverly. "Something *we* haven't told you." She indicated Shelley and herself.

"Oh, I completely forgot!" Shelley's eyes widened. "I saw a light at the lighthouse again Wednesday night. Well, it was actually really, really early Thursday morning, like the middle of the night."

"Another light?" Margaret's eyes went wide.

Diane nodded. "She came and got me, and we went for a walk down the promenade, and I saw it too."

Beverly was regarding them both as if they were lunatics. "You went for a walk at two in the morning?"

"It was a little earlier than that, but not much," Diane said.

Beverly chuckled. "Oh well, then, that makes it so much better."

Everyone grinned.

"So tell us details," Margaret said. "Was it like we saw before?"

"No," Diane and Shelley said together.

Diane looked at Shelley, indicating that she should continue. "It was nothing like that," Shelley said. "This

was not from the Fresnel—the main lighthouse light."
She went on to describe the almost-blinking pattern of
the light.

"But Fred said the building hasn't been open for years,"
Margaret said. "And the door has been locked as long as I've
been living here."

Diane shrugged. "I know what he said. But Shelley and
I didn't have a mutual delusion. We did see that light." She
lowered her voice. "Here's what I think. We should set up
a schedule and take turns watching the entry door to see if
anyone is going in or out."

Shelley rolled her eyes. "I can't just take off in the middle
of the night." Diane turned and looked at her, and Shelley's
face reddened. "Well, I mean, I can, but I can't. I'd be
exhausted the next day."

"I'm willing," Margaret told them. "But exactly what do
you hope to find, Diane? If we do see someone going in and
out, what do we do?"

Diane was silent for a moment. "Fred Little won't be
much help, that's for sure."

"We can't march up to someone in the middle of the
night and ask what they're doing at the lighthouse." Shelley
looked a little nervous. "If someone really is going in and
out, it's someone who probably shouldn't be. They could be
dangerous."

★　★　★

When Shelley got home, Dan informed her that he was going at two to talk with Allan Hoskins again to learn more of his style with the pieces he was building.

Aiden had awakened while she was gone.

"He had some crackers and cheese along with apple juice for a snack," Dan reported, "and he's been outside playing with the puppy ever since."

Shelley glanced through the window in the top half of the back door. "Thanks. Emma still sleeping?"

Dan nodded. "She went down around twelve-thirty."

A few moments later, he left to go over to Allan's.

Shelley walked onto the back porch and shaded her eyes. Goodness, but the sun was bright today. "Aiden," she called. "Come here, please."

Her son and his dog came running toward her.

"Hi, Mommy. You're back." Aiden sounded as delighted as if she'd been gone for a year.

Shelley couldn't help but smile. "I am. Did Daddy put sunscreen on you?"

Aiden shrugged. "Don't remember." And off he dashed.

"You need to come inside and get sunscreen," she called after him.

"Already did."

Shelley chuckled to herself. There was more than one way to get information. While Aiden was occupied outside and Emma was sleeping, she decided to make pretzels. She wasn't sure how they would turn out, but she had watched a cooking show recently in which two top chefs did their best to top each other's pretzel recipes, and the pretzels hadn't seemed that difficult to make. It would be fun to do a special take on a pretzel recipe all her own.

While the first batch went into the oven, she went up and got Emma, who had awakened and was happily cooing to herself in her crib. After changing her and brushing her fine blonde hair, Shelley carried her downstairs and put her in her high chair, where she happily made a sticky mess of zwieback.

Shelley stuck her head out the door. "Aiden?"

"Hi, Mommy." He came charging across the yard, Prize hot on his heels.

"Hey, buddy. Come on inside and let me put more sunscreen on you."

"Aw, Mommy, I don't want more sunscreen."

"If you want to play outside, you need to put more on."

He sighed. "Okay."

She held the door for him, blocking the puppy with her foot when Prize tried to enter. "Stay there, Prize. He'll be right back."

Inspecting Aiden's face and the exposed skin of his neck and arms, she could see that he appeared a little red. "Honey, you need to wear a hat if you want to go back out," she said, as she rubbed sunscreen on him.

"I have to go back out." He squirmed around and looked anxiously out the door. "Prize will be lonely."

"Well, you can't stay out there all day every day."

"Can Prize come in?"

"No." Shelley sighed. She could see this was going to be a never-ending battle. What were they going to do about the puppy? Obviously, Aiden couldn't stay outside for endless hours. All he needed was one sunburn, and her mother-in-law would have a million suggestions on how to prevent it. But Shelley had told him the puppy couldn't come in anymore. Was she wrong to insist on that? She was capping the sunscreen, about to go find Aiden's hat, when she smelled something burning.

Oh no! The pretzels.

She shot across the kitchen and yanked open the oven. Grabbing the tray of pretzels, she pulled it out of the oven and quickly shuffled them onto a rack to cool. But she already could see that it was too late. The pretzels were black on the bottom and an extremely dark, brittle brown on top. Far too burned to eat.

Her shoulders sagged. "Oh...*sugar!*" she exclaimed. It was the closest she ever came to cursing, and she was glad for that because Aiden immediately copied her.

"What's the matter?" he asked.

Shelley sighed. "I made some yummy pretzels, but I burned them."

"I'm sorry." He hugged her leg. Then he ran for the door. "I have to go, Mommy. Prize is sad without me."

"Take your hat." She caught him at the door and tugged the cap down over his fair hair. Then she watched, feeling somewhat deflated. Only a few short weeks ago, Aiden would have been all about helping her with the pretzels. Now he was focused on his relationship with the puppy. She knew it was silly to feel rejected, but that was how it felt. Or perhaps not rejected, but demoted to second place.

She sighed again. She'd known it would happen someday, of course. She just hadn't been expecting it to happen so soon.

Chapter Eighteen

Early on Sunday morning, Beverly settled her father in his easy chair with the television remote, a cup of decaf tea, and his promise not to move until she returned.

Then she met Margaret, Diane and Rocky, and Shelley with both children and Prize for a walk on the beach. It had been Diane's idea, and they were going early so no one would miss her church service. "Well, look at you, missy." Diane craned her neck to see Emma. "You got your first haircut."

"I just trimmed it a little and gave her bangs. That one piece was always in her eyes."

"It's cute." Diane smiled softly. "My daughter Jess had bangs like that when she was a toddler."

Beverly strolled along with her friends, enjoying the cool morning air, the fresh scent of the ocean, and the chat among the group of women to whom she'd drawn surprisingly close in the past two months. *Close* was a relative term, she supposed. She knew she wasn't nearly as open with the other three women as they were with her and each other. But she didn't do girl friendships. This was the closest she'd been to other women since...well, since her college days, probably.

"Beverly, how's your father coming along?" Margaret leaned around Diane to pose the question.

"Very well, I think." Distracted from her thoughts, she paused to consider. "He seems to be on the mend since he was discharged from the hospital. Now that he's no longer nauseated and the dehydration was treated, he's beginning to eat again."

"How is he mentally?" Yesterday afternoon, Beverly had mentioned his episodes of confusion, so Margaret's question wasn't unexpected.

"He's regaining his strength. And his mental facilities also seem to be mending themselves along with the rest of his body. He hasn't had a single episode of confusion since shortly after I brought him home."

"That sounds very encouraging," Diane murmured.

"It is." But to her consternation, she could feel tears threatening, and she choked on the words.

"Hey," Diane said softly. "What's wrong?"

Beverly shrugged, holding up a finger for a moment until she had the tears under control. She *never* cried in front of other people. "I don't know what to do. I'm afraid I may have to put him in a nursing home."

"What?" Margaret exclaimed.

"Why? I thought he was doing better." Shelley moved the puppy's leash to the other side of the stroller before Prize tangled them all into a huge knot.

"He is," Beverly said. "But I don't know how reasonable it is to expect that he can live alone much longer. I can come down most weekends, but that still means he's alone the five other days."

"I guess I didn't realize you were quite so worried about this." Diane stopped to whistle at Rocky so he wouldn't get so far ahead of them.

Beverly sniffed. "I didn't either, until I thought about leaving this evening. At the hospital someone suggested I hire a person to check in on him each day. But I can't imagine how Father would do with someone he didn't know. That's the biggest thing that's stopping me."

Shelley caught her hair as it flew across her face and tossed it behind her shoulder. "What about Mrs. Peabody?"

"But she's almost as old as he is," Beverly said.

"True, but she's in pretty darn good shape." Diane looked thoughtful. "You know, that's a good suggestion. She's physically fit enough to make meals and clean up a kitchen, and she's certainly mentally alert enough to know if he's all right or not. She told me she lives on a fixed income, so I'm sure she could use the money."

"I suspect she'd be happy to do it," Margaret added. "But she might be offended if you offer her money. She'll want to do it just as a neighborly thing."

"There must be some way to get her to accept payment," Shelley said.

They all looked at each other, stymied. Diane laughed. "Well, aren't we just full of brilliant ideas?"

The others all chuckled as well.

"Let's keep thinking about it," Margaret suggested. "Surely there must be a way."

"Prize!" Shelley's sudden exclamation startled everyone. The puppy had made a sudden lunge and had torn the leash from Shelley's hand. She yipped and barked wildly as she ran in circles around them several times, ignoring all of Shelley's attempts to get her to come. Then she took off down the beach.

"Oh no!" Shelley looked frantic. Aiden began to cry.

"Here," said Beverly. She took the handles of the stroller so Shelley's hands were free. She looked at Aiden. She didn't deal with children very much, and she wasn't sure what to do, but Shelley needed to be able to track down that dog. "Aiden, why don't we sit over there on that bench?" Beverly pointed to one of the benches along the promenade. "That way, when Prize comes back, she'll be able to see you."

"Thank you," Shelley said. She began to jog down the beach.

"Come on, Rocky. Let's go help Shelley." Diane followed her.

Margaret settled herself beside Beverly on the bench and hauled Aiden into her lap.

Beverly watched Margaret engage the little boy in conversation. She wished she was as good with children as the others were. It was all she could do to keep the baby girl in the stroller content, she thought, as she shook a stuffed toy in front of Emma, making her grin.

Shelley and Diane were far down the beach by now, with Rocky running ahead of Diane. Beverly put a hand up to shade her eyes so she could see them. Then she saw a small black dot rushing back up the beach toward them. "Look!" She grabbed Aiden's shoulder and pointed. "That's Prize, isn't it?"

Aiden knuckled tears from his eyes and stood on the bench beside Margaret.

"I believe you're right," Margaret said.

As they watched, the puppy approached Shelley and Diane, but she wouldn't get close enough for either woman to grab her. She repeatedly ran within five feet of Diane and Shelley and stretched her front half down to the ground with her back end madly wriggling in the air. But the moment Shelley took a step forward, she would race off again.

"It's a game to her," Beverly observed.

Diane put both hands to her mouth, and Beverly realized she was calling Rocky. As the yellow dog approached, Prize greeted him joyfully, leaping and bouncing around him with her leash dragging behind her. Rocky ignored the display of devotion and went directly to Diane's side, where he took up a sitting position.

"That's it," Margaret said, watching the puppy draw nearer.

Diane and Shelley both stood quite still, even when the puppy came right up and sat near Rocky for a moment before jumping up and running in a big circle again. Shelley knelt beside Rocky and began to pet him. The big dog clearly relished the attention. He rolled over on his back so Shelley could pat his belly.

Prize came up and lay panting beside him. Shelley ignored her.

Beverly held her breath.

Aiden said, "Look! My mommy's going to get my puppy."

"That's right, sweetie." Margaret smiled at him.

And Shelley moved her knee and planted it squarely on the dragging leash. Prize startled and bolted, but with the leash secured, she couldn't go any farther than the end of it.

"Oh, whew." Beverly blew out a sigh of relief as Margaret and Aiden cheered.

Shelley picked up Prize's leash, and the two women and two dogs began to walk back toward Beverly, Margaret, and the children.

"That's one lively puppy," Beverly said.

Margaret shook her head. "Men. I don't know what Dan was thinking. Doesn't he realize that Shelley's already got enough on her plate?"

Beverly eyed Shelley as the foursome approached. She'd never thought much about Shelley's life. She'd never had children and had rarely even spent much time around them. But it was becoming obvious that Shelley worked as hard or harder than she herself did. What must it be like to have your job underfoot twenty-four/seven? It was no wonder Shelley often seemed so giddy and lively when she managed to get away from home by herself.

★　★　★

Dan had another Sunday morning off, so all four of them attended church together in the morning. Why, Shelley wondered, when Dan's hours had been so drastically cut, did they usually need him at the docks on Sunday mornings anyway?

After the service, they went to Dan's parents' place. Frances always had a large Sunday lunch for any of her children and grandchildren who could attend. Shelley went when Dan went, but she'd never had the courage to dive into the huge pool of Bauers by herself.

"Hey, Mom." Dan held the door for Shelley and the kids.

Aiden ran to his grandmother. "Hi, Meemaw. We came to eat."

Frances laughed, lifting him up for a kiss. "Oh, you did, did you? I guess it's a good thing I have some lunch ready then. What if I didn't?"

Aiden giggled. "Silly Meemaw. You *always* have lunch."

Shelley smiled as she regarded the pair. Frances might drive her batty sometimes, but she dearly loved the children.

Several of Aiden's cousins came squealing through the kitchen. They swept him up into their posse and raced off into the living room.

Dan's sister Livvy held out her arms, smiling at Emma. "May I?" she asked Shelley.

"Of course."

Without any children to care for, Shelley felt out of place. Dan's sisters and brothers and their spouses chattered all around her, occasionally tossing a question her way, so she had to pay attention. Her sisters-in-law were nice people, and they always included her in any plans they made as a family. But Dan was the baby by more than six years, so all of his sisters and sisters-in-law were older than she, and most of their children ranged in age between seven and seventeen.

At one point Dan laid his hand over hers and squeezed, giving her a private, reassuring smile. Although she tried not to let him know how overwhelming these huge gatherings were, apparently he recognized her uneasiness.

They stayed for more than an hour, but when Emma's eyelids began to droop and she got fussy, Shelley gave Dan *the Look*.

He stood and corralled Aiden and then returned to the kitchen. "Great meal, Mom. We've got to head out now. Emma's ready for her nap."

Frances frowned. "She can sleep here. You know I have a crib upstairs."

Dan hesitated.

"Thank you, Frances," Shelley said, "but she sleeps better in her own bed." So that Frances wouldn't feel slighted, she added, "And I may just take a nap myself."

Several of her sisters-in-law laughed. Samantha said, "I know how you feel. By the time Joey and Lily were asleep, I was ready to pass out."

"I never napped when my children were small," Frances announced. "I can't imagine how you can keep a house neat and clean if you don't use those naptimes to catch up on housework."

Shelley tried not to bristle. Frances didn't mean to imply that her house wasn't clean, she was certain.

"Oh, give it a rest, Mom," Dan's sister Annie said. "That's a crock, and you know it. I remember you napping."

"I never—"

"Oh yes, you did. Because I used to wait until you were asleep and then get up and go play."

As a wave of laughter rose, Shelley and her family made their escape.

"Don't mind my mother," Dan said the moment they were in the truck heading home. "She likes to have the last word." He laughed. "So does Annie. They butt heads a lot."

Both children fell asleep on the way home. Shelley and Dan were able to get them into their beds and remove their shoes without waking them. As they tiptoed from the room, Dan said, "I want to go over to Allan's this afternoon so he can show me how he turns his table legs. I'm not starting until tomorrow, but he said he'd be in the workshop this afternoon, so I thought I'd go ask a few questions."

Shelley smiled, pleased that he seemed so interested in his new job. "That's fine. I thought we'd have quiche for dinner, and I'm going to chop the spinach and mushrooms ahead of time."

After he left, she did a few chores and folded some of the never-ending stream of clothing the children went through in a week. Afterward, she really was tired, so she stretched out on the couch for a half hour or so until the kids woke up.

She awakened to a cold, wet nose pushing itself against her face. Startled, she instinctively put up a hand, and Prize, who had been on her hind legs licking Shelley's face, dropped to the floor.

Aiden came running down the stairs. "Prize," he called in a stage whisper. "Where are you?"

Shelley cleared her throat.

Aiden's gaze shot to her, sitting upright and clearly awake. "Hi, Mommy. I waked up a little while ago."

"I see. Aiden, what's our rule about Prize and the house?"

He descended the steps and prodded the carpet with a toe, avoiding her gaze.

"Aiden?"

"Prize can't come in the house," he said in a low voice.

"That's right. So why did you bring her in?"

"She wanted to play inside."

Shelley fought the urge to smile. "She told you that, did she?"

"Yes." Inspired, he added, "And she wanted a cookie too, so I got a stool and got her one."

"Well, now it's time for her to go back outside. When Daddy comes home, you need to tell him what you did while I was napping."

Aiden's face fell. "No, Mommy."

"Yes, Aiden."

"But Daddy might get mad at me."

"Why would Daddy be mad?"

Aiden looked away from her. "Because I didn't listen, and I brought Prize inside."

"When you knew you weren't supposed to."

"When I knew I wasn't supposed to."

In an absolutely perfect moment of timing, she heard the back door open.

"Sounds like Daddy's home," Shelley said. "You can tell him now." She got up and walked into the kitchen. "Hi, honey. How did it go?"

Dan looked more relaxed and happy than she'd seen him in quite a while when he came in from Allan's. "Great. I know how to do most everything he needs me to do. He's got quite an operation over there. I didn't realize it."

"Did you..." She saw something that immediately made her forget what she was going to say.

Prize was lying beneath one of their chairs, chewing happily on a low rung.

Shelley let out a short shriek and dove for the kitchen table.

Prize saw her coming and scampered away, but Dan caught her. Aiden came into the kitchen, drawn by the commotion even though he was in trouble.

Shelley was still on her knees by the side of the chair. From the amount of wood slivers and chips scattered around her, Prize must have been at it while Shelley was napping too. She ran a finger over the splintered wood, unable to believe how much damage had been done. "This chair belonged to my grandmother." Her voice quivered. "And now it's been ruined by that—that—*that.*" She pointed to the dog under Dan's arm. She picked up a wet sliver of wood from the floor and tried to fit it back in place, but the rung was too badly damaged, and it no longer fit. Letting the wood fall to the floor, Shelley dropped her face into her hands and began to sob.

It was the last straw. She hadn't wanted that dog, and now look what had happened.

"Mommy?" Aiden's voice sounded frightened. A little hand tugged at the sleeve of the T-shirt she'd put on after they'd arrived home. "Mommy, I'm sorry."

"Aiden." Dan's voice sounded as stern as she'd ever heard it. "Take Prize outside. *Right now.*"

Aiden began to cry.

Shelley knew she should comfort him. But as she thought about the damage to the chair, she could only sob harder. Some of the happiest memories from her childhood had happened while she was sitting in these chairs in her grandmother's kitchen playing games with her sister.

"Outside. Now!"

The sound of Aiden's crying grew distant. Then Dan's arm was around her. Shelley lifted her head, trying to stop crying.

Dan extended a tissue, and she wiped her eyes and blew her nose. "Honey, I'm so sorry." He put his hands beneath her elbows and drew her to her feet, and his voice was rife with disgust at himself. "I'm sorry I ever brought that darn dog home." He drew her against him. "I'll take the chair over to Allan's and fix it. You'll see. I'll make it look as good as new again."

It wasn't new—that was the point. She wanted to scream, but she managed a nod instead.

Dan stepped back. "I'd better go talk to Aiden. He's really upset." His voice firmed. "As he should be. We specifically told him Prize can't come in the house."

She sighed. "He's three years old, Dan. He's just starting to learn about rules. Don't be too hard on him."

Dan nodded. "I think seeing you cry may have scared him straight, at least for a while."

Shelley's shoulders drooped. "Maybe."

Chapter Nineteen

Margaret had a meeting at her church that evening. Our Savior's Sanctuary was one of the oldest churches in Marble Cove. Attached to it was a cemetery with graves dating back as far as the seventeenth century. Among them were several sailors listed as unknown who had washed ashore after their ship had foundered on the rocks in the mid 1800s.

The meeting was a gathering of the youth group and their mentors. Margaret had been active in the program for a number of years. This year she was mentoring Sam Tyler, a fine young man who was a member of the football team at the high school.

At the conclusion of the meeting, she said, "Can I give you a ride home, Sam?"

The young man grinned. He held out a piece of paper and waggled it so close to her face she never would have been able to read it without her glasses.

"What's this?"

"I got my driver's license!" Sam beamed, delighted to share his news. "Dad took me on Friday, and I passed the first time."

"Congratulations!" Having mentored other students, Margaret knew the monumental importance attached to that small piece of paper. "That's wonderful, Sam."

He nodded enthusiastically. "And Mom kept her old car after she got a new one last year, so now I can drive to school and church and everything—with no 'adult' in the car."

She chuckled. "*Everything* covers a lot of ground." She sobered. "Take good care of yourself, and drive safely, okay?"

"Okay. Bye." And off he went, thrilled to be driving home alone.

Margaret said good-bye to a few other people and climbed into her car for the short drive home. As she turned onto the street, she had a direct view of the lighthouse, barely visible now.

Suddenly a light glowed in the gathering darkness.

Margaret gasped. It looked like a light in a window…like Shelley and Diane had described the time they'd seen it at night. Except this light wasn't extremely bright. It did have a vaguely rectangular shape—almost as if someone had covered the window, and light was seeping out from around the edges.

Impulsively, she turned left on the beach road rather than turning right to go home. Keeping her eye on the light, she drove toward the lighthouse. It really did seem to be coming from a window, she thought. Then she did a double-take as a figure passed by the window. As her eyes became accustomed to the sight, the movement was easier to discern. She was almost positive someone had walked across the floor, backlit by the light.

A chill ran up her spine. That hadn't been a trick of the light. There *was* someone in there!

She pulled into one of the gravel parking areas used by tourists. As she glanced back up, the light winked out.

She sat and watched, but no light came back on. She really had seen it, she assured herself. After a few minutes, she began to feel a bit spooked. Even though it was a clear night, it was really dark with very little moonlight. Okay, she was going home. No more sitting out here alone, waiting for heaven only knew what.

She drove home as fast as was safe and hurried into the house. "Allan? Allan! You'll never believe this, but I saw a light in the lighthouse tonight."

Her husband ambled into the kitchen, blinking. "What?"

"You were watching TV from behind your eyelids again, weren't you?" she accused with a smile.

"It was a good show." He grinned. "What's this about a light?"

"I saw a light in the window of the lighthouse tonight." Margaret went on to describe exactly what she'd seen. When she mentioned seeing a person, Allan's sleepy eyes widened.

"Are you sure?"

"Positive." She held up two fingers. "If I were a Boy Scout, I'd take an oath."

"If you were a Boy Scout, I never would have married you," he pointed out, and they both laughed. "So what are you going to do?"

"I'm not sure. Fred already thinks Diane, Shelley, Beverly, and I are a slightly crazy group of amateur sleuths. If I tell him, he's just going to brush it off. I'll tell the others and see what they think."

"My vote goes to telling Fred," Allan said. "Better crazy than meeting face-to-face with smugglers or someone equally unsavory."

"It's not like we would walk up and confront someone." Margaret was indignant. "We do have some common sense."

Allan gave her a pitying look. "My dearest wife, one dose of common sense, split among you four, does not exactly inspire my confidence."

★　　★　　★

Monday morning was beautiful. Shelley took both children to the park just off Main Street. Aiden normally loved the park, but he'd given her a hard time about leaving Prize behind.

"Honey, they don't allow dogs in the park," she'd said.

"Why?"

"Because they might go to the potty, and if their owners forget to pick it up, someone else might step in it."

Aiden had thought that one over. "But we can bring a bag, and you can pick it up."

That had made her laugh. Already he was good at delegating the unpleasant tasks.

A woman walked into the park and settled on a bench with her lunch. Shelley waved, recognizing her from church.

She worked downtown, although Shelley couldn't remember exactly where.

Work. Once again she thought about getting a job. Working part-time wouldn't be so bad. It might actually be nice to get out and see other adults on a regular basis.

It probably wasn't even possible at the moment. In the summer, lots of European kids came over to work. There was an Irish waitress at the Cove, and the girl who'd waited on her in the gourmet kitchen shop might have been French.

Even if she could get work, it would be work in retail at minimum wage. She would barely make enough to cover babysitting, much less help with their expenses.

But the biggest stumbling block to looking for work was right here in front of her. Emma was happily swinging, strapped into a little yellow seat-swing. She squealed and kicked her legs every time she swung forward. Aiden, just beyond them, was busily engrossed in the sandbox with the toys she'd brought along.

She didn't want these little people to be raised by someone else while she worked. Neither did Dan. It was so important to them. Besides, her mother-in-law's reaction to such a newsflash would be a major drama. She would probably have a stroke if Shelley announced she'd hired a babysitter and started working.

Or even worse, she might offer to babysit for them. Dan's sister Annie had let Frances babysit for her children when they were small. Frances had rearranged her house, fed the children things they weren't allowed to have, and generally made Annie so crazy she'd finally hired someone else. It had been a huge hullabaloo at the time, Dan said. No, his mother was definitely not a long-term babysitting option.

On the way home, she took a detour along Main Street. It was so nice to be out of the house.

When she came to the Shearwater Gallery, she spotted Diane at the front of the room, dusting. She waved at Shelley through the window and beckoned.

Aiden went racing ahead. "Where's Rocky?" he demanded.

Diane picked him up and swung him in a circle. "He stayed at home. He doesn't like coming to the gallery."

"How do you know?" Aiden eyes were big.

"He told me. Not in words." She put him down and knelt at his level. "When I make him come to the gallery, he drags his feet. He lies under a table and won't come out to be petted. And when it's time to leave, he suddenly becomes the happiest dog in the world." She looked up at Shelley and grinned. "It's really weird."

Shelley laughed. "Sounds like it." She handed Emma over when Diane rose and held out her arms.

Emma went to her with a happy gurgle. Diane had worn her hair down today, and Emma grabbed fistfuls and began stuffing them into her mouth. "Hey, imp!" Diane swung the baby down from her shoulder to perch face out on her hip. "Is this just a social call?" she asked Shelley.

Shelley nodded. Her own hair was caught up in a ponytail, and then the end was lifted, doubled back and down, and threaded through the center beginning above the elastic band. Tugging from the bottom pulled the tail down to make what her mother had called a "topsy-tail" with pretty rolled sides. It looked nice, but mostly she wore it that way to keep Emma from doing exactly what she'd done to Diane. "We were at the park, so we're going home the long way."

"Someone ought to sleep well this afternoon."

Shelley held up her crossed fingers. "I hope so." She looked around as Aiden ran off to crawl in and out between the legs of Allan's furniture on display, one of his favorite activities. "Where's Margaret?"

"She ran to the post office. She should be back any minute."

Any minute turned out to be about two seconds as Margaret came around the corner, talking to Beverly. She smiled at Shelley and Diane. "Look who I found."

"I assumed you were gone," Diane said to Beverly.

"I changed my mind. I'm still trying to figure out what to do about my dad. At this rate, my vacation days are going to be shot before I ever get around to taking a vacation."

"I had an idea about that," Diane said.

"Great. It's more than I've had."

"I know we'd mentioned Mrs. Peabody, but the consensus was she wouldn't consider it for pay."

The others nodded.

"What if you asked Mrs. Peabody for recommendations for someone local to come in and help? Tell her it has to be done, even though he hates strangers, or you will have to consider putting him in a nursing home. My theory is that Mrs. Peabody will offer to do it at that point."

Beverly seemed to consider it. "Yes, but then I'd be caught between *two* stubborn old—"

"Hold your britches," Diane said as Margaret unsuccessfully stifled a chuckle. "When Mrs. Peabody offers to do it, you'll decline."

"I will?" Beverly's brow wrinkled.

Diane pressed on. "Yes. You'll decline because your father won't accept charity. The only way he'll do it is if you find someone whom you can pay..."

"I see." Shelley always admired Diane, but this was truly brilliant. "Mrs. Peabody will agree to do it anyway, even if she does have to accept payment, thereby saving face."

Margaret rolled her eyes. "You're right. I think it might work. But what a convoluted notion. No wonder you're a novelist, Diane. I could never think like that."

"An aspiring novelist," Diane corrected. "I'm enjoying writing fiction. I just hope I can sell it." Emma began to fuss a little so Diane bounced the baby on her hip. Shelley got her favorite rattle out and handed it to her.

"I'm glad one of us is enjoying her artistic endeavor." Margaret sounded unusually sour.

"Uh-oh. This new style not going so well?" Shelley hadn't much cared for the painting she'd seen the other day, but she wouldn't hurt Margaret's feelings for the world.

"Not going, period." Margaret studied their faces. "I could tell you weren't wild about it the other day, even though everyone was kind and encouraging. And you know what, you were right not to like it. I'm not enjoying what I'm trying to paint now. It doesn't feel like me, if that makes any sense."

"It makes a lot of sense," Diane said softly.

"Usually my painting is a very organic process." Margaret waved her hands wildly, her voice rising.

Shelley looked around to see if Aiden was affected by the change in the older woman's usual manner, but he was busy running two small trucks along the baseboard at the back of the shop.

"Usually I don't have an end product in mind," Margaret said. "I let the work take me where it will. With this, I find myself thinking about my next move constantly. Should I use this brush or that knife? Should that color be darker? I have absolutely hated the whole ordeal. And I hate that painting too!"

The other three were speechless. Normally Margaret was laid-back and placid, comfortable in her own skin.

But before anyone could react, Margaret whirled and dashed out of the shop in a very un-Margaret fashion.

"I'll try to talk to her." Diane handed the baby back to Shelley and started out the door.

After a moment, Diane slowly walked back into the gallery. "She says she's not mad at any of us, but she is upset with herself because I was right."

"Right?" Shelley tried to recall their earlier conversations. Emma was growing sleepy, and Shelley rocked back and forth, back and forth. Finally, the little head fell to Shelley's shoulder and the tiny arms went limp.

"About what's important," Diane clarified. "About her being the one who has to like the finished product. I think it will show in the work if she doesn't like what she's doing."

Beverly nodded. "I imagine you're right, even if I don't have an artistic bone in my body."

Margaret came striding back in the door at that moment. "Okay. Enough of the pity party." She dusted off her hands. "Let's change the subject."

There was an awkward moment of silence. Then Margaret said, "I have something to tell you all. I saw the light in the lighthouse window last night!"

"You did?" A shiver ran up Shelley's spine. She had halfway convinced herself she'd imagined it and had suckered Diane into it as well.

Margaret nodded. "I was coming home from my mentor meeting when I caught a glimpse of it. So I turned onto the beach road and drove a little way toward the lighthouse. It was right there the whole time. After I pulled off the road, I saw someone walk in front of the window. Between the light and the window, I mean."

"Walk?" Diane looked shocked. "Are you certain?"

"I'm positive," Margaret told her. "It was a human figure, plain as day. And then the light went out. Spooked me, if you want the truth. I turned around and skedaddled home."

"I don't blame you," Shelley said with feeling.

"I wonder what it could mean." Diane looked deeply interested. "I haven't heard of anything unusual happening today."

"Maybe because nothing unusual *did* happen." Beverly's voice was crisp. "I imagine it means someone's illegally squatting in the lighthouse or using it for drug smuggling."

"But what if—"

"Honestly, Diane, you've got us all seeing miracles here, there, and everywhere. Well, all but me."

"You saw that light the night we rescued the swimmer." Margaret looked a little hurt, and Shelley wondered if she thought Beverly didn't believe her.

"Well, yes, but there could be a million explanations for that."

Margaret crossed her arms. "Such as?"

"Reflections from headlights, like the detective said. Someone with a spotlight. A shaft of moonlight bouncing off something..." Her voice trailed away. "I don't mean to be a wet blanket, although I guess I'm doing a pretty good job of it." She smiled, trying to joke.

Shelley's heart ached for Beverly. What had happened in her life to make her so resistant to recognizing miracles? Couldn't she simply acknowledge that sometimes God may guide us in ways we don't expect or even notice? At least she'd asked for prayer about her father, or so Diane had told her.

"It's probably a good thing I'm going back to work tomorrow." Beverly offered them a strained smile. "Obviously, I've got too much time to sit around and think."

"What about your father?" Shelley asked. "Do you need us to look in on him until you've spoken with Mrs. Peabody?"

Beverly shook her head. "One of the nurses at the hospital does home visitation, and I managed to convince Father that he needed someone to check on him this week. I probably won't be able to get away with that indefinitely—maybe not even next week—but I'll be back on Friday, so I'll speak with Mrs. P then." She looked at Diane. "Thanks for the idea. If I can get them both to agree to it, it might be a perfect solution."

CHAPTER TWENTY

At home later that evening, Shelley shared the day's events with Dan. "Beverly has started having doubts that seeing that swimmer and rescuing him was a miracle."

Dan considered that as he polished off the last of his Tubby's ice cream, a unique maple flavor called Tree Hugger produced by a small ice cream stand in Wayne, on the other side of Augusta. His brother Hal, who lived in Augusta— the one Dan had been visiting when he first saw Shelley— brought tubs of several hand-scooped flavors packed in dry ice a couple of times a year.

Prize, lounging nearby, watching him intently, clearly hoping for a drip or an offer to share.

"My thinking on miracles has changed a bit since your accident," Dan said in his slow, deliberate manner. "By all rights, you shouldn't have walked away from that smashed hunk of junk last month." He put his arm around her, as they sat idly swinging on the porch after putting the children to bed. "I used to think miracles were things that happened in the Bible and maybe sometimes to other people."

"Me too. My accident made the word *miracle* so much more real to me." Shelley put her head on his shoulder. "What made me trust Diane that day? I barely knew her."

"She's a good sort." Dan nodded once to emphasize his point.

"And she and Margaret have experienced their own personal miracles. I don't know what you'd call a mysterious rescue from drowning or a complete recovery from a terminal cancer diagnosis if it isn't a miracle."

"Ayuh."

After sitting for a bit longer, they headed for bed. While Dan put Prize in her kennel on the porch, Shelley went up to check on the children. Both were sleeping soundly. As the puppy began to howl, interspersed with occasional barking and whining, she hoped Aiden didn't wake up. Last night, Aiden had sobbed in bed until he exhausted himself. The puppy fussed intermittently all night long. Shelley imagined that every time Prize awoke and found herself alone, she made more noise. And Shelley felt bad.

She couldn't forget Lee Waters' words about pack animals and puppies suddenly finding themselves alone with no siblings. But what was she supposed to do? Prize's howling when they kept the kennel inside was loud enough to wake Aiden—as he'd proved when he'd gone down and gotten the puppy.

Dan came upstairs just as Shelley climbed into bed. He was rubbing an agitated hand at the back of his neck. "I sat with her for a little while, trying to get her to settle down. But she's having none of it."

Shelley smiled sympathetically. Dan was such a soft touch. He was the same way with the kids. Instead of giving Aiden one chance and then using consequences for problem behaviors, he patiently explained why the actions had been wrong and then sent him to time-out in the corner. Until Aiden cried. At which point, Dan would get him and cuddle him on his lap.

Shelley sometimes had to actively restrain him if Emma fussed in her crib. Shelley could tell the difference between sleepy time fussing and distress. But every little peep bothered Dan.

"Let's try to get some sleep," she said. "I'm sure she'll settle down. We made it through last night. Maybe tonight will be better."

It was. But it didn't start well. They dropped off to sleep, only to be awakened several times by a mournful howl or a pathetic little *come get me* bark from outside. Prize was probably whimpering between those barks, but since the kennel had been moved outside, Shelley couldn't tell. Finally, after a long, frustrating hour had passed, the puppy grew quiet. Shelley fell instantly into a deep sleep.

She awoke in the morning with a smile. Over the baby monitor, she could hear Emma babbling along with the musical mirror toy attached to one side of the crib. Every so often there would be a *clunk* as she flailed until she hit the large red button to restart the music.

Dan was already climbing out of bed. "I'll get her. Would you like to sleep in?"

Shelley shook her head. "No, I'll start breakfast. What's your work schedule today?"

Dan's eyes clouded. "I'm at the office from ten until two. Then I'll grab some lunch and go over to Allan's for a few hours."

She nodded, rising and drawing on her robe. "All right. You want lunch at two, then?"

Dan nodded, already half out the door, and Shelley had to grin. That man loved his kids.

She washed her face, brushed her hair, and then padded from the room on bare feet. The floors were cool. As she passed Aiden's door, she realized it was closed, and she frowned. He didn't like his door closed. She was a little surprised he'd been able to fall asleep that way.

Quietly, she turned the knob and stepped into the dim room. An odd thumping startled her for half a second, and then shock gripped her. Prize was lying snuggled against Aiden's side, wearing a silly doggy grin. The thumping was her tail beating a rhythm on the mattress. It was just like last time.

"Prize!" She started across the room and then gentled her voice as she quickly realized she couldn't blame the puppy. Prize's tail had been wagging but now it was down and still, and she wouldn't look up. "It's all right, baby." Shelley picked her up and carried her from the room, stroking her head. "You're a good girl. You just belong to a young man who has a little trouble with rules, that's all." She had almost reached the bottom of the stairs when she heard a sound behind her.

"Mommy!" Aiden stood at the top of the steps, looking as guilty as a small boy could. "Where's my Prize?"

Shelley turned around, so he could see the puppy in her arms. "Prize is on her way back outside where she belongs. And you, sir, need to come down here and explain to your father and me why you are still breaking the rule about the puppy staying outside."

She turned and marched down the steps, carrying Prize back to her kennel. When she had attached the line to the puppy's collar, she came back in and prepared fresh food and water to take out to her.

After she came inside the second time, Dan was in the kitchen securing Emma in her high chair. Aiden came slinking in, and she silently pointed to his seat at the table. Dan helped him up before going to the cupboards and taking out cereal bowls, utensils, and juice glasses.

Shelley sliced up half a banana into baby-sized pieces and gave it to Emma, setting the other half in front of Aiden. She poured juice, added cereal and milk to the bowls, got out a chewable vitamin for Aiden, and took her seat. All without saying a word.

She was barely settled in her chair when Aiden couldn't take the silence any longer. "Mommy, we can talk about Prize now if you want to."

Across the table, Shelley saw Dan hide a grin, and she gave him a warning look. If Aiden thought they were amused by this behavior, he'd never stop. "What about Prize?"

"About her sleeping with me."

Shelley set down her spoon. "Aiden, there is nothing to talk about. This can't go on. We told you Prize can't be in the house. She may not sleep with you."

"But Prize is afraid of the dark." His big blue eyes were focused first on her and then on his father. "She's really, really afraid, and sleeping with me makes her feel brave."

Shelley looked at Dan. He had the same stricken look on his face that she suspected she did. Was Aiden that afraid of the dark?

"All right, buddy." Dan rubbed his back. "We can talk about it later."

Aiden looked confused. "You're not going to holler at me?" His tone was tentative and somewhat skeptical.

"Well, we're not very happy with you," Dan said, "but we aren't going to holler."

After breakfast, Aiden asked to go outside with his dog, and Dan sent him out the door after applying sunscreen and telling him to keep his hat on.

Dan cleared the table while Shelley cleaned up Emma, who had managed to get banana up her nose, in her hair, and even in one ear. "I know you're mad," he said, "but I didn't have the heart to yell at him. If he's that scared of the dark, think how much courage it took for him to come downstairs alone and open the back door in the pitch black."

"I know. I had no idea he was that afraid of the dark. We need to get a couple of nightlights. Put one in his room, one in the hall, and maybe one in the bathroom."

Dan nodded. "I can do that today on my way home."

"Honey," Shelley said quietly. "You know the dog has to go."

Dan froze. His eyes widened. "As in permanently?"

She nodded. "I cannot handle having her chew up our possessions. She can't sleep in our son's bed. She's a dog. She smells. And Aiden is ignoring us and doing what he likes."

Dan wouldn't look at her. "All right." Abruptly, he turned and started out of the room. "I've got to get ready for work."

"Dan—" But he was gone. She might have won the battle over the dog, but she sure felt like she'd lost one with her family.

⋆　　⋆　　⋆

As she assisted a customer in the gallery on Tuesday, Diane watched Margaret whenever the other woman wasn't looking. Margaret doggedly kept at her painting. Despite her outburst, she had started on a second canvas in what she called her *new style,* but she wasn't herself. Normally, she'd be pleased as punch to be moving on to a new project.

"What's she working on now?" asked the man who had been examining the paintings on the walls of the gallery. Diane had noticed that he seemed to particularly like Margaret's paintings of the lighthouse. She couldn't blame him. If she sold this book, she was going to reward herself with one of those paintings.

"I don't know," Diane said in answer to the client's question. And it was true. Margaret was fanatically private about her work these days.

To forestall a request to look over Margaret's shoulder, Diane said, "She's rather secretive about her pieces until she's finished. Have you seen this view of the Marble Cove coastline she did? She used photos she took from a boat as reference."

The man and his wife dithered for nearly half an hour longer over which painting they liked the most, ultimately choosing one with the lighthouse at sunrise. "They're all wonderful!" the wife said.

Margaret appeared not to have heard a word, although Diane knew their voices carried perfectly well to the back of the gallery.

After she rang up the purchase and carefully wrapped the painting in layers of brown paper to protect it, the couple happily carried their new treasure away.

"I thought they'd never leave."

It was so unlike Margaret that Diane turned to stare at her.

"I only meant they seemed to have a lot of trouble deciding which painting they liked," she amended.

Diane tilted her head. "You're starting to worry me, Scrooge."

Margaret didn't even smile, which worried Diane even more than the curmudgeonly comments. "I didn't want to show them what I was painting because I was afraid they wouldn't like it." She sighed. "I miss painting seascapes. I miss painting landscapes. I miss painting Marble Cove-scapes."

"Then why don't you paint them?" To Diane, it seemed very simple.

"Because they're not *real* art."

"They are so."

"You know what I mean."

"What I know is that art critic has scarred you for life." Diane frowned. "You have real talent, Margaret. I think you should paint what you enjoy."

Margaret was silent for a moment. "Maybe we should change the subject," she said finally. "How is your writing going?"

Diane shook her head. "I've sort of hit a wall."

"How so?"

"About two weeks ago, I was working on plotting the last section of the book." She went on to tell Margaret the story of Rocky and the index cards and was rewarded by the first genuine chuckle she'd heard from her friend all day. "Ever since then, it's like I'm stuck. I can't remember what order I had all the cards in, and I had worked so hard to find just the perfect sequence. Now I can hardly bring myself to face plotting again, so I've just been writing scenes I have in my head. I'll worry about putting them in order later."

Margaret shook her head. "Being creative stinks sometimes."

Diane laughed. "Yes, but it sure beats doing any other type of work. I've had more fun writing this book than I ever did writing for a newspaper."

CHAPTER TWENTY-ONE

After Dan came home from work and had his lunch on Tuesday, he and Aiden went into the living room. When Shelley checked on them later, they had built an elaborate Lego structure.

"Mommy!" Aiden jumped up when he saw her, threatening to overturn the entire thing. Only a lucky catch by Dan saved it. "Daddy played Legos with me."

"I see that. Daddy keeps his promises. So what are you building?"

"It's a firehouse." He threw himself flat on the floor to point at a small red fire truck parked inside a garage at the bottom.

"It's a beautiful firehouse." Shelley smoothed his hair, and then she turned to Dan. "Can I talk to you for a minute?"

"Sure." Dan rose. "I'll be back in a minute, buddy." He followed Shelley into the kitchen, the happiness fading from his eyes.

"Dan, we need to take the puppy to the shelter today. I can take the kids to the park if—"

Dan's Adam's apple worked, as he gulped. "Shel, I don't think I can give her away."

Shelley's eyebrows rose almost to her hairline as a swift wave of anger welled. "You brought her."

"I know." Dan looked utterly miserable. "And believe me, I'm sorry for it. But I can't—"

"Never mind." She cut him off with a sharp gesture. "Emma's waking up. You take the kids to the park, and I'll deal with the dog. Then you can go over to Allan's." *While I spend the rest of the afternoon trying to comfort Aiden.*

"Are you sure?"

She looked around the room. "I don't see anyone else volunteering for the job. So yes, I'm sure." She set her jaw, working hard not to say anything she would regret later. "Don't tell him. When you bring them home from the park, it'll be done, and I'll be home again. I'll tell him."

"We'll tell him together." Dan took a step toward her, raising his arms as if he intended to embrace her. Then he caught a good look at her face, and his arms dropped. When he hesitated for a moment, she turned away without meeting his eyes. He heaved a sigh and went back to the living room.

Shelley took deep breaths, so angry she wanted to snatch something up and heave it across the room. Why did she have to be the bad guy just because Dan was too much of a softie to fix the mistake *he'd* made?

Moments later, he and the children were heading out the door to the park.

"But, Daddy, I want to take Prize."

"Prize can't go to the park, remember? Park rule."

"Stupid rule."

"Aiden. We don't use that word in our house. Not even for things like that..." And then they were out of earshot.

Shelley stood in the kitchen for a moment, her heart aching. It wasn't that she didn't *like* the dog. Prize was pretty cute. But she just wasn't working very well in their lives right now. Maybe someday when Aiden was older.... Anger flared again. Dan should be the one doing this. She steeled herself and went to get her handbag and the puppy's leash to take Prize to the animal shelter.

Prize whined in the car. Shelley had tied her leash to a backdoor handgrip, so she couldn't bounce around or get beneath Shelley's feet. Every so often, Shelley glanced in the mirror to make sure the puppy was all right.

The animal shelter was outside of town along the highway that passed Marble Cove. It was a pretty large structure, chiefly because one of the ways they met their budget was by charging tourists steep prices for kennel spaces for the beloved animal companions they brought along on vacation. Pets weren't allowed in most rental properties, but it was surprising how many people would pay outrageous fees just to keep them close by.

As she waited at the stoplight at the intersection with the highway, a powerful wave of doubt swept over Shelley. Was she doing the right thing? Aiden was going to be heartbroken when he found his puppy gone. Maybe they could just tell him she had run away.

No. She tightened her fingers on the wheel. If they were going to follow through with this course of action, they weren't going to lie to their son about it.

The light changed. She glanced over her shoulder at the little dog, who had stopped whining. She lay on the back seat, head on her paws, looking at Shelley with huge, trusting brown eyes. *You don't give away members of your family,* those eyes seemed to say.

Shelley reached for her resolve and drove on. There was a knot in her throat, and she swallowed repeatedly. In all too short a time, she was pulling into the parking lot.

The shelter was a pretty gray brick structure with white trim. Several fruit trees and tidy, colorful gardens greeted visitors.

The place was hopping this morning. Folks from "away," the Mainers' term for anyone not born and raised in Maine, were arriving to pick up their pets for the day, to personally feed them, or to throw balls and Frisbees in the large enclosed yard.

Shelley parked and opened the back door, crawling across to untie the leash from the far side. Backing out of the car, she tugged at the leash to get Prize moving. No deal. The puppy huddled against the door, looking terrified. The barking of dogs in the kennels behind the building was probably scaring her.

If she was frightened now, how was she going to feel when Shelley handed the leash to a stranger and walked out the door . . . when Prize was shut in a concrete run behind bars, all alone? Tears stung Shelley's eyes. Resolutely, she picked up the pup and headed indoors, snuggling the puppy against her. Prize was trembling, involuntary shivers shaking her small form. It was as if she knew what was about to happen.

A middle-aged lady with kind eyes stood behind the counter. "Hello. Can I help you?"

Shelley nodded. "I have to . . . I have to give up our puppy." She winced. It sounded so cold.

"All right. I need to get some information from you." The lady's face was pleasant but expressionless. She reached for a form and began to fill in the date. "Your name?"

Shelley answered all the woman's questions. Her chest felt so tight it hurt. Prize whimpered, and she realized she was holding the puppy too tightly. Forcing herself to relax her grip, she stroked Prize's silky back.

"Do you know what kind of mix she is?"

"Beagle and cocker spaniel, we were told." She rested her chin on the soft little head.

The clerk smiled. "That explains why she looks like a beagle with a wavy coat. She's adorable."

"Yes." Shelley's voice was soft and sad. "She is."

"Reason for surrender?"

Shelley felt herself flushing. She bit her lip to maintain her composure. In a matter of moments, she would be handing the puppy over. "She chews on everything. Every time I take my eyes off her, she's chewing something she shouldn't be. I can't watch her every second—I have two small children. And my son lets her sleep in his bed, even though I told him not to, and now his sheets smell like dog all the time."

The woman's dark eyebrows rose. "Anything else?"

Shelley nodded. She could no longer hold back the tears that threatened. "She gets under my feet…I broke my good cookie jar when she tripped me." Why did none of her reasons seem important? "My son loves her," she said brokenly. "But I just can't deal with having everything in my home ruined. She chewed up a chair I got from my grandmother. We tried keeping her outside, but she howls at night. And now my son stays outside so much during the day, I'm constantly afraid he's going to get sunburned. And I— Oh, never mind."

She handed Prize to the woman and picked up the pen, scribbling a nearly illegible signature on the form the woman had set before her. She started to rush out the door but then turned. "She'll find a new home, won't she?"

The woman shrugged, rubbing her cheek on Prize's head. "I wish I could promise you that, but I can't. She's precious, and she's a puppy, so probably. But there's no guarantee."

Shelley couldn't hold back her sobs any longer. Blindly, she grabbed the door handle and pushed out into the warm summer morning.

A voice said, "Honey, do you need help?" but she shook her head and plunged for the car. Inside, she jammed the key into the ignition and turned on the engine. Taking deep breaths, she calmed herself somewhat and buckled her seatbelt.

But when she looked back over her shoulder to back out of the parking spot, her gaze fell on the empty back seat. She started to cry again.

Lord, I don't know what to do. I feel like the lowest lowlife, taking my son's puppy away. And I feel even worse leaving her at a shelter.

Realizing she couldn't possibly drive, she put the car back in park and let the tears flow. Those weren't the only reasons she was upset, she acknowledged. She had gotten used to seeing that little black, brown, and white face waiting to be fed, panting after she'd run through the yard with Aiden, flopped on her dog bed upside-down with her ears sticking out.

She took a deep breath and gripped the gear shift again, but her hand simply wouldn't grasp the knob. Suddenly, a light bulb of clarity went off in her head.

What was she doing? She wouldn't dream of sending away her children if they were a problem, so why was she giving up on this innocent little dog? Dan had been moved to bring the puppy home for a reason, but Shelley had treated him as if his ideas were of no value. She hadn't been fair to Dan, *and* she hadn't been listening to God. If God thought they needed a dog, they needed a dog. She leaned forward and banged her head against the steering wheel several times. *Okay. I'm listening.*

She couldn't explain it, but when she opened her heart, an overwhelming sense of rightness and urgency seeped into her heart. *Go get her. She needs you. And you need her.* Abruptly Shelley knew what she had to do.

Bursting out of the car, she rushed back into the shelter. She prayed it wasn't too late.

"Ma'am?"

The kind-faced lady behind the desk smiled at her. "Yes?"

"I can't—I'd like to take my puppy home."

The woman's face sobered. "What's changed?"

"Pardon?" Shelley stared at the lady.

"Why have you changed your mind? This puppy is very young. Her problem behaviors are mostly just puppy things, and that's not going to change overnight."

"I know." Panic rose. "We'll find some way to work it out. I can't give her up."

The woman looked sympathetic. "I'm glad you feel that way. But you have signed the papers. Look, you think you want her now. But if things don't change, you're very likely to be right back here again in a few days or weeks or months. Besides, it's against shelter policy to give them back."

Shelley sucked in a breath of dismay. In her mind she saw Prize being led out to be destroyed. What had she done?

Before the sobs could overtake her again, the woman smiled. "But I didn't record your paperwork yet. I had a feeling you were going to regret your decision." She bent, and when she straightened, she held Prize in her arms. "I kept her here under the counter just in case. Once you surrender them, you have to adopt them and pay the fee."

Relief poured over her. Could her act be undone? But a fee? As Shelley opened her mouth to admit she couldn't pay, the woman raised a hand.

"So we're just going to forget you ever signed her over, okay?"

"Thank you. Thank you so much." Shelley could feel tears rising beyond her ability to control. She took Prize into her arms and hugged the poor thing so tightly she thought she might hurt her.

The woman smiled knowingly. "There might be a few things you could try that would help with your situation."

"Like what?" She couldn't imagine that it was possible to keep a puppy from chewing.

"The biggest thing I'd suggest is using what we call a tie-down. Get a couple of inexpensive leashes and loop them beneath a leg of furniture in several places where you spend most of your time at home. The kitchen, the family room, places like that. Clip her to the leash when you're in that room. Make sure she has plenty of her own things that she's allowed to chew on nearby. That way, you can watch to be sure she's not gnawing on your furniture, and she can't sneak off when you're distracted. It's also good for helping the animal bond with you. Soon she'll want to be where you are all the time."

A tiny ray of hope pierced Shelley's heart. "That sounds like it could work. But I move around the house a lot during the day."

"In that case, use yourself as the tie-down." The woman took a leash from a display on the wall and showed Shelley how to loop it around her waist or through a belt loop, so that the puppy was actually attached to her. "See? Where you go, she follows."

"I have a three-year-old and a nine-month-old," she said. "This could be a real challenge."

The clerk laughed. "I didn't say it would be easy." She turned and opened a file cabinet, extracting several sheets of paper. Then she reached for a folder and put the papers in it, along with two business cards she picked up from a holder on the counter.

"Here's more information about how to use tie-downs, as well as some suggestions on how to deal with inappropriate chewing and getting on the furniture. You can use liter-size soda bottles to save your chairs and table legs. Just cut off the top and set the leg in it. She won't be able to get her mouth around that. And even if she does start to mess with it, you'll hear her in time to prevent damage." She handed the folder to Shelley. "My contact information is on one of those cards, and the name of a good dog trainer is on the other. I would strongly suggest you start this little one in obedience classes."

"Isn't she awfully young?"

"Not at all. They have classes for babies now. 'Puppy Kindergarten,' they call it. It's a great way to start instilling good habits in your puppy." She tapped her fingers on the counter. "What was your other concern? Oh, right. Sleeping with your son. Maybe you could work out a compromise. Lay a dog bed on the floor right beside your boy's bed, and keep a tie-down there so she stays there all night. Tell your son she can sleep near him, but not in his bed."

"That's a great idea. Aiden can pet her, but his sheets won't smell like dog. Speaking of that, do you have any suggestions for keeping the whole house from smelling like dog?" Shelley grimaced.

The lady laughed. "If I did, I'd be rich." She tapped her lips, thinking about the question. "Sprinkle baking soda beneath your couch cushions. They make scented powder you can put on your carpet before you vacuum, but I'd be careful with that. The kids might be allergic to it." She set her hands on the countertop. "Bathe her or get her groomed once a month. A professional grooming is best because they'll use bath products that won't dry out her skin, and they'll also clean her ears and trim her nails."

"That sounds workable." Shelley felt buoyant with hope. She walked to the display of pet paraphernalia and discreetly picked up the price tag on a leash.

"Can I interest you in a couple of leashes?" the lady asked.

Shelley studied the leash, but then she shook her head. "Maybe I can use rope or something. We just don't have the money for extras right now."

The woman studied her for a minute. Then she raised a finger. "Wait right here." She walked to a heavy door and hurried through it, leaving Shelley alone in the office with Prize.

"You're okay, baby girl," Shelley said. "We're almost ready to go home, I promise." Was it her imagination, or did Prize seem calmer? She laughed at herself. What was she thinking? *She* was calmer. She'd probably been vibrating with nerves that had alerted the puppy that something was very wrong. She must be totally insane, she decided. This was one more stressor in her life than she needed...but her family was going to keep the dog.

A few minutes later, the clerk breezed back through the door, which closed with a *thunk* behind her. She extended a large paper shopping bag to Shelley. "Here."

"What's this?"

The clerk smiled. "A couple of leashes, a dog bed, and some sterilized bones and chew toys. Don't worry, everything's been thoroughly disinfected if it isn't new."

"I can't take these," Shelley protested.

The woman nodded. "Please do. A lot of them are donations from grateful pet owners who appreciate our setup. We also have a lot of things left behind that folks never claim. And occasionally, if a pet passes away while on vacation, the owner leaves everything because they can't handle the memories."

"That's so sad." Shelley cringed at the thought of a pet dying in a strange place, even a nice one like this.

"A lot of people bring their animals *because* they're old, and they don't want to leave them with strangers. This way, they're close if their furry baby takes a turn for the worse."

Shelley understood. "That makes a sweet kind of sense." She hefted the shopping bag and tucked Prize more securely beneath her chin. "Thank you so much. If you hadn't been here, I might have made a terrible mistake."

"That's why we're here, dear."

As she drove homeward with Prize in her spot on the back seat, a sense of peace stole over Shelley. The puppy had come into their lives for a reason, she felt certain.

The lighthouse came into view as she turned onto the beach road and headed for Newport Avenue. She thought of Diane's certainty that the mysterious lights preceded miracles in more than one life in Marble Cove. She believed Diane was right.

The trip home was far faster than the trip out had been. At the house, she quickly untied the puppy and grabbed her purse and the shopping bag.

Dan met her at the door. He looked so sad. "How did that go?"

She smiled and moved aside so Prize could bounce into the house. "Pretty good."

"What?" He looked stunned. "I thought—"

"I couldn't do it. I think I experienced the same feeling you had the day you brought her home. Plus, there was a lady there who gave me lots of helpful advice."

"Mommy! Did you take Prize for a walk? I missed her."

Shelley looked down into the shining face of her beautiful child. She imagined what his face would've been like if she'd had to tell him Prize was gone. *Thank You, Lord, for changing my mind.* "She's back now. I think she missed you too."

With a whoop, Aiden rush out the back door, the puppy close on his heels. "Come on, Prize. Let's go play!"

Shelley turned to Dan. "I owe you an apology. Instead of thinking about why you might have been moved to bring home a dog, and what a blessing it could be, I only saw the negatives. My mind was on things, not the happiness of our son. I'm sorry I treated you unfairly."

Dan smiled, the slow smile that always made her heart speed up. "I accept your apology, if you'll accept mine for not speaking with you before making such a big decision."

"Of course." She kissed him. "I think we can make this work, Dan. I really do. It's going to take some work, and you are going to have to be firm with her too."

He studied her face for a minute and then put a hand to her forehead. "Are you feverish?"

Shelley laughed. "Nope. I'm just fine. Keeping that dog outside isn't going to work. I felt guilty every time I tied her out there alone."

Dan smiled gently. "A little dog hair in Aiden's bed is a small price to pay for a happy child."

"Not *in* his bed. *Beside* his bed." She held up the dog bed. "We'll put this down right beside Aiden, and she can sleep there. I mean it, Dan." She shook a finger at him. "You have to back me on this. I am absolutely not kidding about keeping her off the furniture."

"I will, I promise." Dan pointed out the window. "Look. That is one happy little boy out there. You did the right thing, honey. And I think Aiden will be happy enough with this compromise that he'll listen."

"Me too. Now you need to call the vet. This puppy needs her shots."

Dan winced. "I'm sorry. I know that's going to be expensive."

"It's okay." She grinned at him. "You're not getting steak for quite a while."

Chapter Twenty-Two

Two hours later, Shelley wasn't feeling quite so chipper. Dr. Spangler, the local vet whom Diane thought was a cutie, had had a cancellation in his schedule, so Shelley had taken Prize over that very day. After paying nearly a hundred dollars for an exam, vaccines, and worming, she felt distinctly green around the gills. Still, she wasn't changing her mind.

She had barely gotten the gate to the backyard open when she heard a car crunch on the gravel of the driveway.

"Good afternoon!" sang her mother-in-law.

Shelley managed a smile. "Good afternoon."

Dan came out from the yard carrying Emma. Aiden and Prize were right behind him.

"Hi, Meemaw." Aiden ran to her for a hug.

"Hi, sweetie." Frances lifted him off the ground; then she set him down and stared at him. "My goodness, boy, what have you been doing? You've got a tan like a dockworker. Does your mama make you play outside every day?"

Aiden giggled. "No, silly Meemaw. I play outside with Prize."

Dan pointed at the puppy before his mother could ask. "Prize, remember?"

"Oh." Frances looked concerned. "Shelley, have you read about the effects of overexposure to the sun? Especially in fair-skinned people?"

Shelley nodded. She opened her mouth but Frances forged ahead.

"This child needs sunscreen every time he goes out, and you should reapply it every two hours. And he needs a hat."

"I wear sunscreen," Aiden said indignantly. "All the time."

Shelley appreciated the vote of confidence from her son. "And a hat."

"He isn't wearing one now," Frances pointed out, as Aiden raced off again.

"He's only been out for a few minutes," Dan said in an exasperated tone. "Did you come over here to criticize our parenting skills?"

"Of course not." Frances smiled. "I stopped in to see my grandbabies. And you two."

"The story of my life," Dan said dryly. "Since we had kids, we're always going to be second-place finishers, Shel."

Shelley chuckled. She appreciated Dan's standing up for her.

Frances also laughed, and the momentary awkwardness passed. As she followed them into the house, she said, "I also stopped by to remind you about your Uncle Lester's eightieth birthday party. You don't have to stay long, but it would be nice if you stopped by to say hello."

"We plan to." Shelley pointed to her lighthouse calendar. "I've already got it written in." She turned to take off Emma's little bonnet.

"All right. Oh my goodness."

"What?" Shelley looked around, alarmed by the shock in her mother-in-law's voice.

"I can't believe you cut her hair." Frances sounded as if she'd just learned someone had died. Frances lifted her out of Dan's arms and held the baby at arms' length to stare at her.

Shelley and Dan both looked at Emma. Shelley frowned. "I just gave her some bangs. That front lock was hanging in her face all the time."

"Oh, but she looked so sweet when you gathered it all up on top of her head."

"It's hair, Mom. It'll grow." Dan sounded as if his patience was a bit forced.

"I know." She sighed. Deeply. "I just wasn't prepared for it, that's all. She's my little sweetie-pea, and all of a sudden she looks so grown up."

Dan laughed. "She's only nine months old. I think we've got a few more hours before she's grown."

"Oh, you." His mother playfully swatted him with her handbag. "You know what I mean." Her eyes softened as she looked at her granddaughter again. "You're so lucky to be just starting this adventure. It seems as if they're grown and gone in the blink of an eye."

Shelley knew Frances genuinely loved her grandchildren. She was very good with them, always ready for imaginative play or a silly game. It had probably been a sad day for her when she'd had no more little ones of her own around.

"Already I miss Aiden's baby days," Shelley said. "It's fun watching him grow, but Emma has reminded me of how I love having a baby around."

"Well," Frances said with a gleam in her eye, "you don't have to stop, you know."

"Maybe not," Dan said, grinning at Shelley, "but until my job security improves, we don't need another mouth to feed." His smile faded.

"Shelley, have you thought any more about getting a job like you said?" Frances said.

Shelley's eyebrows rose. The way she recalled it, Frances had done all the talking. She nodded. "I've thought about it."

Frances regarded her expectantly, but Shelley wasn't about to give her any details.

"I think it would be good if you could contribute a little something. I was home with my own children all their growing-up years, but a little time away wouldn't hurt, I don't think."

Dan looked at Shelley. Neither one of them said a word.

"What?" Frances asked.

"Our financial situation is fine, Mom. Shelley isn't looking for a job."

"Oh, but—"

"Frances." Shelley was unable to hide the annoyance in her voice. "Could we please change the subject?"

"Of course." With an overly reasonable tone, Frances managed to make Shelley's request sound completely *un*reasonable.

"You mentioned feeding extra mouths, but you've already got one." His mother pointed out the window at the puppy. Shelley could only marvel at the flawless shift of topics to criticize. "What on earth possessed you to get a puppy?"

"I thought it would be good for Aiden." Dan sounded defensive.

"As if poor Shelley needs one more thing to deal with. Why, I'd have given your father a piece of my mind if he'd brought home a dog."

Although Shelley had made peace with their new addition, it still was nice to hear that someone understood why she'd been so stressed.

Then the back door opened, and Aiden clattered in, closely followed by Prize.

"Aiden Daniel Bauer!" His grandmother's stern tone stopped Aiden in his tracks. "You take that dirty dog out of here right now."

Aiden looked uncertainly from her to his parents. "Can Prize come in for a little while?"

"Yes," Dan said.

"Woohoo!"

"That's the most unhygienic thing I've ever heard of," his mother announced as boy and dog scampered past her. "Dogs carry all kind of germs and diseases. Besides, dogs can be vicious. What if it bites Aiden or Emma? My children were never, *ever* allowed to bring an animal inside the house."

"Which might explain why all of us have at least one indoor pet now," Dan said to Shelley.

"And I read that allergies are a growing problem today. The children are sure to develop them if you continue to let Aiden bring that dog indoors."

Right then and there, Shelley knew there would be no more discussion about where Prize would live and sleep. Her children hadn't shown a single sign of an allergic reaction to the puppy. Prize was an indoor dog, and as the shelter worker had suggested, she would be sleeping beside Aiden's bed at night.

"We appreciate your concern, Mom, and we'll take it into consideration," Dan said. "What's Dad up to today?"

Bless her husband, Shelley thought. He successfully distracted his mother from her rant about pets in the house, *and* he hadn't made a single promise to honor one of her ridiculous suggestions.

★   ★   ★

Beverly decided to come back to Marble Cove a day early. She was so worried about her father that she was less than effective at work. Fortunately, she still had some leave as well as a boss who was very supportive of family problems.

Still, she thought as she drove toward Marble Cove on Thursday evening, this constant running back and forth was getting stressful. Not to mention gas money and wear and tear on the car. Augusta wasn't just a few miles away, and though she disliked driving at night, she would be forced to do just that if things didn't change, especially in the winter when the days were so much shorter.

As she got closer to home, she could see the familiar outline of the lighthouse, an inky silhouette against the darkened horizon.

Wait. What was that? Adrenaline raced through her system. Had she seen a light?

Now that was just silly, she admonished herself. Diane and all her miracle talk had her primed to see things that weren't there.

And then it winked on again. Beverly braked and slowed, pulling off the side of the road. She couldn't take her eyes off the small, steady glow. It was up near the very top of the lighthouse, as if someone was standing on the widow's walk with a flashlight. It wasn't the same as any of the lights Diane, Shelley, and Margaret had described. It certainly wouldn't be enough to warn a ship of dangerous rocks, but it was perfectly visible from the close vicinity of the Marble Cove community.

The light appeared to shift back and forth. Once. Twice. And then she realized that what she was seeing was a person—or at least a figure that looked very human—as it moved back and forth on the gallery walk.

There! She knew it. The lights they all had seen were man-made, just as she'd suspected. She grabbed her cell phone and took a picture. After saving it, she hit Diane's number.

*   *   *

Shelley and Margaret arrived at Diane's house that evening mere minutes before Beverly did. When their city friend got there, Shelley could hardly believe the change in her.

"I saw the light," Beverly said the moment she walked in. "Well, I saw *a* light." She had a spot of color in her cheeks and looked more animated than normal.

"Tell us about it." Diane closed the door behind her and ushered her in. "Would you like something to drink?"

Beverly accepted a glass of freshly squeezed lemonade and reached for one of the cookies Shelley had brought along. "I saw a light tonight. I took a picture, but it didn't turn out well enough in the dark to tell what it is."

Shelley leaned forward. "What did the light look like?"

"As I was driving toward town..." Beverly went on to tell them what she had seen. She showed them the blurry photo on her phone, but they agreed not much could be seen. "Someone was up there walking around. I'm certain of it." She turned to Diane. "I'll help with a stakeout if you like. We need to figure out who's using that building and for what." She must have seen the look Diane couldn't hide, because she crossed her arms defensively. "No, I'm sorry. I still am not convinced there's anything miraculous about it. But I'm certain I saw someone up there with a light tonight."

"There's one way to find out." Diane's voice was brisk and peppy.

"You're serious about watching the lighthouse?" Margaret looked doubtful. "A real stakeout? It sounds so cloak-and-daggerish."

"What are we looking for?" Shelley wasn't so sure about the notion of a stakeout.

"People going in or leaving the lighthouse." Diane said.

"Yes, but what do we do if we catch them?"

There was silence as everyone contemplated that.

"I hate to be a wet blanket," Shelley said, "but if someone truly is doing something illegal, he might be carrying a gun. I don't know about you, but that scares me."

"Me too." Margaret raised her hand as if she were a student in a desk. Shelley glanced at her, a little concerned. Margaret still seemed quieter than normal, as she often had since her gallery opening and art critic's that review.

"We'd be foolish to actually approach anyone we saw," Beverly said. "What if we just went and observed? If we see someone, we'll take a picture on our phones and then call Detective Fred Little."

"That sounds like a plan I can endorse." Diane grinned. "Want to start tonight?"

"Tonight!" Margaret shook her head. "I can't start tonight. I'm going to have to explain this to Allan in great detail so he's convinced it's not dangerous."

"I'll take tonight," Diane said. "I can probably do the whole night if no one else wants to start this soon."

"How many nights are we talking about?" Shelley asked.

"Let's see what happens tonight and maybe tomorrow night," Diane suggested. "Then we can decide what we want to do next."

"I could take a shift tonight," Beverly said. "How about if I relieve you at two, Diane?"

"Make it two thirty." Diane glanced at her watch. "By the time I get over there, it'll be eleven, and if you stay until six, that would be three-and-a-half-hour shifts for each of us."

"All right. Where should I meet you?"

While the two women made arrangements for the location of the stakeout, Shelley thought about whether she could participate. When Diane and Beverly concluded, Shelley said to Margaret, "I could take the second shift tomorrow night if you could do the first. Dan's schedule has changed so they don't need him on Sunday mornings all the time anymore. He can get up with the kids if I need to sleep in a little."

Margaret hesitated. "I suppose I could take the first shift tomorrow evening."

"*If* we still need to observe tomorrow night," Diane said. "Who knows? Maybe Beverly and I will have this mystery solved before morning."

"That would be great." Diane took a cookie from the plate Shelley had brought over, and she bit in. Her face lit up. "Shelley, these are terrific!"

"Thank you." Shelley smiled, but then the concern she'd been mulling over returned, and she decided she might as well get her friends' take on her mother-in-law's employment idea. "I have a question for all of you."

All three older women turned to her expectantly.

"I don't think it's any huge secret that Dan and I are having some financial worries. You all know how his hours have been cut."

Her three friends nodded.

Shelley took a deep breath. "I've been thinking of getting a job." She grimaced. "Well, toying with the idea, at least. More in a *sore tooth you can't quit touching* kind of way."

Diane chuckled. "Something you don't really want to deal with but you may not have a choice?"

"Exactly." She fidgeted with the zipper on the light cardigan she wore. "Dan and I had agreed that I would stay home with our children. That's important to both of us. But Dan's mother keeps making these incredibly nosy, pointed comments about my helping support our family. I can't help thinking maybe she's right."

"Do you have a certain type of work in mind?" Beverly leaned forward, her expression encouraging.

Shelley shook her head, her shoulders slumping. "Not really. All I've ever done is retail. I didn't go to college, and I don't have a talent like Margaret has."

"That's not true." Diane sat up straight and pointed at the platter of cookies.

"She's right." Beverly nodded. "You are a terrific cook, Shelley."

"Baker." Everyone looked at Margaret. "She is a good cook, but if you're thinking what I'm thinking, her baking is what she should focus on. Her desserts and such."

"My...?"

"Have you ever thought of a baking business?" Beverly asked.

"It wouldn't necessarily have to be baking only," Diane said to Beverly. "She could also do casserole meals or even catered parties for the summer crowd."

Shelley was beginning to see where this was headed. "What about a cookie business? There's nothing like that anywhere around. If they were good enough, people from away might buy them by the dozen to take home."

"Yes!" Diane began to reel off ideas with her customary enthusiasm. "If it really takes off, you could even sell and ship them through a Web site."

"I do love baking cookies," she said hesitantly.

"And you're incredibly good at it." Margaret sent her an encouraging smile. "There's no question in my mind that if people found out about your cookies, they'd be buying them."

Beverly nodded. "If you decide to give it a try, I'll be glad to help you budget, calculate costs and prices, do the small-business paperwork and get approval from the health department. A lot of paperwork is involved in setting up a business."

"But it could be so exciting," Diane said. "I could help you make fliers for realtors to hand out with their vacation information packets. And you could put coupons in the local tourist publications."

"You would need a logo." Margaret regarded her seriously. "I could help you design one and paint you a sign."

"Oh my goodness." Shelley had never considered anything like that, but she was excited by the idea. "That certainly gives me something to think about."

They kicked around a few more ideas, with Diane and Beverly getting into a spirited debate over which of Shelley's cookies would be the best for a grand opening.

Margaret stood, and the chatter died down. "I'm going to head home. It's been a long day." She smiled, but her heart didn't seem to be in it.

After she departed, Diane looked at the other two. "I'm really starting to worry about her. She's been subdued ever since that review."

"I know." Shelley rose too. She had to get to bed; the kids were up early every morning. "Adelaide told me her mother is sad a lot. So I'm sure Allan and Addie are seeing the same thing we are."

Diane put her hands on her hips. "I wish I knew how to help her. I'm not good at sitting back and doing nothing."

"We'd never have guessed," Beverly said in a dry tone.

All three of them laughed, and then Shelley walked across the street to her own home. Her mind was racing.

"Hey." Dan was watching television. "Is it foggy tonight?"

She shook her head. "No. It's pretty clear." She nearly sat down and shared Diane's suggestion and everyone's comments right then and there, but she didn't. She wasn't ready to reveal her thoughts to Dan. After the way he'd flipped out over her last idea, she honestly didn't know how he might react. However, he had eventually come around to it.

Still, he probably wasn't going to like this one. He was dead-set against having a working wife. But the best thing about this was that she could work right out of her own home, so it wasn't as if she'd need to leave the children. In fact, the more she considered it, the better the whole idea seemed.

CHAPTER TWENTY-THREE

"Psst! Diane."

"Over here," came a hushed reply.

Beverly edged around a boulder, trying to stay low. It seemed the worst part of this surveillance might be getting in and out without being seen. Finally, she spotted her friend sitting on an insulated blanket in the sand.

Diane wore a black watch cap and a dark turtleneck sweater beneath a parka. She had pulled the neck of the sweater clear up over her nose, leaving only a small strip of her face visible around her eyes. A low boulder in front of her would prevent anyone from seeing her.

Beverly sank down on the blanket beside Diane. "Have you seen anyone?"

Diane shook her head, clearly disgusted. "No one and nothing. Not even a shred of movement." She picked up a black canvas bag and settled the strap over her shoulder. "I'm going to bed. Call me if you see anything." She offered Beverly a pair of binoculars. "Need these?"

Beverly shook her head. "I brought my own, thanks. Although I probably won't use them unless I see something. I'm afraid light might reflect off the lenses. If there is someone up there, I don't want to spook him into hiding or doing anything rash."

Diane looked chagrined. "I never thought about the reflection. I used my binoculars a number of times."

Beverly shrugged. "I doubt that anyone saw you."

"All right," Diane said. "Good night." The white flash of her teeth signaled a grin. "Or should I say 'Good morning'?"

Beverly groaned quietly. "Don't remind me."

The next four hours passed so slowly that Beverly actually checked her watch to be sure it hadn't stopped. Twice. It was still and quiet, with only the rhythmic wash of waves coming ashore, one after another. Very hypnotic, she decided, shifting her legs to the other side. It would be easy to nod off.

But she managed not to, and as the first hints of rosy light began to appear on the horizon, she slipped away from the sandy spot behind the boulder and made her way home.

*　　*　　*

Diane yawned as she walked into the Shearwater Gallery the following morning. She hoped they wouldn't need to do too many night-time stakeouts. Getting to bed at two-thirty in the morning was not her idea of fun. She might have been able to do it when she was twenty-four, but thirty years later, it was a struggle.

She wasn't sure who had gotten the worse end of the deal, she or Beverly. Her friend had gotten up at two-thirty and watched the lighthouse until shortly before sunrise. Beverly had texted her shortly after six, telling her she hadn't seen a thing. And neither had Diane, making their first night a total bust.

"Oh, good morning." She was more than a little surprised to see Allan Hoskins in the gallery this morning. "Where's Margaret?"

Allan frowned. "I don't know. She was already gone when I woke up this morning. She left a note asking me to send Addie over to Shelley's and open the gallery."

"Did she say when she'll be back?"

Allan shook his head. "No. And that's not like her. But she hasn't been acting quite like herself lately."

"Ever since that pretentious critique, you mean." Diane rolled her eyes in disgust.

"Exactly." Allan's eyes were tired and sad. "I keep telling her she does beautiful work, and she should ignore that woman. But her feelings were really hurt."

"I know. She hasn't seemed right since then. Has she shown you the piece she did in her new style?"

Allan shook his head. "She hasn't said a word about her work in over a week. I didn't even know she'd painted anything new." His tanned, craggy face looked dejected. "She always talks about what she's painting. Or at least, she used to."

Without saying a word, Diane walked to the back of the gallery. She picked up a canvas that was facing the wall and turned around, holding it up against her.

"Oh," Allan said. "*Hmm.* That's . . . different, isn't it?"

"Yes. I think it's quite good in a much more modern way, but it's not to my taste."

"Mine either," he said. "But she can paint houses for all I care, as long as it makes her happy. I don't think she's happy painting that way." He indicated the moody, modern picture Diane still held.

"Do you think she's going to be gone for more than a day?"

Allan shook his head. "She didn't pack a bag, as far as I know. And she wouldn't just take off overnight without telling me."

Diane hoped he was right. Tonight Margaret was scheduled to take the first shift watching the lighthouse. And she was worried about her friend.

⋆　　⋆　　⋆

Beverly saw Mrs. Peabody come out on her front porch early that afternoon with a watering can that looked as though it weighed more than she did. Still, the old woman hefted it high in the air and watered a gorgeous fern she had hung on the porch.

Beverly grinned as she waved. "Mrs. Peabody! Hello."

"Hello, dear." The white-haired woman set down the can and waved energetically. "How are you?"

"I'm fine." Actually, Beverly was exhausted. She'd been awake since two in the morning, and since she hadn't been able to fall asleep until nearly eleven last night, she was functioning on only three hours of sleep.

"And your father?"

Beverly walked across the street. "He's doing well. Tired, but that's to be expected. And he's eating well. He's himself again." She hesitated, wondering what the best way to approach the topic was. "Mrs. Peabody, I have a dilemma. I'm hoping you can help."

"Of course, dear. What can I do?"

"You know my work keeps me from being here all the time. I can manage weekends, but I would like to find someone to look in on Father during the week. Just to check in and say hello each day, maybe have lunch with him, be sure he eats, that sort of thing."

Mrs. Peabody nodded. "I think that's a very wise idea. I shudder to think what could have happened if that sweet little Shelley Bauer and the new neighbor and I hadn't noticed that he hadn't been out and about."

"I agree. And in the winter, it's an even bigger problem, because no one is out very much like we are at this time of year."

"It shouldn't be too difficult to find someone." Mrs. P cocked her head, reminding Beverly of a bright-eyed little bird. "There's a place in town—Eldercare, I believe it's called—that has folks who do that type of visitation."

"I know. The problem is, he won't consider anyone he doesn't know."

"That is a problem."

Beverly sighed. "Yes. I don't know what I'm going to do."

"I could look in on him if you like."

"Really? Oh, Mrs. Peabody, that's a very kind offer, but I couldn't let you do that. Besides, it would really tie you down. He's going to need someone to come in every weekday for a bit."

The older woman's faded blue eyes twinkled. "Tie me down? My dear, you must have an inflated view of my social calendar. It would be my pleasure to look in on Harold five days a week. I can make him a little lunch, or even have him over to luncheon at my home when he's feeling up to it. And while I'm visiting, I could wash up his dishes and straighten up a bit, if you think that wouldn't be overstepping."

"That wouldn't be overstepping at all." Beverly was quite sincere. "But truly, I can't accept. He would never allow me to let you do that without at least paying you a little bit."

Mrs. Peabody was silent.

Beverly's heart sank. Diane had been so sure this plan would work. Perhaps she should have waited until Diane was with her to discuss this. If there was a more persuasive woman on the planet than Diane Spencer, Beverly had yet to meet her.

"Well, I suppose if you insist..."

Beverly tried not to smile too widely. "Oh, I do." She'd done it! Quickly, she named an hourly fee that was not outrageously generous but not stingy either.

"That's an awfully big salary for a little bit of nothing." Mrs. Peabody looked doubtful.

"Yes, but if I pay you any less, he will know you're just doing it out of the goodness of your heart," she reasoned. "And I'm afraid he'll balk if he thinks we're just humoring him."

"I see what you mean." Her neighbor nodded slowly. "In that case, I suppose I can accept it."

"That's wonderful." Beverly meant it sincerely. "I won't worry a bit with you to keep an eye on him. Oh, thank you, Mrs. P."

"You're very welcome, dear." The old woman cleared her throat. "Are you going to be cleaning on the weekends?"

Beverly nodded, unsure where this was going. She'd noticed that her father's house needed some serious attention, and she'd resigned herself to spending her weekends scrubbing, dusting, and vacuuming. But she couldn't have Mrs. Peabody trying to do much actual cleaning. There were limits to the old lady's energy, as spry as she seemed.

"I have a suggestion, if you don't mind. If it doesn't suit, that's okay, but it seems to me you're going to be burning the candle at both ends every weekend if you drive down here to care for your father and cook and clean."

Beverly nodded wryly. "Funny, but that exact thought has occurred to me."

"I have a sixteen-year-old granddaughter who could use a little pin money. She's a good worker, and if I looked over her shoulder a bit, you'd get your money's worth. She could clean for your father one day a week after school."

"That would be terrific." Beverly meant it. "Is it the girl with the long brown hair I've seen helping you with your flowers?" That girl was about the right age—a pleasant, slender little thing with gray eyes and glasses.

Mrs. Peabody nodded. "Belinda is her name. A good girl. Quite a bit quieter than I was at that age, but she's a good worker. I'm sure she'd do a good job."

"This all sounds too good to be true," Beverly said. "You can't imagine how much you've relieved my mind."

"It'll be good for your father to have someone to talk to for a bit each day."

Beverly hid her smile. *To listen to* was more like it. Mrs. Peabody could segue flawlessly from one topic into the next without ever drawing breath, it seemed. "Thank you so much, Mrs. P. Now I know who to come to when I need great ideas."

Her elderly neighbor preened, clearly pleased with the compliment. She tapped her temple. "I might not be a spring chicken anymore, but this old brain is as sharp as ever."

Beverly didn't doubt it for a minute.

CHAPTER TWENTY-FOUR

It was a glorious, gorgeous day.

Margaret sat on a smooth expanse of rock at Birch Point Beach State Park near Owls Head, another small resort and fishing community not far from Marble Cove. Lucia Beach was a pocket beach protected by rocky headlands on each side. It was a quiet little getaway overlooked by most tourists.

The pencil she gripped in her fingers fairly flew over her sketchpad as she roughed in the cobblestone and sand beach in the foreground. Then she moved on to the white rock ledges along the northeastern side of the beach. In the distance lay Ash Island, separated from the mainland by water of a deep, pure blue, sparkling today as sunlight bounced off the wavelets.

As soon as she finished her preliminary sketch, she opened her case of supplies and reached for her creamy art sticks, thick chunks of color she favored when she was in a hurry to lay down larger areas in certain hues. She breathed in deeply, reveling in the pine-scented ocean breeze.

As she lifted her pencil to take a break, a movement on the ocean caught her eye. Narrowing her gaze against the sun, she was delighted to see a humpback whale breach out in the deeper waters of Penobscot Bay. It was still a little early for calving, and this was the first one she'd seen.

Tucking the pencil behind her ear, she stretched her arms above her head. Then she propped her hands behind her on the boulder, leaning back on her arms as she watched for more whales. For the first time in almost two weeks, she felt the old sense of excitement pulsing in her veins. She wanted to get back home and paint, to translate the gorgeous vista before her into a completed canvas that would share her vision with the world. Or at least, with people who stopped in to visit the Shearwater Gallery.

She trekked back to her car and grabbed the lunch she had purchased in Owls Head earlier in the day. Carrying it back to "her" spot, she contemplated the view as she ate. The light was a little strong, but she could work with that.

Polishing off the cookie, she put away her lunch bag and opened the trunk of her car. She hadn't gone anywhere without a portable easel and a stool in a long time, thank goodness.

Without allowing herself to dwell on what she was doing, she set up her equipment where she'd been sitting and placed a fresh canvas on the easel. She was thankful she had several toned canvases in the trunk in case she ever came across a scene she felt she had to paint immediately. Toning was the process of lightly covering the entire surface of a white canvas with a more subdued, neutral color. She had found that white was particularly difficult to work with outdoors, the stark color creating too strong a contrast.

First, she used a charcoal to sketch her subject. She had put away the drawing pad on which she had done the earlier sketch. That was mostly to refresh her memory if she couldn't finish in one sitting.

The realization made her laugh. Apparently her subconscious had decided she was going to paint today, because she hadn't had any intention of painting when she first took a seat. In fact, the selection of Lucia Beach had been completely random. Her only requirements were that there be few people around and surroundings that would stir her soul. The unique contours of the beach certainly fit that bill.

Anyone wondering if there was a God could hardly fail to believe after witnessing the way the protected little pocket was carved into the rocky coastline or perusing the varied rocks produced during eons of geologic upheaval. The very boulder on which she sat bore a series of long vertical scratches that carved the surface in the same direction, reminders of the glacier that had once inched across its surface.

When she had finished her preliminary work, a sense of relief filled her. Quickly she chose a deep blue to lay down as a foundation for the water portion of the canvas and began to work.

She deliberately didn't let herself think about anything but the exact colors, the types of strokes, the placement of paint on the canvas. When she stopped, she had a good start on a gorgeous study of the area in which she sat, facing out to sea. She had even added a humpback whale among the waves. She studied it, feeling anxiety rise.

She loved it, but would anyone else? It was her old style, true, but it also contained some elements of the new effects with which she had experimented. Who cared? She *really* loved it! A sense of peace filled her. For days she had been agonizing over whether to paint what she loved and what sold or to paint culturally significant pieces that would receive critical acclaim. At last she had her answer.

She painted for nearly three hours, barely taking a break. Finally, with a regretful look at the light and shadows that had changed with the angle of the sun, she put away her things and cleaned the paint from her hands. Time to go home.

Allan and Adelaide arrived at the house at nearly the same instant she did. Addie greeted her happily and went off to feed the cats as Margaret turned to her husband. When she smiled at him, she saw the brief flash of relief Allan couldn't mask, so she leaned in and gave him a quick buss across the cheek. "Thank you for holding down the fort today. I just...I just had to get away."

Her husband's eyes were understanding. "You're welcome. The gallery wasn't too busy. We sold one of your paintings and that cherry sideboard I just finished last week. It's a good thing Dan is interested in working with me, because there's no way I can finish enough stuff to keep up with the demand if sales continue as they have been."

Margaret nodded. "That's a wonderful problem to have. Which of my paintings found a home?"

Allan smiled. "The most recent one you completed. I wasn't sure we should sell it, but Diane said you had told her you didn't care what she did with it."

"It sold?" Margaret was astonished. "But it was...it was..."

"Rather modern compared to the bulk of your work, but striking in its own right and very well executed. I hung it this morning just to see what kinds of comments it would get, and it was hardly on the wall long enough for anyone to see it."

"Thank you." She'd known that it was technically adequate, but she certainly hadn't felt it was particularly memorable.

Allan gave her a brief hug. "The woman asked if you'd be doing any companion pieces. I took her name and e-mail in case you want to contact her."

Margaret had to grin. "Not a chance. That painting had the distinction of being the least enjoyable project I've ever done."

Allan studied her without saying a word. He stared for so long that Margaret finally asked, "What? Is my face dirty?"

Her husband shook his head. "You've barely smiled in two weeks. It's good to see you looking happy."

Margaret absorbed the comment. "I'm feeling happier than I was for a while. Today I drove up to Lucia Beach and painted, and it went well."

"Good."

"I've come to some conclusions."

Allan looked interested. "Which are?"

"I don't care what one pretentious critic says," she told him. "I focused far too much on the *art world*." She made quotes in the air to emphasize the term. "It's taken quite a while for me to believe I'm a talented artist with a certain flair and style. My joy in my work stems from celebrating that, not in trying to suppress it. Never again will I try to force myself into someone else's idea of what I should be painting. I can't please everyone." She laughed. "Although as I think back over the gallery opening and the number of paintings we sold, I realize that my work pleases quite a few people."

Allan smiled broadly. "Quite a few indeed. The only person I've ever heard say anything negative was that one single 'art critic.'" It was his turn to use quotes in the air. "Unfortunately, she has a bigger mouthpiece to air her opinions than most folks do."

★   ★   ★

Before dinner in the Bauer household, Shelley stuck her head into the family room. Adelaide, Margaret's daughter, had been there most of the day, and Aiden was worn out. He lay on the couch on his side watching *Sesame Street*, one small hand trailing over the edge to rest on his puppy's head. Prize lay directly below him, tethered to a tie-down leash that was too short for her to be able to clamber onto the couch.

Dan sat in the easy chair with Emma in his lap. He had worked from noon to four today in accordance with the flexible new schedule he'd been given. Shelley hated to admit that the first thing she did when he got home every day was search his face for signs that he had more bad news.

"Dan," she said. "Could you come out here please?" Butterflies fluttered madly in her stomach.

Moment later, Dan appeared in the kitchen. "I put Em in the playpen. She seems happy enough for the moment."

"It won't last long. She'll be getting hungry soon."

"So what's up?" Dan leaned against the counter.

Shelley twisted her hands together. "Why don't you sit down?" She sank into the chair Prize had gnawed on last Sunday.

"Uh-oh." Dan searched her face as he took the seat opposite her. "This sounds serious."

Shelley was so nervous she couldn't even make a joke. Last time she'd mentioned something about work to Dan, he'd gotten completely bent out of shape. Granted, that had been about work for him, not her, but she already knew how he felt about her working.

She took a deep breath and let it out slowly. "It is serious. It's about me working."

Dan opened his mouth, but she held up a hand, and he paused.

"At least let me explain before you object. It's not quite what you're thinking."

"What is it?" He sounded wary, and she understood he was doing his best not to be dismissive right off the bat.

"I've thought and thought about looking for work," she said. "But the reality is that I'm not qualified to do much of anything that would earn more than minimum wage. And that would make no sense at all. I would barely make enough to pay for childcare."

Dan nodded. They'd been over this ground before.

"But what about working from home?" she asked. "If I was able to work at home, I could manage it without childcare. So any money I make would be income."

He tilted his head. "But only after Uncle Sam takes his cut. And believe me, for self-employed people, it's a hefty chunk."

She nodded. "I know."

"So what is this job?"

"Baking," she said simply. When he didn't interrupt or comment, she hurried on, telling him about her friends' suggestions for opening a baking business and the assistance each of them had offered. "You know how I love making cookies and other sweets. And bread—oh, I love making bread."

"You sound excited about this."

"I am," she admitted. "What do you think?"

Dan hesitated. "Starting up a home business might be more expensive than you think. Have you researched it?"

"Not much. But Beverly said she would help me."

Dan was silent.

"If I work up an estimate of what it would take to get started, will you at least listen to me?"

"Of course." He sounded defensive.

She sat back and crossed her arms. "I feel like you already have your mind made up and you're going to be against this idea no matter what I say."

"That's not true." He hesitated. "I mostly feel really strongly about the kids being raised here, in their home. If you can juggle that and a home-based business, you should try it."

"Really? You think I should do it?"

"I think you should explore it further. It might be a lot more complicated than you expect."

"Maybe not," she said hopefully. She realized she had braced herself for a negative reaction so thoroughly that she was having a hard time believing he wasn't going to shoot her down. "Thank you!"

Aiden, apparently recovered from his fatigue, raced through the kitchen, Prize at his heels. He'd unhooked the puppy from her tie-down, and the pair of them headed for the back door. "Mommy, I'm going to play in the yard."

"All right. But just for a few minutes. We're going to eat supper soon."

Dan grinned as Aiden slammed out the door. "He's doing well with remembering to help with Prize, eh?"

Shelley nodded. "This morning he and Adelaide were playing in the living room, and I completely forgot about Prize because Emma was fussing. He hooked her to the leash by the couch all by himself."

"Good." Dan glanced out the window—and then he was on his feet, headed for the door. "Aiden! Get off that picnic table."

Shelley shook her head as Dan stood at the screen door watching until Aiden followed directions. "Thanks," she said. "He's determined he's going to climb that tree one of these days."

CHAPTER TWENTY-FIVE

On Saturday morning, Shelley and Beverly met Diane and Margaret at the gallery at opening time. The group had decided to meet after their second night of surveillance to decide what their next move should be.

"I'm so glad you're back," Diane said to Margaret. "I was worried yesterday."

Margaret looked sheepish.

"Back from where?" Shelley asked.

"I went off on my own to do a little soul-searching." Margaret smiled, and Shelley was relieved to see the return of her usual merry twinkle.

"And what was the result?" asked Beverly.

"Did this have to do with that critic's rotten review?" As usual, Diane went straight to the heart of the matter.

Margaret nodded. "I've been upset about it. No, not upset. Devastated, if you want the truth."

The others exchanged glances.

"We knew it had really hurt your feelings," Diane said.

"I tried a different style." Margaret spread her hands. "And remember I told you how I felt about *that*."

Beverly laughed. "And quite emphatically too." Her tone softened. "So I take it you've found a new perspective?"

"I have." Margaret explained the revelation she had had during her day away. She hurried back to her work area. "And here's the result." She backed toward them with a large canvas and turned to unveil it dramatically.

Shelley was stunned when she saw it. A view looking out toward an island from a sheltered beach, with a whale just sliding back beneath the waves. It was a lot like Margaret's usual style, but the colors were slightly more dramatic, the perspective just a little different. Shelley couldn't really say what the difference was, but it was definitely a new and improved Margaret Hoskins piece.

"Holy bananas!" Diane laughed. "Margaret, this is amazing. It looks like your work . . . and yet there's something a little different."

"It's you with a really pretty new twist," Shelley told her and was pleased to see Margaret blush at the compliment.

Margaret set down the canvas against the counter, leaning face out, as she explained the revelation she'd had during her time away. As she did so, a customer wandered into the gallery. Diane slipped away momentarily and welcomed him, inviting him to browse.

Beverly had just finished telling Margaret that she too found the new piece very compelling when the customer approached Diane.

"Excuse me," he said. "Sorry, ladies."

"No problem," Diane assured him with a smile. "We would chat all day if no one stopped us. How can I help you?"

The gentleman pointed at the newly completed painting propped against the counter. "I'm interested in this painting. It's absolutely stunning. But there's no tag. I don't know how much it is."

Diane beamed. "That's because it just came in this very morning."

The man grinned. "Guess it's my lucky day."

"Give me a moment," Diane said, "and I'll have a price for you."

Quickly, she beckoned to Margaret, and the two women slipped into the back room for a moment. They soon returned, and Diane approached the client, quoting him the price on which they'd decided.

"That's great," the man said. He pulled out a charge card. "Can I take it with me?"

Margaret winced, hurrying forward. "Hello." She shook his hand firmly. "I'm the artist. If you're leaving the area today, you can take it, but you'll need to be very careful, because oils take a little time to dry thoroughly. If you're here all week, I'd strongly recommend you leave it here for a few days and pick it up toward the end of your time in Marble Cove."

"That works just fine for me," the man assured her, "so long as you put a 'Sold' sign on it. I'm here until Saturday. Do you have any similar works?" He gestured around the room. "I didn't see anything else quite like this."

Margaret smiled, a warm and genuine smile Shelley was pleased to see. "No, that's the only one in that style I have available right now."

The man snapped his fingers regretfully. "I was hoping for a companion piece." He fished in his pocket and withdrew a business card. "If you ever have anything similar, I'd love to see it."

Margaret accepted the card in a calm and serene manner Shelley wasn't sure she'd be able to manage if someone loved her work that much. "I don't work on commission, but I'll be happy to keep you in mind if the spirit moves me to do anything like that." They shook hands just as Diane returned with the charge slip to be signed.

The moment the customer was down the street and out of earshot, the gallery erupted in cheers.

"If I had champagne, I'd pop the cork right now," Diane declared.

Everyone laughed, and the moment grew lighthearted.

Beverly briefed them on her chat with Mrs. Peabody. "It worked like a charm," she told Diane.

"That's terrific. What did your father say?"

Beverly looked a little sheepish. "I haven't talked to him about it yet."

"Beverly!"

"I know, I know. But that's going to require some thought. He's liable to be as mulish in his own way as Mrs. P was about taking payment."

"Make him think he's doing it for her," Shelley said.

"What?" All three of the others turned to her.

"Make him think he's helping her. Poor lonely soul, it would be good for her...that sort of thing."

Beverly nodded her approval. "Another good idea."

Margaret cleared her throat and looked around. "I have a proposal to make."

"Regarding?" Diane's eyebrows rose.

"Our stakeout team. I don't know about the rest of you, but only getting half a night's sleep just about did me in. I'm exhausted."

"Me too," Beverly volunteered as the others nodded.

"What if each of us takes a shorter shift? Say, every two hours from ten until six the next morning. It might help a little. I also think instead of doing it every night, maybe we should skip a night or two in between."

"That's probably a good idea," Shelley said. "If we get a decent amount of sleep we might be able to manage a week or so."

"A week." Margaret groaned.

The others laughed.

"I hear you," Diane said. "I sure hope whoever's behind that light—no pun intended—shows his face soon."

"Me too." Shelley shivered. "I didn't like sitting out there in the dark alone. I *really* didn't like it. I was certain there was an ax murderer right behind me. I almost took the dog along, but she'd be no help at all unless I needed her to lick somebody to death."

Diane laughed.

Margaret frowned. "I thought you were getting rid of the puppy. Isn't that still the plan?"

Shelley shook her head. "I tried. I just couldn't do it. I wouldn't have been able to live with myself if I'd left her at the animal shelter. She's staying, and we're trying some new tricks to keep her off the furniture and stop her from chewing the house to pieces."

"Do you have a kennel for her?" Margaret asked.

Shelley shook her head. "We borrowed one from Dan's sister, but she's already growing out of it. I just use leashes to keep her where I want her, but I'm waiting for the day she realizes she can chew through them."

"I have a friend whose dog just passed away," Margaret told her. "She wants to give away the kennel. She kept it in the kitchen, and it looks like new. Are you interested?"

"Absolutely." Shelley clapped her hands, delighted. "But I can't take it for nothing. Ask her how much she'd like for it."

Margaret waved a hand in denial. "She won't take money, I'm certain. She just wants to get rid of it because it's a sad reminder of her little guy."

"Then...I gratefully accept."

"Great. I'll get it and drop it off after work this evening, all right?"

"Sounds good." Shelley glanced at her watch. "I'd better get going. Emma was fussy last night. Either she's getting sick or she's teething again."

*　　*　　*

Diane left the gallery at noon and walked home. She took Rocky for a short walk and then shut him firmly out of the office, where she once again was laying out index cards. This time, though, she wasn't doing it in the living room. She'd learned her lesson.

She had been working steadily and had a rough draft of nearly two-thirds of the book done. The final section, however, continued to elude her. She'd been ignoring it for the past few days, hoping her subconscious was busy working it out while she avoided writing.

This afternoon she finally couldn't avoid it any longer. If she wanted to submit this to an agent any time soon, she absolutely had to have at least a first draft ready to go if it should be requested.

She sighed, reluctantly getting out the index cards she'd salvaged after Rocky's mad romp near the beginning of the month. She discarded some that were no longer necessary because she'd already written those scenes. The ones that were left...*Ay-yi-yi*. Rocky had made such a mess of her plotting that she wasn't even sure where to start.

Idly she plucked an index card from the top of the pile. Reading it, she wondered why she had thought this scene was such a good idea. She was sure it was going to be tedious to write, which probably meant it would be tedious to read.

Tedious...that was it! The pacing was off. It would be dull reading because there wasn't enough action, and the clues she'd inserted for her heroine, who was trying to solve a mystery, had been spread out too much. She crumpled up the index card that had started the brainstorm and tossed it over her shoulder. She didn't need that scene at all!

Painstakingly, she began to sort the cards in piles of like colors. Then she took each of those single-color piles and read through all the cards, discarding some and putting the rest back into an order that made sense to her, given the story she had written to date.

Finally, she took all the cards, now in order, and laid them out on the floor, just as she had the day Rocky sabotaged her efforts. Slowly she began to pick and choose between the various colors, creating an imaginary chronological timeline of events.

It took well over an hour, but when she finally finished, she leaped up and did a silly little victory dance right there in her office. She couldn't remember how she'd had all this ordered before, but she was certain it wasn't as tightly knit and compelling as the plot she'd just completed.

She almost opened the door to grab Rocky and thank him. Then common sense took over. Grabbing a pencil, she numbered each card so that no matter what, she would be able to put them back in the correct order.

Then, and only then, did she open the door and let her big, sweet goof of a dog into the office. When the door opened, he practically rolled into the room. Apparently, he'd been lying against it, and the sudden release of support was his undoing.

Diane began to laugh. "If I sell this book, buddy, I suppose I'm going to have to thank you for your plotting assistance."

★   ★   ★

"Father?" Beverly approached her dad, who was sitting at the kitchen table doing a crossword puzzle. He'd been a crossword fanatic ever since she could remember. In fact, some of her earliest memories were of him frowning ferociously at the *New York Times* crossword puzzle.

"Yes?"

It was good that he was a little distracted, she decided. She picked up a dishrag, dampened it and began to wipe off the countertops, which her father had left littered with crumbs. "I have a proposal for you."

"Shoot."

"I was talking to Mrs. Peabody the other day, and frankly, I'm a little concerned about her." She glanced over her shoulder at him.

Her father lifted his head. "Why? She seems pretty chipper to me."

"Oh, she is. It's not her health that concerns me."

"Well then, what's the problem?"

"I believe she is living on a very limited income." Beverly turned back to the sink. She rinsed out the dishcloth, hung it up and began to put away the dishes she'd washed earlier that morning and stacked in the drainer. "Extremely limited, in fact. I felt bad about it, and then I thought of a way to give her a little extra money without making it seem like charity." She took a deep breath. "I'd like you to consider having Mrs. P come in and cook for you occasionally." She crossed her fingers. "Maybe lunch on the days when I'm not here."

Her father grunted. "Woman talks a blue streak."

Beverly grinned as she sorted cutlery. "Yes. Yes, she does. Do you think you could handle it? I'd really love to find a way to help her."

"I suppose I could do that."

Yes! Behind her father's back, Beverly did a silent fist pump. "And there's one other thing. Mrs. Peabody has a granddaughter I'd like to hire to come and clean the house once a week. She'd only be here a few hours, and she's a very nice girl. She's saving up for college." She tacked on that last one, knowing how much her father valued education.

"A house cleaner. Good idea." Her father nodded. "I should have thought of that myself. Place is getting to be too much for me, and I don't want you to have to spend your weekends cleaning. Does my new housecleaner have a name?"

"She does. It's Belinda."

"Belinda. Pretty, old-fashioned name. When can she start?"

Really, Beverly thought, as she called Mrs. Peabody a little later to make arrangements for the coming week, the whole thing had been far easier to talk her father into than she'd expected. She'd have to remember to thank Diane.

Chapter Twenty-Six

Across the street in the Bauer home, Shelley was walking the floor with a screaming baby. As she walked and patted, she waited for the doctor to call her back. Emma was running a fever of 102. It had gone down some when they gave her baby ibuprofen, but as soon as that wore off, the fever had come back. Emma had had ear infections before, and Shelley feared that's what this was.

Dan had to work from ten to two, and she had barely gotten home from her powwow at the Shearwater Gallery that morning when he was thrusting the unhappy baby at her and hurrying out the door.

To distract herself, and to keep from getting as upset at the crying child, she thought about Margaret's kind offer from earlier that day. A larger kennel would be enormously helpful. There were times when Shelley simply couldn't watch the puppy every second, even with the tie-downs.

Now that they'd decided to make Prize an indoor puppy, Shelley felt even guiltier having to tie her outside every time they went away. But it had been their only choice. She couldn't be left alone to chew up the entire house. A kennel she could store underneath the desk in the kitchen was the perfect answer.

Somehow, Shelley doubted that Margaret really had a friend who was giving away a perfectly good kennel. But she honestly couldn't afford to go and buy one, so she had decided she would accept the offer gracefully—and make the Hoskins family a batch of her double chocolate chunk cookies. Everyone who tasted them practically drooled.

In fact, if she decided to pursue this cookie baking business venture, that particular offering would definitely be on the list. Along with the ever-popular chocolate chip and no-bakes...and some sort of sugar cookie...maybe something for the fruit lovers, and another something for those who liked nuts...a brownie...maybe some cake balls. Last Christmas, she'd seen really darling ones with inverted ice cream cones atop them, decorated like smiling elves, and they were always a delight.

Perhaps she should develop a list of about twenty recipes and start trying them out on her Sunday school friends and her neighbors. Even the other mothers at the park were fair game, she thought with a smile.

The telephone rang, startling Shelley out of her reverie. She looked down at Emma and realized the unhappy little scrap had fallen asleep against her shoulder.

Carefully, she bent her knees to reach for the phone without waking Emma. "Hello?" It was a half-whisper.

"Shelley Bauer, please."

"This is Shelley."

"Oh, hi, Shelley." The voice was familiar, and the smile Shelley could hear in it probably was reflected on the pleasant face of the pediatrician's receptionist she'd known since Aiden's birth. "Hang on a second. The doctor wants to talk to you."

Half an hour later, Shelley was on her way to the emergency clinic. The doctor would meet her there. Since it was Saturday, of course he didn't have office hours. She winced, thinking of the cost of this visit. Oh well, at least Dan still had insurance. Thinking of that brought back the worries she'd been trying to hold at bay. What were they going to do when they were no longer covered?

Dan had employment now, she reminded herself. And Allan Hoskins needed so much help he was ready to give Dan more hours whenever he wanted. But he hadn't worked for Allan for even two weeks, so it was hard to know how much income that would generate. She was going to have to look into independent insurance plans. Perhaps Margaret would have some ideas about where to start.

As it turned out, the doctor was certain Emma had another ear infection. Shelley groaned at the diagnosis. She'd suffered through two prior bouts with ear infections, and all she'd been able to do was give Emma some eardrops that supposedly helped with the pain. She wasn't looking forward to that again. Last time she'd been up all night. At least this time she was planning on getting up during the night anyway.

★   ★   ★

"Diane?" Shelley's whisper was louder than she'd intended. The noise from the surf probably masked their chatter, but why take chances?

It was four-fifteen in the morning. Ahead of her, Rocky scrambled to his feet and stood poised to alert. "Quiet, buddy." Diane put a hand on his back. "Over here, Shelley." Diane pitched her voice low as well.

Shelley moved forward. Even though she'd been expecting to see her friend, it still was a bit scary. They had agreed not to use flashlights, just to exercise extreme caution when walking the path out to the rock formation not far from the lighthouse door.

"Hey," Diane said. Rocky surged forward.

Shelley ruffled his coat. "I'm a little late, sorry. Emma's sick." She set down the bag she carried and watched as Diane slung her backpack over her shoulders. "I've been up with her all night, but Dan has her now. I shouldn't be taking such pleasure in waking my poor husband to help with the baby, should I?"

Diane's teeth flashed white as she grinned. "He's only working part-time, right? He can nap tomorrow. You, on the other hand, work full-time from dawn to dusk every day."

Shelley yawned. "And believe me, it feels like it." She made a shooing motion. "You go on home now. I'll call if I see anything. I guess there's been nothing so far?"

Diane shook her head. "Not a flash, not a pinpoint, nothing." She sighed. "We might as well go back to our normal routines. Seems like we saw it more often that way."

"I think that's a good idea. Maybe we can all keep our phones close at hand, so if one of us sees something she can quickly call the others."

Diane yawned. "Let's talk about it tomorrow." She waved one hand and turned away. "See you."

"See you tomorrow."

As Diane and Rocky vanished into the inky night surrounding her, Shelley turned and took a thick blanket from her bag. Leaving it folded, she placed it on the insulated blanket Diane had left behind for her. Then she pulled out a small stadium seat with a back, something she'd realized after her first uncomfortable shift would be invaluable. She took a seat, eyeing the black bulk of the lighthouse looming ahead of her. Cowardly as it was, she secretly hoped nothing happened on her watch. Up close and personal like this, spying on someone doing who-knew-what in the building didn't seem like such a good idea.

She yawned. What a day. She could feel the tension draining out of her. Unfortunately, so did every drop of energy. Fatigue swept over her. Her eyelids fluttered, and she blinked rapidly. *No sleeping, Shelley.*

She turned her head and stared into the darkness to her right and then repeated the process to the left. Each time she began to feel her eyelids drooping, she changed position. She checked her watch. Yawned again. Changed position. Checked her watch again. Four-twenty. Oh, mercy, she'd only been out here fifteen minutes. This might just be the longest two hours of her life...

She startled herself awake, jerking her head up from where it had drooped down to her chest.

Must stay awake...Blink, girl, keep those eyes alert—or at least open. Must stay awake...must stay...must...

★   ★   ★

Diane couldn't sleep. Which was utterly ridiculous. She should be exhausted. Margaret had taken the first evening shift of their surveillance effort tonight. Then Beverly from midnight to two, and Diane from two until four. Shelley was taking the dawn shift.

She tossed and turned in her bed and glanced at the clock at least two hundred times. The hands crept slowly toward five, and finally the first tiny lightening of the darkness began. During daylight hours she could see the lighthouse from her bedroom window. At night, she could only imagine what it would have been like to see that sturdy sentinel standing guard and warning off unwary ships.

Dawn wouldn't truly arrive for another hour. If smugglers or drug runners or vagrants or whoever were using the lighthouse for unsavory purposes, they hadn't been around in a couple of days. And they probably weren't going to come now, since it was so close to—

A light winked on, startling her into sitting upright. She slid her feet into her slippers and crossed to her window, nearly too excited to breathe. It was the same light she'd seen several weeks ago. The small yellow square seemed to float in the air, but she knew it was coming from the lighthouse.

The light blinked twice, and Diane sucked in a sharp breath. Were people walking around up there? She reached for her phone and hit the camera feature. When it came on, she took a picture—but to her dismay, all she got was a dark photo with a little light somewhere in the middle. The lighthouse wasn't distinguishable, nor were any other features.

Come on, Shelley. Why don't you call? Diane couldn't call her, because she didn't know if Shelley's phone was set to vibrate or if it would announce to the world that someone hiding in the rocks was receiving a call.

She had Beverly and Margaret both on speed-dial. She called Margaret first. "Hi, it's Diane. Meet me outside as soon as you can find shoes. The light is back!" She barely waited for a mumbled acknowledgement before she did the same thing to Beverly.

Quickly, she threw on sweatpants and a sweatshirt and stuffed her feet into her low Bogs. "Sorry, Rocky," she said, as she rushed out the door and closed him in the cottage, "not this time."

Margaret joined her in the street almost immediately, and they hurried on to the Wheelands' home, where Beverly was already standing outside.

They could see the light glowing against the black lighthouse silhouette as they moved. It flickered once.

"There," Beverly said. "Is that a person?"

Whatever it was didn't happen again. All that remained was the steady square of light shining out into the night.

Diane was pretty certain Marble Cove had never seen three grown women move as fast as they were moving down the promenade along the sand to the line where the black boulders began.

"Mute your phones," Diane hissed. "We don't want them to ring. Shelley was supposed to call me, but she hasn't yet."

"I hope she's all right," Margaret said breathlessly.

Worry tightened Diane's throat. Had she placed a dear friend in danger? If anything happened to Shelley, she wouldn't be able to forgive herself. They scrambled along the trail through the dunes and out to their hiding place.

"Shelley!" Diane's whisper was harsh with fear. They could see the younger woman now, sitting in her chair unmoving, her head slumped forward. One arm hung over the edge of the stadium seat and her fingers lay limply against the rock.

Diane skidded to a stop on her knees in front of Shelley and reached to place her fingers against the pulse in Shelley's neck. Her skin was warm, thank the Lord, and—

A scream rent the night air.

Shelley shot out of the stadium seat, knocking Diane backward onto her fanny.

Beverly said, "Sh-sh-sh!"

"It's all right." Margaret made frantic gestures to indicate that everyone should settle down.

"You scared me to death." Shelley had a hand at her throat. "What—Oh no! I fell asleep." Chagrin colored her tone as awareness returned. She whirled to look at the lighthouse.

Incredibly, the light was still on. This close, it was obvious to them all that it was some kind of lantern flickering slightly.

And then a dark shadow moved between it and the window, making the light appear to blink for a moment.

They'd made enough noise to wake the dead, Diane thought. No wonder whoever was in there was looking out. "There's someone in there, and I'm going to find out who." She ran forward before any of them could catch her. "Hey," she shouted up at the lighthouse, "we know you're in there." Reaching the door at the base of the old structure, she began to pound with a fist on the heavy wooden door. "Come out here."

"Diane." It was Margaret's voice. "The light just went out."

"They must still be in there, though. Someone call Fred Little."

Beverly whipped out her phone. All of them had entered the detective's number in their phones in case they discovered smugglers, or worse, using the lighthouse.

By now it was after five, and the sky was definitely lightening.

"I am not moving from this spot," Diane shouted. "Whoever is in there isn't getting past me." And she meant it. The mystery of who was in the lighthouse had been building since she'd moved to Marble Cove, and she was determined to find out what was going on.

It seemed to take forever for Detective Fred Little, who also happened to be another Newport Avenue neighbor, to arrive. Although the sun wasn't showing on the horizon yet, it was definitely more light than dark.

"Detective!" Diane beckoned from the position she still held in front of the door. "We saw someone in this building, burning a light, less than an hour ago."

"Somebody in there, eh?" Fred sounded more than skeptical.

Diane had encountered his attitude before, and it drove her crazy.

"Fred." Margaret's voice was calmer than Diane's. "All four of us saw light coming from that window right up there." She pointed, and they all looked up. The window was clearly visible now as dawn approached. "And someone walked between the window and the light source. We *all* saw it. And this isn't the first time. Every single one of us has seen lights of some kind out here."

"You thought you saw the Fresnel flashing too," he reminded them.

Diane thought his tone sounded more than a little indulgent. "We *did* see it," she corrected him. "There was nothing imaginary about it."

"Lights don't just go on and off by themselves." Fred tramped off to the right as he spoke. "Let me take a look for any way someone could get in besides through there." He indicated the sturdy wooden door. "The key to that baby is locked in a safe in the municipal office. There is no possible way anyone got that door open."

Diane began to follow him, but Fred held up a hand. "No civilians allowed. You ladies just wait here."

"That takes nerve," she said indignantly, as the detective disappeared around the side of the building. "After we alerted him to a problem, he...he..."

"Treats us like civilians." Margaret's tone was sympathetic but there was a twinkle in her eye.

Most of the annoyance rushed out of Diane like helium from a balloon. "Yeah. Just like civilians."

"Hey, hey, Shelley, what's wrong?"

Diane looked at Beverly, who was looking at Shelley.

The youngest of their group stood a little apart from the rest of them fighting tears. "I'm sorry," she said in a voice barely above a whisper. "I let all of you down."

"Let us down...?" Diane was mystified. "Do you mean because you fell asleep?"

Shelley nodded.

Margaret smiled and moved to Shelley's side, rubbing her back. "If I'd had the night and day and night you had with that poor sick baby, I'd be comatose right now. Don't you feel bad for a minute, honey."

Diane nodded. "My goodness, Shelley. That could have— and would have—happened to any one of us if we had gotten as little sleep as you have. Besides, what harm did it do? We saw the light, we blocked the door, and we called Fred. What more could you want?"

Shelley shrugged. "I just wish I'd been doing my job and seen it right away. How did you guys see it anyway?"

Diane raised her hand with a rueful grin. "I couldn't sleep. And I just happened to look out my bedroom window that faces this direction."

They talked among themselves for a bit longer. Finally, Detective Little appeared from around the left side of the old building.

Diane studied his face, but she couldn't glean any inkling of what he was thinking. "Well," she demanded, "what did you find?"

Fred put his hands on his hips. For the first time, Diane realized he was wearing his jacket, badge, belt, and weapon over...pajama pants? The pants in question were a dark blue and green plaid, very much like ones her husband Eric had worn.

"There is nothing around here to indicate that someone's going in and out," he told the assembled women. "And there's no other way in or out, anyhow. From the way you fussed, I thought at the very least I'd find a dead body. But no, you dragged me out of bed before dawn to investigate...*nothing.*"

"But we really did see a light," Diane said.

"And there was someone moving around in there." Margaret sounded surprisingly pugnacious. "Honestly, Fred Little, do you really think I'd roust you out of bed in the middle of the night unless I thought it was something serious? There was at least one person in there."

"All right, all right." Fred sounded harassed. "So you think you saw someone—"

"We *did* see someone," Beverly corrected.

"It must have been a reflection from something," he said. "Lights from a ship off the coast or the moonlight flashing off the window, maybe. I'm no scientist, but it almost had to be some kind of reflection."

"All four of us have seen lights," Shelley told him. "And they're not reflections. They're not even all the same."

Diane pointed at the sky. "No moon. Or at least, not enough to give any kind of light. There was only a sliver of silvery moon tonight."

"Well, I didn't find anything," Fred said irritably. His eyes narrowed. "I'm not even going to ask what the four of you were doing skulking around out here in the middle of the night." But it was a clear invitation for an explanation.

No one spoke.

"Keeping secrets from a law enforcement officer is probably not the wisest course you could take." He sounded more than a little disgruntled. "Now if you don't mind, I'm going home and try to get a little more sleep. I suggest you do the same."

After the deputy stomped away, the four women stood facing the lighthouse as dawn crept across the sky with stealthy fingers of pink and gold.

"I don't know what kind of vanishing act went on here, but I am absolutely certain someone was in that lighthouse tonight." Diane looked at her three friends, wondering if they were annoyed that she had pursued this so far.

Beverly cleared her throat. "I can't say for sure if any miracles are going on here, but someone is up to something."

"The fact that it might be man-made doesn't rule out the existence of miracles associated with it. God uses people for his purposes all the time." Margaret wasn't usually the one who argued this point.

"I'm not getting into the middle of your wrangling over miracles," Shelley said, "but I know what I saw, and I saw someone in there tonight. As for miracles, Beverly, you can believe whatever you choose, but I *know* my children probably wouldn't be alive today if it wasn't for the miracle that led Diane to my assistance. God was with me that day."

CHAPTER TWENTY-SEVEN

By midday on Sunday, Emma's ear infection had improved markedly.

Dan had let Shelley sleep in a bit this morning after she'd finally returned home. She was pretty sure he thought she and her friends were insane, but he admitted he'd heard a lot of stories about lights in the lighthouse over the years. Then he took Aiden to church while she stayed home with Emma. They often went to Sunday lunch with Dan's family, but he called and begged off this week because of Emma's illness. Shelley was rather ashamed of how relieved she was not to have to go.

She would bake something for her mother-in-law as a silent apology, she decided. Frances Bauer had a sweet tooth and always enjoyed tasting Shelley's creations.

After lunch, Emma went down for a nap. Dan went out to his workshop, while Aiden, sun-screened and wearing his hat, played in the yard with Prize. Shelley was grateful for a few moments of solitude. She sat down with her recipes to see what she might make for her mother-in-law.

Carrot cake appealed to her. But rather than baking one large cake, Shelley thought about how she could present it in a form that would fit in better with a cookie business. Cupcakes, perhaps, decorated with tiny icing carrots like she'd seen in fancy magazines. In fact, she probably should plan to have a cupcake on hand all the time. They were all the fashion.

She studied the quantities in the carrot cake recipe she had gotten from her grandmother, tweaking amounts in a manner she thought would produce an even tastier result. Then she jumped up and began to put together the ingredients.

She could see Aiden outside through the wide picture window. He was playing happily in the sandbox while the puppy snoozed in a patch of shade beneath a nearby tree.

Shelley put the cake in the oven and cleaned up her baking dishes and utensils. A few minutes later, she sat down at the kitchen table to make a few more notes about the altered recipe. If it turned out to be exceptionally good cake flavor, she wanted to be sure she could do it again.

She was startled out of her concentration by the sound of barking. It was Prize, barking with all the shrill vigor of her little lungs. Shelley glanced out the window, but she couldn't see Aiden or the puppy. Concern rose. Prize didn't bark very often.

She went to the back door. "Aiden?" she called through the screen. She still couldn't see him, but she could see Prize barking frantically beside the tree near the picnic table.

And then she saw the bucket lying on its side at the very edge of the table. Fear squeezed her heart. She had a very clear mental image of Aiden placing that bucket on top of the picnic table and climbing atop it to reach the lowest tree branch.

Shelley raced outside. Prize's barking drew her around the picnic table—and that's when she saw Aiden lying motionless on the ground. Prize barked and ran in circles, racing in to lick Aiden's face and backing off again to bark some more.

"Aiden!" It was a shriek as she hurried to his side. "Honey?"

The little boy was unconscious. There was a large gash at his temple from which blood flowed.

"Dan!" She screamed for her husband again, trying to remember what she should do. Put pressure on the wound to try to stop the bleeding? There seemed like an awful lot of blood. Her breath hitched as she put a hand against Aiden's temple and pressed gingerly.

"What happened?"

She looked around to see Dan racing toward her. "Call 9-1-1," she shouted. "Aiden fell off the picnic table. I think he was trying to climb that tree again. He's got a cut on his head, and he's unconscious." Even from a distance, she saw the sudden fear on Dan's face, as he reversed course and sprinted back to the house.

Behind her, she heard a familiar voice. "Shelley, what can I do to help?" Shelley nearly sobbed with relief, as Diane joined her. "I was walking home from church when I heard you yell."

"Get me a clean dish towel. And please bring me the portable baby monitor. I forgot it." Shelley continued to hold pressure on the bleeding wound. Beneath her hand, she could feel a goose-egg that seemed to grow larger by the second.

Dan ran across the yard toward them, clutching the cell phone in his hand. "They're still on the line." He held up the phone. "The EMTs are on the way."

Diane hurried back out of the house, dish towel in hand. "I got it out of your kitchen drawer," she said. "I hope it's not a good one."

"It doesn't matter." Shelley whipped it from her hand, folded it into a pad, and resumed pressing against the wound.

Aiden stirred and whimpered. "Mommy?"

"Right here, sweetie." Shelley bent over him, adrenaline still racing through her. "You hit your head. Just lie still."

Within moments, Shelley could hear the screaming siren. As the emergency vehicle drew to a halt in front of the house, Dan ran out to meet them.

Shelley glanced at Diane, realizing that this was the second time her friend had seen her through a crisis. "If they want to take him to the hospital, would you stay with Emma? She's still sleeping."

"Of course."

Shelley tried to smile. "The last time I left my kids with you, I was a basket case of nerves. This time, I know Emma couldn't be in better hands."

Diane smiled. "I'll take good care of her." She laid her hand over Shelley's. "'Be of good courage, and He shall strengthen your heart, all you who hope in the Lord.'" She smiled. "That's from the thirty-first Psalm."

"Thank you." Shelley managed a genuine smile. As the emergency medical technicians hustled across the yard with their red boxes and Dan right behind them, she silently prayed their son's injuries weren't serious.

The EMTs talked to Aiden as they checked him over before carefully lifting him onto a backboard and securing him. He started to cry when he realized the straps prevented him from moving, and Shelley moved in to reassure him. She rode to the hospital in the ambulance with him, while Dan followed in her car.

At the hospital, Aiden was examined thoroughly. A doctor reassured Dan and Shelley that he didn't appear to have broken any bones but he had a concussion and the cut on his head would need stitches. They wanted to do a CT scan to rule out any brain or spinal cord injuries. Then Aiden was whisked away.

Dan and Shelley walked outside to have better cell phone reception so they could call Dan's family. He was afraid his parents might hear it from someone before he could tell them.

"Be of good courage," Shelley repeated to herself. "And He shall strengthen your heart, all you who hope in the Lord."

"What?" Dan had just finished talking to his mother, who had promised to call the rest of the family.

Shelley shared the Bible verse with him. "Diane said it to me right before we left for the hospital." She smiled. "I've been clinging to it ever since."

"She always knows just want to say, doesn't she?"

"Well, those weren't her own words, but yes, she usually does. I've been very blessed to have met her." *Thank You, Lord, for bringing such an amazing woman into my life. Women,* she corrected. He had seen her need, and He had provided Margaret, Diane, and even skeptical Beverly to lighten her heart and make her everyday concerns seem more manageable.

"She's with Emma, right?"

Shelley nodded.

"I wonder if she brought Prize in."

"Prize!" Shelley was horrified that she had completely forgotten the puppy who had alerted her to her son's emergency. "Dan, she was wonderful. I might never have known Aiden was hurt if it wasn't for Prize. I heard her barking and barking. She wouldn't leave him. I can't believe I forgot about her."

"So did I," Dan said. His phone rang, and he checked the caller ID. "It's my brother. I'd better tell him everything's going to be okay."

"I'm going back in now," she told him. "Before you come in, would you call Diane? Check on Emma, and ask Diane to bring Prize inside and give her water . . . and a doggy treat."

Dan nodded. "That dog is getting a steak dinner tonight. I don't care what it costs."

Inside, Shelley didn't have to wait long before Aiden's bed was rolled back into the ER cubicle. There was an ice pack over the lump on his head, and his eyes were closed.

"Hey, baby. Mommy's here."

Aiden's eyes fluttered opened briefly at her voice.

The doctor came into the cubicle. "He's all right. No skull fracture or any sign of spinal trauma."

Shelley sagged with relief.

"We'll get him stitched up now. He must have fallen from some height."

"There was so much blood." Shelley shuddered. "I couldn't seem to get it to stop."

The doctor nodded. "Head wounds often bleed profusely and can look worse than they are, but it's a good thing you found him when you did. If he'd lain there for any length of time, he could have lost a lot of blood."

"Our dog barked." She glanced tenderly down at her little boy. He was dozing, which was probably just as well. He wasn't going to be happy when he realized they would be sewing his head with a needle.

The curtain moved aside, and Dan entered.

Shelley looked up at him and smiled, but the smile faded as she saw the expression on his face. "What is it?"

"Prize is missing."

★   ★   ★

Shelley could barely make herself sit still on the short ride home. She sat in the middle of the back seat, right next to Aiden's car seat. As they turned onto Newport Avenue, she craned her neck, hoping to catch a glimpse of Prize running around in a neighbor's yard.

Diane had probably found her by now. Prize would be inside waiting for them—probably curled up in Aiden's usual spot on the couch, the little sneak. But Shelley wasn't sure she could ever bring herself to fuss at the dog again. Prize had proven she was much more than simply a living toy for Aiden. When something went wrong, the little dog had stayed with him and sounded the alarm.

Dan parked, and she hurried to unbuckle Aiden's seatbelt. Then Dan opened his door and lifted him out.

"Daddy?"

"Hey, buddy. I'm going to take you inside to rest now."

"My head hurts."

"I guess it does. You fell out of that tree." Dan paused. "It's a good thing you have that hard head, or you might have been hurt worse."

Aiden smiled, a lopsided, slightly loopy effort that made Shelley and Dan exchange an amused look. "I don't have a hard head. Silly Daddy."

Shelley hurried ahead of them to open the back door, but Diane beat her to it. She had Emma on her hip.

The baby gurgled and reached for Shelley. "*Mamamama!*"

"Hello, pretty girl." Shelley kissed her. "You look like you're feeling much better after that nap." Over the baby's head, she looked anxiously at Diane. "Prize?"

Diane's expression gave her the answer. "No. Margaret, Allan, Addie, and Beverly are out looking. Fred Little promised to keep an eye out for her. Even Mr. Wheeland and Mrs. Peabody are looking for her."

Tears filled Shelley's eyes. "I can't believe this. How are we going to tell Aiden?"

Dan cleared his throat from behind her, reminding her that not only was she blocking the door, Aiden might be listening.

She scooted inside, and Dan carried Aiden on into the living room.

"I'll go out and start hunting for her now," Diane said. "She can't have gotten far."

"How did she get out?" Shelley was so careful about keeping the gate closed, for Aiden as much as the dog.

"The EMTs must have left it ajar. Dan was already in your car, and I never thought to check. Actually, I completely forgot about the poor little thing for a while. Emma woke up for a few minutes after you left, and she wasn't particularly thrilled to see me instead of you. It wasn't until after I'd gotten her to go back down that I remembered Prize."

Shelley felt even worse. "So she could have been gone for quite a while by now."

Diane nodded reluctantly. "I'm sorry, Shelley."

"You have nothing to apologize for. Things happen sometimes. I'm going to start praying for her safe return." She jiggled Emma, who was squirming to get down.

"I can search and pray at the same time, and you'd better believe I will. Someone will call when we find her." Diane turned and hurried off.

Shelley followed Dan into the living room. He had laid Aiden on the couch. She put Emma in the playpen, where she happily sat up and grabbed a book, holding it upside-down and turning the thick pages with relish.

Dan straightened. "If you want to stay here with them, I'll go out and join the search."

Shelley nodded. "Good idea. I'll man the phone."

Dan bent over Aiden and very gently kissed the tip of his nose. "See you, bud."

"Where are you going, Daddy?" Aiden mumbled sleepily.

Dan hesitated. "I have some work to do."

Aiden accepted that. Dan kissed Shelley and Emma and left the house.

Shelley put one of her son's favorite movies on, but after a few moments, she realized his eyes were closing again. The doctor had said sleep was fine so long as they checked his pupils every thirty minutes. She set her phone alarm so she would be reminded.

She didn't quite know what to do with herself, so she baked. She let Emma crawl around the kitchen and explore, while she made blueberry muffins from scratch and checked on Aiden when her alarm went off. Then it occurred to her that she should call the animal shelter and alert them in case someone brought Prize in. Her heart sank, as she realized she probably should call the vet for the same reason. If someone brought Prize to the vet, it was very likely because she'd been injured, a prospect Shelley couldn't bear to contemplate.

Instead, she thought of the chain of events that had allowed the puppy to save Aiden today. She hadn't wanted the dog. She'd kicked it out of the house, and she'd even taken it to the pound to get rid of it. She'd punished her son for sneaking the puppy into his bed, when she should have been thanking God that he had such an open, accepting heart.

But God apparently knew Prize was going to be needed. It was nearly miraculous that the dog had been right there with Aiden, given her attitude toward the puppy.

Right now, she couldn't even recall exactly why she'd been so adamant that the dog not come in the house. Her reasons seemed so superficial. Yes, there'd been a little hair. Nothing that a vacuum and a tape roller couldn't remove. Yes, she put things in her mouth and chewed. So did other babies, regardless of species, and they all grew out of it.

Lord, I apologize. You did everything but hit me over the head with a dog bone to make me see that Prize was meant to be with us. But I refused to listen. Please don't let it be too late. And please help me to see your Word in my everyday world. If you have to hit me over the head, so be it.

The phone was ominously quiet. She thought about dinner, but it was hard to plan when she had no idea when Dan might return. Checking in the refrigerator, she saw there was some leftover broccoli quiche, a white sauce that could be used on spaghetti, and several servings of chicken-corn soup she'd made one evening. All of it could be reheated fairly quickly, so tonight would be leftovers night.

She checked on Aiden several more times, fed him some of the soup, a biscuit, and applesauce, and she fed Emma.

Then she gave Emma a bath, but it was hard to take her usual joy in her daughter's squealing and splashing. She let Aiden sit in a shallow bath and quickly washed everything except his hair. It was too close to the nasty, sutured lump on his forehead.

After Emma was in her crib, Aiden fussed for his father a bit.

"I'm sorry, honey," Shelley said, "but Daddy can't come home yet. I promise he'll come in and kiss you when he gets here, even if you're sleeping."

"You promise?"

Shelley nodded soberly.

"Okay." Aiden made a face after he nodded his head too vigorously. "Owweeee."

"Let's get you settled," Shelley said. "What book do you want to read?"

"*Harry the Dirty Dog.*" The classic children's picture book had been popular since Shelley herself was small, and it was Aiden's current favorite.

They read the book together.

"Mommy," Aiden said when they were done, "I want Prize to sleep with me. You should let me have Prize because I'm hurt."

Shelley's heart contracted. She had feared this very thing. "Prize is...already sleeping, honey. Why don't we let her alone tonight? If she sleeps with you, she'll wake up every time I come in to check on you. Remember I said I have to do that all night long?"

Aiden sighed. "Yes." His eyes were already closing again.

Shelley kissed him on the forehead and smiled, but on the inside, she was crying.

Dan came home at ten, his face pale and fatigued. Shelley took one look and knew the puppy hadn't been found.

"Did you eat?"

He nodded. "Diane bought burgers and milkshakes and drove around handing them out to all of us who were looking."

"Would you like anything else?"

Dan shook his head. "I just want to go to bed. Maybe someone will find Prize tomorrow. Our phone number is on her ID tag, so it's possible we'll get a call."

"I hope so." Shelley started for the door. "I'll be back in a minute."

"Where are you going?"

She paused, one hand on the knob, and looked back at him. "I want to be sure the gate is open. If Prize comes back on her own I want her to be able to get in."

They went to bed with heavy hearts. After praying together as they usually did, Dan pulled Shelley close and fell asleep within minutes.

She lay awake for a very long time.

CHAPTER TWENTY-EIGHT

Shelley awoke very early and very tired. She and Dan had taken turns checking on Aiden throughout the night. Several times he had asked for Prize, and their excuses about why the puppy couldn't come to him were wearing thin. And Shelley didn't like lying to him, even if it was to keep him calm.

Yawning, she found her slippers and lightweight summer robe. Even in June, it was cool enough here in the early hours to want a second layer. She thought of dear old Mrs. Peabody, wearing her wool jacket. She wouldn't discard it until July first, no matter how warm it might get. And it came right back out of the closet on the first day of September—no exceptions.

Thinking of Mrs. Peabody reminded her of the kindness of her neighbors, so many of them out searching for Prize yesterday afternoon and evening, and her spirits fell even further.

"Mommy?" The little voice floated out to her from Aiden's room. "Where's my Prize?"

Shelley heaved a sigh, turning and walking into her son's room. Aiden was still pale and heavy-eyed. His sleep also had been interrupted quite a bit. "Good morning, sweetheart. How does your head feel?"

"Hurts. I want my Prize."

"Soon, Aiden. Prize doesn't want to take a chance on bumping your head and making you hurt more." Wow. What a whopper. She just didn't know what to say to her son. How could she tell him his puppy was gone?

"I want her *now.*"

"I know." Shelley leaned over the bed. "Look at me, please." She checked his pupils, satisfied that he seemed to be doing fine. "You'll be feeling better in a day or so." She gently stroked his hair. "Why don't you go back to sleep for a little while? It's still really early."

Aiden stared up at her, his blue eyes filling with tears. "I want Prize," he mumbled, as he turned over on his side and grabbed the blanket with the silky edge that he'd loved since he was a baby. He lay there quietly talking to himself. "I want my Prize. I want my puppy..."

Shelley backed out of the room feeling like a criminal. What were they going to do? She walked into the bathroom and turned on the tap, letting the water warm up a bit before she washed her face. Finishing, she groped for the towel on the handrail and moved to the window as she patted her skin dry. Dan had installed a thermometer right outside the bathroom window so she could see what the temperature was. As on so many mornings, the day started with a low-hanging fog draped over the town. But she could already see the sun burning through it. By nine, it should be a pretty day.

Downstairs, she started coffee. She crossed to the back door and opened it, as she often did first thing in the morning before it got too warm.

Prize was curled up on the mat outside the door.

Shelley gasped.

The puppy scrambled to her feet and stared at Shelley, an anxious little whine rising from her throat.

"Prize!" Shelley flung open the door.

Alarmed by the sudden movement coupled with her name—was she in trouble?—the puppy skittered backward.

Shelley stopped abruptly. "Oh, baby," she said, "I'm so sorry. I didn't mean to scare you." It broke her heart that the puppy didn't immediately run to her. She got down on her knees and patted her lap. "Come here, girl. I know a little boy who is going to be tickled to pieces to see you."

Prize's ears came up. She cleared the space between them and launched herself into Shelley's arms.

With her arms full of warm, wriggling puppy, Shelley buried her face in the soft fur and let it soak up her tears. Prize began to wiggle after a moment. Shelley lifted her into her arms and carried her into the house. "Where were you all night?" When she set the puppy down, the little dog immediately ran to her water bowl and began slurping water like a camel at an oasis.

Shelley opened a can of puppy food and put a portion in a bowl. Prize ate it so fast that Shelley was afraid she might throw up. Shelley put a lid on the can and set it in the refrigerator. Then she turned to the puppy. "Well, come on. I know someone who wants to see you."

As if the puppy knew exactly what she had just said, she took off through the house, claws scrabbling momentarily on the vinyl floor in the kitchen. She scampered through the living room and up the stairs.

Shelley followed as fast as she could. She arrived in Aiden's doorway just in time to see Prize take a flying leap onto Aiden's bed. Shelley was astonished. She had never seen the pup jump that high before.

"Prize!" The little boy sat up, delighted to see his beloved puppy. He threw his arms around her, and the dog put her head on his shoulder.

Shelley felt tears rise. An arm slipped around her shoulders, and she turned to smile up at Dan. "She was outside the door when I went downstairs."

Dan closed his eyes momentarily. "Thank You, Lord." It was a sentiment that Shelley fully appreciated.

Aiden lay back down in his bed. "Come on, my Prize. Come on, girl. Lie down here with me." He patted a spot beside him.

The puppy moved to Aiden's side, scratched up the sheets to make herself a suitable bed, turned around three times, and flopped down with a heavy doggie sigh.

Aiden looked at his parents. "Thank you, Mommy. Prize missed me."

Shelley chuckled. "I know. She missed you a lot. Why don't you try to sleep a little more?"

"Okay."

Emma also was still sleeping, so Shelley and Dan went downstairs. As she walked through the living room, something occurred to her. "Hold on."

She rushed to the closet where she kept cleaning supplies and old blankets. Pulling out a large sheet, she hurried back to the living room.

"What are you doing?" Dan looked puzzled.

She smiled. Snapping open the sheet, she said, "Grab the other end of this, will you?"

When Dan complied, she lifted the sheet in the air and let it gently land on the couch. Adjusting it to cover the whole seating area and armrests, she tucked it in to hold it in place. "There."

Dan grinned. "Does that mean what I think it means?"

Shelley nodded. "I'm covering the couch so Prize can be up on it if she likes. She can cuddle with us when we're watching TV."

"What about the tie-downs?"

"She's still a puppy, and we're still going to use them sometimes. But when we're with her, she doesn't have to lie on the floor anymore. Ever."

Peace stole through her and filled her heart. Somehow, in the middle of the chaos of her life, she had found a little grace. Sometimes, she realized, she just had to let go of her preconceived notions and listen to God's plan for her life. He had reasons for everything and everyone He sent into their lives.

Thank You for returning Prize to us, Lord. She was eager to call everyone with the good news. What a relief! She would cherish and care for the little life from now on, she vowed. Dogs had been fashioned by God to be man's closest companion, not to be discarded if they weren't perfect.

Much like people in her family, Shelley realized, thinking of her mother-in-law. Dan's mother meant well. She loved Shelley in her own way and wanted the best for all of them. Shelley just needed to learn to let a little more of what Frances considered best roll off her back, especially when it related to their family finances.

Then something else occurred to her. She had been so preoccupied thinking about whether to take on a baking business and fussing about what to offer that she had totally neglected the most important thing. She couldn't do this without God.

Right there in the doorway of her son's room, she bowed her head and asked God to be with her in her new venture.

ABOUT THE AUTHOR

Best-selling author Anne Marie Rodgers has published more than forty novels since 1992, the last nine for Guideposts Books. She was the launch author for Guideposts' *Stories from Hope Haven* series and has been a finalist for the prestigious RITA Award. Anne Marie has been involved in animal rescue efforts for many years. Currently, she volunteers at Centre Wildlife Care, rehabilitating injured and orphaned wild animals, and serves as the coordinator of the Orphaned Kitten Program in State College, Pennsylvania, where she and her family make their home. She considers irises, beaches and babies of any species some of God's finest creations.

A CONVERSATION WITH
ANNE MARIE RODGERS

Q. What was your favorite scene to write in Finding Grace?

A. Diane's mishap with Rocky destroying her carefully laid out plotting was lots of fun to write. Although I've never had this particular problem happen, I am owned by several large dogs who have been known to race through a room from time to time, leaving disaster in their wake.

Q. What details from your own life did you incorporate into the story?

A. The scenes with the puppy were quite familiar after my experiences raising puppies for Guiding Eyes for the Blind. I am continually astounded by the amount of chaos one small furry creature with angelic eyes can create. On the other hand, writing about Margaret's artistic endeavors was total fiction. I can't even paint a wall, much less a landscape.

Q. What's the first thing you do when you sit down to write a book?

A. You mean after I break out the chocolate? I brainstorm...think of all the things that could possibly happen and decide what direction I want my conflict to take.

Q. *What's a good cure for writer's block?*

A. Sit yourself down and do not permit yourself to get out of your chair until you've written your desired number of pages. Write stream-of-consciousness if you don't have your story in your head. Write "I WILL finish this book!" over and over again if that's all that comes to mind, but whatever you do, don't stop writing.

Q. *What's a misconception about being a writer?*

A. Our time is not as flexible as people assume. I have set work hours because I need large blocks of time to immerse myself in my fictional world. It's not easy to simply pop in and out of Marble Cove repeatedly.

Q. *What advice would you offer to aspiring writers?*

A. Talking about writing will never make you an author. Take the plunge and start putting your words on paper. Every day.

Q. *Have you ever witnessed an inexplicable occurrence, even a miracle?*

A. Absolutely. My younger daughter was pinned in an automobile after a crash that demolished the vehicle. The door wouldn't open and there was glass everywhere.

The next thing she remembers, she was standing on the side of the road with fairly minor injuries—and not a single scratch from glass. To this day we have no idea how she managed to get out of that car. (Well, we do, but He's too modest to confirm His assistance.)

Q. Tell us about your work with animals.

A. I am a wildlife rehabilitation volunteer. I have taken courses in Capture and Transport (i.e., how to get a skunk out of a window well without being perfumed) and Basic Wildlife Rehabilitation. In a typical shift at Centre Wildlife Care, I might syringe-feed infant squirrels and skunks; bottle-feed raccoons, foxes, fawns and groundhogs; prepare food for large birds such as hawks, owls, and herons; and/or tube-feed baby opossums and rabbits. Every thirty minutes, our extremely vocal contingent of baby songbirds must be fed. Turtles need to soak for an hour; adult convalescent critters' cages need to be cleaned; and other animals require medication or other medical attention. Our educational menagerie must be cared for, and there is an endless supply of laundry to fold and dishes to wash. And then I come home in time to bottle-feed the orphaned kittens waiting in incubators at my house and take phone calls about more babies who need the services of the Orphaned Kitten Program, which I coordinate. My life is quite literally a zoo, but I wouldn't change a single thing about it.

Baking with Shelley

Shelley's Double Chocolate Chunk Cookies

½ cup unsalted butter
½ cup granulated sugar
½ cup brown sugar
1 egg
1 teaspoon vanilla
1½ cups all-purpose flour
¼ cup cocoa powder
½ teaspoon baking soda
½ teaspoon baking powder
½ teaspoon salt
½ cup white chocolate chips
½ cup semisweet chocolate chips
¼ cup chopped walnuts (optional)

Preheat oven to 350 degrees. Cream the butter and both sugars in the bowl of an electric mixer. Add the egg and vanilla, and mix thoroughly. In a separate bowl, sift together the flour, cocoa powder, baking soda, baking powder and salt, and add to the butter mixture. Beat on low speed until thoroughly combined. Stir in the chocolate chips. Form the dough into one-and-one-half inch balls. Place the balls two inches apart on foil-lined baking sheets. Bake ten to twelve minutes, until just set. Makes about two dozen cookies.

From the
Guideposts Archives

This story by Royal Krantz of Richmond, Virginia,
originally appeared in
the November 1982 issue of *Guideposts*.

It was near dusk when I heard that unearthly scream from the woods nearby where I was working. I don't spook easily, but I could feel a cold ripple of fear.

I'd come alone from town to our isolated farm to tinker with some tractors. "I'll probably stay overnight," I'd told my wife Doris.

Now, as I picked up my wrench, the weird cry came a second time—not human, not animal. And it was louder, closer.

That did it. I had to get out of there. I jumped into my truck and barreled down the lonely back road toward home. Then, rounding a curve, I came upon a scene as startling as the scream that still echoed in my head. A truck was carelessly parked at the side of the road—the door open, motor idling, lights on. Beside it lay the body of a man.

I braked hard and pulled in behind the truck. *He's had a heart attack*, I thought to myself. But bending over the unconscious figure—he was in his twenties—I could see blood pulsing from a wound in his left thigh.

I don't have any medical training, but I knew this boy was bleeding to death. I tore off my belt. As I cinched it tight around his leg like a tourniquet, another car stopped and the driver hurried up to me. "Help me get him in my truck," I told him. "Call the rescue squad, and I'll drive ahead to meet them."

Later, we learned that Jeffrey Brumfield's rifle had jolted off the seat and fired into his leg, piercing a major artery. Doctors barely managed to save his life—and shattered leg.

Jeffrey might well have died, they said. But I had heard an eerie scream eight miles away from a victim who had blacked out.

Read on for a sneak peek of the next exciting book in
Miracles of Marble Cove!

It seems only a miracle can save Margaret's gallery—
and her dream.

Seaside Summer
by Pam Hanson & Barbara Andrews

The secret was in the light. Margaret Hoskins stepped back from her watercolor of Marble Cove's lighthouse to get a better perspective on her latest painting of the historic landmark. She was pleased with the gleaming white of the tower and the sandy gold of the beach, but the contrast between sea and sky still needed some work. Getting the glow of the sun just right wasn't easy, but she was satisfied with the progress she'd made so far.

Nothing she did pleased her more than scenes of Orlean Point Light, and the latest had special meaning for her. It showed a bright beam of light emanating from the high tower, something that supposedly hadn't happened in many years, not since the lighthouse had been decommissioned. Of course, she and her three friends, Diane, Shelley, and Beverly, knew better. They'd recently seen the light in times of crisis.

Now, though, it was time to walk to the Shearwater Gallery, her new business in the small town of Marble Cove, Maine. Margaret decided to take the painting with her. Her husband, Allan, had made a beautiful oak frame and stained it to complement the golden sand of the beach. The more she studied the work, the more confident she became that it would soon be ready to add to the other works on display. She wrapped the painting in heavy brown paper and covered it with a black plastic bag to protect it from the elements on her walk to the gallery.

Margaret walked rapidly down the quiet streets of the quaint old town with one eye on the sky watching for potential bad weather. She took a moment to look at the darkness overhead before unlocking the door to the art gallery. If it weren't for the mild temperature, the dismal gray sky and steady rain could have been a harbinger of late fall storms.

Bad weather on the first of July was a sign of hard times to come. She knew that Marble Cove relied heavily on tourists, but the town was unusually quiet today. Unless the weather improved drastically, the Fourth would be a total wash—literally! Margaret worried about the economic impact on her neighbors and friends, but she was also afraid that a bad summer would ruin any chance she had to make a go of her Shearwater Gallery. Locals had been enthusiastic about her opening, but she knew success depended on selling to visitors.

Margaret glanced out at the depressing weather one more time and saw a figure hurrying toward the gallery. As soon as she recognized her friend Diane Spencer, she held the door open for her.

"You didn't need to come out in this awful weather," Margaret said with a welcoming smile.

Margaret felt fortunate to have Diane as a new friend. A recent widow, Diane had moved to Marble Cove from Boston because she'd loved her family's vacations there. She was only fifty-four, young to be alone on her own, but Margaret admired the way she filled her time with long walks on the beach, hiking on woody trails, and working on her first book, a cozy mystery novel.

"A little rain can't keep me from helping you," Diane said, flicking back her damp shoulder-length brown hair. "I love seeing your gallery take shape. In fact, I have a lead on a still-life painter who might want to consign some work with you."

Margaret smiled at her tall, slender friend, glad to see her on this otherwise dreary day. Diane removed her rain-splashed London Fog coat and wiped her feet on the rubber doormat. "I love coming here. Your paintings of Marble Cove give me ideas for the settings in my book." She spotted the bagged painting leaning against the wall. "Have you brought something new to hang?"

"It's a new lighthouse painting, but it's not quite ready yet. I tried to put in the light as the four of us saw it. I'll show it to you, but first let me make some tea."

Margaret flipped on the overhead lights and led the way to the cozy area in back. It was a more recent addition to the building, and was divided into a work area and a restroom. She had a long worktable, a hot plate, her desk, a computer, and some comfortable chairs concealed from the display room by a partition her husband had built.

"I'm delighted to have you here. I can't remember when I've seen such a dreary day on the first of July. I hate to hold you up on your writing though," she said, putting the teakettle on one of the two burners.

"You're not. I'm at a good stopping point. Anyway, no one is lining up to publish a first book. I like to think that the longer I work at it, the better it will be."

"From what you've told me, the plot is exciting and unusual, and I don't even know what the final twist will be."

"I'm not entirely sure myself—"

"Did you hear that?" Margaret asked, interrupting her friend.

Diane was silent for a moment, then frowned in agreement. "Yes, I heard a sort of creaking, but it's stopped now."

"I should be used to the moans and groans of this old building," Margaret said. "Unfortunately, it's the best we can afford right now."

"It has charm," her friend assured her. "Visitors love to wander in and out of historic buildings. Your gallery wouldn't have the quaint ambiance tourists love if you built a new place."

"That's true," Margaret said, taking two tea bags from a box of Earl Grey. She stopped right before dipping them in the mugs. "There it is again. I'm sure I heard something this time."

"Yes, I heard it too, but I don't have a clue what it could be."

"Me neither, but I guess there's nothing I can do about it. Everything in town is so saturated from this endless rain. It could be swollen wood or any number of things." Margaret dangled the tags of the tea bags over the edges. "I meant to get some cookies to keep here, but it slipped my mind."

"Tea is just fine. There's something cozy about having a cup with a friend."

"I agree. It's a warm rain, but looking out at it makes me feel chilly."

"Maybe—"

Margaret's words were cut off by a crashing noise, and the lights in the front of the store went dark.

"What on earth!" she cried out, trying not to panic as she rushed to the door and stared into the gloom.

"Oh, my goodness!" Diane said standing behind her. "It's the roof."

"It fell in!" Margaret said in horror.

Diane put her hand on her friend's arm to hold her back. "Wait, don't go near it! More may fall."

Margaret could scarcely breathe, and the suspense was almost as bad as the shock of hearing part of the building's roof collapse. After several anxious moments, it seemed safe to get a closer look at what had happened.

"It's mostly ceiling plaster," Diane said as the two women cautiously inched forward.

"Thank heaven we weren't standing under it," Margaret said, staring at a big pile of debris.

Margaret put her hand on Diane's arm to hold her back, knowing that her friend was a retired journalist and still had the curiosity necessary to be a good reporter. "Don't go too close," she cautioned.

"Rainwater must have leaked through and softened the plaster until it fell," Diane said.

"We had an inspection before we moved into the building. The roof was sound. But maybe the last storm weakened it. I hope our insurance covers it. I bought the most economical package I could find to keep costs down."

"Certainly some of it will be covered." Diana moved closer toward the big pile of plaster and picked up a slab of what used to be the ceiling. "Oh, this is nasty stuff."

Margaret looked with dismay at the bare boards that were all that was left of the damaged portion of the ceiling. She backed away from the debris pile and cautioned Diane to do the same.

"I'd better call Allan," she said, backing toward the relative security of her office space.

She used the cell phone still in her purse, so rattled that she had to punch the number in twice. It seemed to ring forever before he picked up.

"Allan, part of the roof of the gallery collapsed. It's a mess. There's a big pile of plaster in the middle of the room."

"I was just getting ready to take Adelaide to the community center. I'll drop her off and be right there. Maybe you'd better get out of the building."

Her husband's voice calmed her.

"Diane is with me. We'll wait at the Cove until you get here."

Margaret was doubly glad for her friend's companionship as they walked to the local gathering spot. The small restaurant was nearly empty, and she chose a window table to watch for Allan while Diane went to the self-serve counter for tea.

"It doesn't seem real, the ceiling falling like that," Margaret said as the two of them sipped herbal tea. "Even if our insurance covers the cost of repairs, I'm afraid I'll have to stay closed until they're done. That could be the end of my gallery."

"Surely not. You're off to such a good start, selling several paintings your first month. You really are a good artist. People are already beginning to realize that."

"I'm also a good bookkeeper," Margaret said with an ironic smile. "I've been crunching the numbers. Only a really good summer can put the gallery in the black. And look." She gestured at the overcast sky outside the window. "I've heard that several bed-and-breakfasts have cancellations. It's not looking good for the Fourth."

"Allan is probably there by now," Diane said. "You two will want to inspect the building, so I'll head home now."

"Thank you so much for your support," Margaret said. "I don't usually overreact, but I was already worried about the gallery's finances. I guess I'm afraid that this is the straw that breaks the camel's back."

"You're going to be a famous artist someday," Diane said with a kind smile. "We'll laugh together about the day your ceiling fell in."

Margaret hurried over to the gallery, telling herself over and over that she wasn't going to cry when she saw her husband. Nothing upset him more than her tears, and she didn't want to distress him any more than necessary. He was waiting just inside the door of the gallery.

"I'm sorry, sweetheart," he said before she could speak. "I guess the old roof just couldn't take another Maine storm, but it's fixable. We'll get a roofer over here and let him recommend someone to plaster the ceiling."

He was carrying a big tin tub that he put under the leaking roof to catch as much rainwater as possible.

"I'm not sure the insurance will cover all the repairs," she mumbled.

Although Allan had been an accountant, he'd left all the finances of the gallery in her hands. She was afraid he had no idea how bad the situation was. They'd made some sales, but not as many as they needed to cover the payments on the gallery.

"This should qualify as an act of God," he said. "You'd better call your insurance agent right away to be sure it's covered."

"I'll do that," she said. "I just hope it stops raining soon."

She didn't want to tell him that losing part of the summer could be disastrous for the gallery. He would find out soon enough if she couldn't make a go of it.

"Let's see how fast we can get the repairs done. As far as the weather goes, I've never seen a summer when the sun didn't shine at least some of the time," he said.

Margaret smiled and turned her head away so Allan wouldn't see the tears in her eyes. She appreciated his calm attitude, but sooner or later he would have to realize that Shearwater Gallery was in big trouble. She didn't want to believe that her long-held dream of opening it could be shattered in a single season, but the prospects looked bleak indeed.

A NOTE FROM THE EDITORS

We hope you enjoy Miracles of Marble Cove, created by the Books and Inspirational Media Division of Guideposts, a nonprofit organization that touches millions of lives every day through products and services that inspire, encourage, help you grow in your faith, and celebrate God's love in every aspect of your daily life.

Thank you for making a difference with your purchase of this book, which helps fund our many outreach programs to military personnel, prisons, hospitals, nursing homes, and educational institutions. To learn more, visit GuidepostsFoundation.org.

We also maintain many useful and uplifting online resources. Visit Guideposts.org to read true stories of hope and inspiration, access OurPrayer network, sign up for free newsletters, download free e-books, join our Facebook community, and follow our stimulating blogs.

To learn about other Guideposts publications, including the best-selling devotional *Daily Guideposts*, go to ShopGuideposts.org, call (800) 932-2145, or write to Guideposts, PO Box 5815, Harlan, Iowa 51593.